D0055767

THE
NEPTUNE
CHALLENGE

ALSO BY POLLY HOLYOKE

The Neptune Project

THE
NEPTUNE
CHALLENGE

POLLY HOLYOKE

DISNEY · HYPERION

LOS ANGELES   NEW YORK

Copyright © 2015 by Polly Holyoke

All rights reserved. Published by Disney • Hyperion, an imprint of
Disney Book Group. No part of this book may be reproduced or transmitted in any
form or by any means, electronic or mechanical, including photocopying, recording,
or by any information storage and retrieval system, without written permission
from the publisher. For information address Disney • Hyperion,
125 West End Avenue, New York, New York 10023.

First Edition, May 2015
10 9 8 7 6 5 4 3 2 1
G475-5664-5-15060
Printed in the United States of America

Library of Congress Cataloging-in-Publication Data
Holyoke, Polly.
The Neptune challenge/Polly Holyoke.—First edition.
pages cm
Sequel to: The Neptune Project.
Summary: "Nere and her friends, all genetically engineered to
survive in the ocean, go on a rescue mission"—Provided by publisher.
ISBN 978-1-4847-1345-7 (hardback)—ISBN 1-4847-1345-1
[1. Genetic engineering—Fiction. 2. Environmental degradation—Fiction.
3. Ocean—Fiction. 4. Undersea colonies—Fiction. 5. Survival—Fiction.
6. Science fiction.] I. Title.
PZ7.H7435Nc 2015
[Fic]—dc23   2014041793

Reinforced binding

Visit www.DisneyBooks.com

SUSTAINABLE FORESTRY INITIATIVE   Certified Sourcing
www.sfiprogram.org
SFI-00993

THIS LABEL APPLIES TO TEXT STOCK

FOR JOSEPH, MY PATIENT
AND LOVING LIFELONG DIVE BUDDY

THE NEPTUNE CHALLENGE

chapter one

SOMETHING NIBBLED at my nose. Forcing my eyes open, I spot a persistent little yellowtail rockfish swimming in circles over my face. Impatiently, I brush the fish away and check my dive watch. I groan when I see it's only 5:00 a.m. We don't have to be up for another hour, but I know I won't be able to fall asleep again. Even though I'm finally safe at my father's colony, I'm still wired from all the nights I spent in the open ocean alert for predators.

Staring at the black rock ceiling over my head, I punch the small pillow built into my sleeping hammock, then turn over on my side. The light in our dorm cave is dim, but I can see Bria curled up like a little kitten in the hammock next to mine, her fine brown hair drifting about her face. Ree sleeps on the other side of Bria, her speargun within easy reach. I'm not the only one still adjusting to Safety Harbor.

I unclip its fastenings, slip from my hammock, and tug on my seasuit, grinning when I realize my friend Lena is sleeping with her mouth wide open. She wouldn't like it if the boys at the colony could see her now. Beyond Lena, dozens more girls sleep in hammocks tied in neat rows.

Trying not to think about how many girls I have to live

with now, I pull Bria's blanket up around her shoulders and swim to the surface to watch the sun rise. Even without travel fins, I cut through the black sea easily. Popping my head out of the water, I draw in a breath of air. It feels dry and strange in my lungs.

Since surviving the Neptune transformation two months ago, I mostly breathe water now, but I still surface to watch sunsets and sunrises whenever I can. They're one part of my old life on land I won't give up.

Our Safety Harbor inlet is calm this morning. Small swells lift and lower me gently. Already the sky overhead is starting to gray, and clouds along the horizon blush pink and red. I can just make out the hardy spruce trees that cling to sharp outcroppings along the shore. The morning is quiet except for the rush of the nearby surf and the cry of a gull winging its way across the dawn sky.

Mariah, the leader of my family's dolphin pod, finds me bobbing on the swells. Her little calf, Tisi, swims a tight circle around me while her daughter Sokya rushes up and flips water in my face.

:what worries you this morning?: Mariah asks as she cranes her head out of the water so she can see me better. At forty, Mariah is a grandmother several times over. Her teeth are a little worn, and her right side is scarred by an old shark bite, but her eyes are still bright with intelligence.

Mariah is also amazing at reading my moods.

:There're so many people at Safety Harbor,: I try to

explain while I rub Sokya's favorite spot, in front of her dorsal. The slick, rubbery feel of her skin is familiar and comforting. :And they all think Dad's awesome and great at running things. I'm afraid they expect me to be just like him. That Janni girl wants me to join her Sea Rangers and help fight the Marine Guard and sharks, but I just want to work with dolphins.:

:you led us safely here through many fights and many miles of sea,: Mariah reminds me.

I wince, remembering the dangerous journey my friends and I had to make from the southern sector to reach my father's colony. I hadn't really led everyone here safely: two of our group died on our trip to Safety Harbor, and we lost sweet Pani, one of Mariah's granddaughters, all killed by Marine Guard divers sent by the Western Collective to capture or eliminate us.

:We never would have made it here without your help,: I say to Mariah.

:I helped the most,: Sokya declares. She leaps out of the water and lands on her side, dousing me with a wave.

:we helped each other on that journey,: Mariah replies, and I reach out and gently scratch her melon.

Moments later, Tobin surfaces nearby. Even wet, his hair glints cedar red. His green eyes light up when he spots me and he swims closer. Sokya and Mariah both rush to greet him. All the dolphins in our pod like Tobin.

"Hey, Nere, you're up early," he says with a smile.

"I couldn't sleep in." I smile back at him.

"Me neither."

We say little as we float together and watch the skies brighten from gray to lavender to blue. Just being around Tobin and the dolphins relaxes me. I let my mind drift.

Suddenly, on the very edges of my awareness, I sense a mental touch. :Nere!: I think I hear someone call me. The contact is faint, but I sense the caller's desperate urgency.

"Did you hear that?" I ask Tobin.

"Hear what?"

"I thought I heard someone calling my name telepathically."

"I didn't hear anything, but you have a longer range than I do."

I keep listening hard, but the call doesn't come again.

When the sun touches the tops of the waves and burnishes them bright gold, Tobin clears his throat. "It's great out here, but I'm way ready for breakfast. If we don't eat now, we'll be late for our jobs."

"Yeah, we'd better go." I glance uneasily toward the strait. I'm sure I didn't imagine that call, or the need in it.

:I will come and help you teach the young ones later,: Mariah promises before she swims away with Sokya and Tisi in her wake.

I slip beneath the surface and follow Tobin as he heads for the mess cave. Safety Harbor is really just a narrow inlet several miles long lined with caves and smaller coves along the northern side of the Queen Charlotte Strait. Despite the scorching temperatures farther south, the waters here are still cold and so rich with nutrients, the steep rock walls of the colony are covered with scarlet corals, feathery pink sea fans, and white sponges.

More kids are awake now and heading for breakfast just like Tobin and me. I smile when I see Robry ahead of us in line, rubbing his dark brown eyes, his black hair still tangled from sleep. Even though Robry's only ten, he's growing up to look amazingly like his big brother. My heart twists when I think of Cam, my best friend I had to leave back home.

Inside the mess cave, one of my father's helpers in scuba gear supervises our food prep, and the other watches to make sure we don't mess around too much. At breakfast things are usually pretty calm, but there are over three hundred of us here now, and during lunch and dinner the mess cave can get a little wild. When I pass through the food line, the kids on breakfast duty hand me a fresh piece of salmon in a food pouch and a container of wakame mash.

Luckily, Ree and Thom, two of our friends from the southern sector, are already there and eating together, so Robry, Tobin, and I swim over and join them. Most of the kids at Safety Harbor are friendly, but I'm not great at hanging out with new people.

:*Buenos días*, boss,: Ree greets me. Because of her strong nose and dark eyebrows, I think she looks like a fierce Mayan princess.

:I'm not your boss anymore. Janni's our boss now, and that's fine by me,: I reply absently. I'm still listening for that mysterious telepathic call again.

Ree glances over at Janni, a strong, stocky girl who's chief of the Sea Rangers, an elite group chosen for their skills in fighting and sea survival. :Janni does look pretty tough,: Ree admits admiringly.

As if she can feel us looking at her, Janni turns our way. She nods to me but doesn't smile. She was really nice when we first arrived, but for some reason she's been less friendly toward me recently.

:So who's going to try out for the Sea Rangers?: Ree asks everyone.

:I am,: Thom declares. :I'm gonna go crazy if I have to spend another day firing spear darts at targets.: Tall, with a craggy face and big hands, Thom grew up with a band of guerrillas determined to topple the Western Collective, so he's more used to action and fighting than the rest of us.

Bria and Lena come over and join us. Bria seems bright and cheerful as always, but Lena looks like she's still half asleep.

Ree nudges Thom while she sends Lena a teasing grin. :Hey, I thought you were going to sleep through your classes and work shifts today, Sleeping Beauty.:

Thom looks away uncomfortably. I know he won't join Ree's teasing because he has a huge crush on Lena.

:If you say another word to me before I've woken up, I'll cut your braids off,: Lena threatens Ree.

:Someone woke up on the wrong side of her hammock this morning,: Ree says, her black eyes dancing.

:Hey, Ree,: I say to distract her, :isn't that the guy you thought was *muy guapo* when we were training at the Gymnasium yesterday?:

Ree whips around to look, and Lena sends me a grateful smile as she starts nibbling at her salmon.

:Here's Safety's Harbor's newest hero,: Tobin greets Penn.

:Hi guys,: Penn says. A little older than the rest of us, Penn is part Chinese. Yesterday he became one of the most popular kids in the colony when he figured out a way to stream music into our ear receivers, the tiny implants that help us communicate with my dad's non-telepathic helper staff.

:Penn, you'd really be my hero if you can find a way to make seaweed taste better.: Lena opens her food container and glares at her wakame mash. She scoops out a portion with her fingers and closes the box before the rest floats away.

:Sorry,: he says with a smile and a shrug. :I'm better with computers. I'd probably poison everyone if you turned me loose in the kitchen.:

:Is Lena complaining about the food again?: asks Kalli, swimming over to join us after finishing her breakfast shift. Skinny and smart, with brown skin and a quick smile, Kalli already seems to know everyone in Safety Harbor.

:Lena's right. Breakfast shouldn't be all green and mushy,: Bria says as she frowns at the portion of mash she's holding in her fingers.

:It's not so bad,: Robry says seriously. :It's full of minerals, vitamins, carbs, and fiber we can't get from fish.:

:Thanks for the food lecture, Dr. Cruz.: Lena rolls her eyes at him.

:At least we're not really having SEE-food for breakfast,: Robry replies with a mischievous gleam in his eye. :Oops, now we are.: He opens his mouth so wide that Bria and Lena can't help but see the green mash all over his teeth. A small piece of seaweed floats out of his mouth and hovers over their table.

:Eww! That's disgusting,: Bria shrieks, but I can tell she's trying not to giggle.

:If your breakfast is so disgusting, I'll have it,: Tobin says with pretend eagerness and grabs for his little sister's mash container.

:No way. This is *my* breakfast,: Bria declares, and Tobin winks at me.

:You could sign up to join the cook crew,: Kalli suggests to Lena, who's starting to look a little green herself. :They're always looking for people to help out.:

:I just might do that,: Lena surprises me by saying. :I liked cooking back home. Someone has to do something to make the food around here edible.:

:Go for it, Chef Lena!: Ree grins at her.

As soon as we finish breakfast, we check the screens set into the dark rock walls by the cave's entrance. I'm scheduled to help out at Dolphin Bay this morning.

:Looks like most of us have a local sea-life class this afternoon,: Penn points out.

:They probably want to teach us not to pet the anemones,: Thom says glumly.

:I wish they wouldn't treat us like total sea newbies after we survived our little thousand-mile trip here.: Kalli shakes her head.

After grabbing our fins from the dorm caves, we thread our way through dozens of other kids swimming to their morning jobs and classes located in caves and coves throughout the colony. Tobin and Thom swim along with me, since they're heading for the Gymnasium—a wide sandy cove where the Sea Rangers teach fighting and survival skills— which is right next to Dolphin Bay.

I smile when I spot a red Irish lord sculpin below us on the floor of the inlet. The small, shy fish is trying to hide in a mass of scarlet soft corals surrounded by a rainbow of purple, pink, orange, and blue anemones. We've just reached the deep channel that leads to Dolphin Bay when I feel that distant mental touch again.

:Nere, I need your help.:

This time the contact is strong enough that I know exactly who it is. I catch Tobin's arm before he can swim on.

:Tobin, I know who's been trying to reach me. It's my brother, James, and I think he's in trouble!:

chapter two

I CLOSE MY EYES and concentrate on reaching out telepathically to my big brother. :Are you okay? How can we help?:

:I'm hurt and I'm adrift in a small boat. I—I keep blacking out.:

:Where are you?:

:Five or six miles southwest of Safety Harbor. There's a small rocky island covered with trees just east of me.:

:Hundreds of islands around here look like that.: I can't keep my fear and frustration from my mental voice.

:This one has a tall rock on one end that looks like a tower. Nere, you gotta find me before the Marine Guard does.: His mental voice is so weak, I can barely hear him now.

:We will,: I promise him. :Hang on.:

I open my eyes to see that Tobin and Thom are watching me. :What's up with your brother?: Tobin asks.

:He's injured and he's stranded in a small boat somewhere south of here. He cut out his locater chip more than a year ago. If the Marine Guard finds him, they'll send him off to a prison camp for sure. We gotta tell my dad. Come on.:

As we hurry back toward the home caves, I call the pod, and soon eleven excited Pacific white-sided dolphins are dipping and swirling around us. I ask Sokya for a tow, and after she darts in close, I catch hold of her dorsal fin. Seconds later, we're flashing through the water *way* faster than I can swim on my own. I glance over my shoulder and see that Tobin and Thom are getting towed by their dolphin partners, too.

Mariah swims up beside us with Tisi, and I tell her about James contacting me.

:we will find your brother. now our pod will finally be together again.:

I *so* hope she's right. James had good reasons to stay behind in the Channel Islands, but things must have gotten even worse down south if he was desperate enough to make his way here.

People look startled and curious as we race past.

:Kalli, have you seen my dad?: I call as we speed by her.

:Yeah, I'm pretty sure he was heading topside. What's going on?:

:Tell ya later.:

We find my dad in the shallow sea cave that leads to the colony's surface buildings. After I pop my head out of the water, I see he's in the midst of taking off his mask and flippers.

"Hey, Dad," I call out to him. His face lights with a smile when he sees me.

"Good morning, sweetling. I looked for you in the mess cave, but I must have just missed you."

A pang shoots through me as he speaks. After he and my mom staged his death so he could come here and build Safety Harbor, I thought I'd never hear Dad call me "sweetling" again.

"James contacted me," I say, "and he's hurt." Quickly I fill him in. My dad's smile fades as I talk, and his brows draw together.

"I don't think we can risk sending a boat for him until nightfall," he says reluctantly. "The strait is crawling with ships this morning. I don't know what's happening out there, but something big's going on."

"Then send us," I say. I glance at my two friends, and they both nod eagerly to show they're in. "We'll swim under the surface and the pod will help us find him. Tobin's a good medic, and he can treat James until you can send a boat for him tonight after it's dark." At least I hope Tobin can keep him alive until then.

"But the Marine Guard might pick you up on sonar."

"Dad, that was a threat we faced every day on our way here," I say, not even trying to hide my impatience. Sometimes I think he forgets we managed to survive for weeks in the ocean with no help from adults.

He swims closer and places a hand on my shoulder. "I know, but I just got you back," he says, his gaze steady.

"*Please*, James sounded so weak, and you know Mariah's the best at search and rescue."

"All right." He drops his hand and takes a deep breath. "If you survived a voyage from San Diego up the Western Collective to Canada, you can probably survive a few hours out there in the strait. You three hurry and get your travel gear, but you're going to take two of our best Sea Rangers with you. They know the waters around here."

I sigh in relief, and the dolphins whisk us back to the dorm caves. Within minutes, Thom, Tobin, and I are ready with seapacks and spearguns, and we meet up with Janni and Rohan, the two Sea Rangers my dad chose to accompany us. Rohan, a quiet Indian boy, nods to Tobin. They're already friends because Rohan is a medic, too.

:I need to inspect your spearguns and seapacks before we cross the perimeter,: Janni announces abruptly.

Thom, Tobin, and I glance at one another. Does she really think we don't know how to take care of our equipment? James might not have time for this! Biting back a protest, I hand her my speargun.

She looks it over. :These bands will need to be changed soon.:

:But not yet,: I say.

:Not yet,: she admits grudgingly and moves on to my seapack. What is up with her? Just as Janni finishes inspecting all of our gear, my dad approaches us. Beside him is Vival, the stern-faced woman in charge of the Sea Ranger program.

"Because Janni knows these waters best, I'm placing her in command of this expedition." Vival speaks to us through a transmitter in her dive mask. Neither she nor my dad is a telepath.

"But, Nere," my dad adds through his own transmitter, "you're in charge of dolphin communications and their search. I want you to save James, but you can't risk getting caught and revealing the existence of this colony to the Western Collective, the Canadians, or anyone else. Good luck."

He swims forward to give me a hug. I try to hug him back, but it's hard to embrace someone wearing a wet suit, a dive belt, and an oxygen tank. I give Janni a sideways glance afterward. She doesn't look happy about my father's orders.

:You guys ready?: she asks. We nod, and she signals a Safety Harbor dolphin to give her a tow. We pair up with our own dolphins, and soon we're speeding toward the shimmering silver wall of bubbles that stretches across the narrow mouth of Safety Harbor. That wall protects the entire colony from sharks, other predators, and scavenger fish. As we cross it, all I can see are bubbles, and they tickle my face and hands.

Then we're through the wall and heading west. Drawing in a deep breath, I realize this is the first time I've been outside the perimeter since we arrived at Safety Harbor a week ago. I tighten my grip on my speargun and look around carefully for any sign of danger. Visibility is good today, which means we can see almost forty feet ahead through the clear green water. A small school of mackerel flows past us, sunlight glinting on their stripes and silver scales. We pass a tall yellow-brown forest of kelp, and I almost smile when I spot several harbor seals watching us curiously out of their big, dark eyes.

As we travel swiftly below the surface, I relay to Rohan and Janni everything James told me about his location.

:It sounds like he's probably near Tegan Island,: Janni says. :That has a big rock spike on its south end. We'll start our search there.:

A few minutes later, the dolphins sense a ship. My heart beats faster as we scatter and dive deep to avoid sonar detection. Luckily, the ship continues up the strait without slowing, but soon we encounter three more ships traveling together in a convoy, and we have to dive and hide again.

After we turn to avoid a fifth ship, Janni shakes her head. :I've never seen this much boat traffic out here.:

:At least they don't seem to be hunting us for a change,: Rohan points out with a serious smile.

I try to reach out to James, but he doesn't respond to my mental calls. His range is so limited, I'm surprised he reached me in the first place. But sometimes when telepaths are desperate, they can broadcast their thoughts more strongly. Tobin must sense how worried I am, because he and Mali move up beside me.

:Hey, we'll find your brother, and he'll be okay,: Tobin reassures me.

:I hope you're right. James can be a real pain sometimes, but he's the only brother I've got.:

:Why didn't he come north when you did? All you've ever really told me about James is that his Neptune transformation failed.:

I choose my words carefully. James has some secrets I can't ever tell. :It didn't completely fail. He had some strong telepathic abilities he inherited from my mother, and the transformation intensified those. The problem is, his ability to shield didn't switch on. So James hears every thought of every person near him, all the time.:

:Being around other people must drive him crazy after a few hours.:

:That's why he was happier living all by himself out in the Channel Islands.:

:That still had to get pretty lonely after a while,: Tobin says, shaking his head.

I try to reach out to James again a few minutes later.

:Nere?: I hear him reply, but his mental touch is much fainter than before.

:We're coming, but is there some way you can mark your boat? I don't want to risk swimming up to the wrong one and having someone spot us.:

:Th-thought of that already. Look for a gray dinghy with

the motor hanging below it. Since it conked, I'm using it as a sea anchor.:

:Where are you now?:

:N-not sure. Think I've drifted a long way from that island.:

:Hang in there. We *are* going to find you.:

Quickly, I relay to my human companions what James just told me. When we reach the island, we risk surfacing, but there's no sign of James's dinghy. I choke back a sob. The wind is picking up, and it could have pushed his light little boat miles from here by now.

We duck back under the waves. Janni pulls out a chart and calmly assigns each of us an area to search while my dolphins swim around us in circles, squeaking and whistling in their excitement.

:we will start soon?: Sokya asks me repeatedly. The pod loves to look for people. Her brother, Densil, who is much more steady and thoughtful than Sokya, swims up beside me.

:we will find your brother in time,: he promises. :I will be happy to see him again.:

:Thanks, Densil,: I say, leaning into him for comfort. :I know you'll find him, and he'll be glad to see you, too.: But will my brother be okay?

The moment Janni finishes our assignments, I divide the dolphins into teams and send them off to search with their human partners. Mariah tows me while Laki races ahead of us, using her ability to echolocate to search the seas ahead for any sign of a small boat. The minutes tick by like hours, and James still doesn't respond to my calls. What if he's bleeding to death at this very moment? I've already lost my mother; I can't lose James, too.

Finally, an endless half hour later, Sokya contacts me, and she sounds very pleased with herself. :we found the boat. my team wins!:

chapter Three

:*NICE JOB, SOKYA,*: I reply to my enthusiastic dolphin friend. :I'll give you lots of fresh squid when we get back to Safety Harbor.:

I contact Rohan, who's working with Sokya's team. :Have you found my brother?:

:The dolphins located a small boat with an outboard dangling below it. I'm surfacing to check it out.:

I'm certain enough that Sokya and Rohan have found the right boat to ask Mariah and Laki to take me to it. What if Rohan's too late to help James, I can't help wondering as we race through the sea.

:James is still alive,: Rohan finally reports to all of us. :He's dehydrated, he has a nasty gash on his arm, and he has a fever. I'm guessing he's been adrift for a while without water.:

:Is he going to be okay?: I ask, fighting to keep my mental voice steady.

:I think we can get him fixed up, but it's a good thing the dolphins found him when they did. Janni, we're maybe a quarter of a mile from Gull Island.:

:There's a small cove along its southern side,: Janni

replies. :If we can beach his boat there, the Marine Guard is less likely to spot it.:

The moment my dolphins and I reach the dinghy, I head straight for the ladder on its stern. Mali and Ricca are swimming nearby, which means Tobin must already be here.

I scramble to the top of the ladder. Both Rohan and Tobin are kneeling beside James, and tears sting my eyes as I gaze at my unconscious big brother. Tobin is gently cutting away a bloody, filthy bandage on his arm, and Rohan is setting up an IV. Beneath his bristling beard, James's skin is gray, and his lips are dry and blistered. He's even thinner than he was when I saw him several weeks ago.

Tobin glances at me. "I know he doesn't look great, but I think he's gonna make it."

"He must be strong to have hung on this long," Rohan adds encouragingly.

I *so* want to help, but I'm afraid I'll just get in their way. "Guess I'll leave you guys to it."

Feeling useless, I climb down the ladder. Janni and Thom are both beneath the boat now.

:We need to get the dinghy over to the island before the Marine Guard finds it,: Janni says. :It's time to put the dolphins to work again.:

Grateful for something to do, I pull two dolphin towlines from our seapacks. The lines are knotted into a series of loops, and with Thom's help, I tie them both to the bow of the dinghy. While we uncoil the towlines, Tobin slips back into the water and Janni cuts the line to James's broken motor.

The dolphins must see this as another exciting game, because they all crowd around me eagerly, including some of the older and more mellow females in the pod like Kona and Mona.

:I want to pull,: Sokya says imperiously.

I choose six, including Sokya, Mona, Densil, and Kona, and they race to poke their beaks through the loops. I ask my friends to head straight for the entrance to the cove on the nearby island. With six strong dolphins pulling, the dinghy surges forward.

:a boat comes,: Mariah warns me, :and it sounds like one of the fast ones with the dark bottom.:

I swallow hard. She means it sounds like a cutter, the swift ships the Marine Guard uses for patrolling.

Trying not to panic, I share Mariah's warning with the rest.

:Densil, Sokya,: I call to them. :You've got to pull faster. The Marine Guard may be coming.:

:Whoa!: I hear Rohan's startled exclamation as the dolphins surge forward. :It's like there's a real motor on this thing now.:

The dolphins swim so rapidly, they are leaving Janni and the rest of us behind. I ask Mariah to send some of the pod back to tow us, too.

:Rohan, if that boat spots us, you jump overboard,: I hear Janni call out. :There's no point in both of you getting caught.:

:Roger that.:

I wish Rohan could stay with James, but I know the dolphins can pull the dinghy faster without his extra weight. :Mariah, is that ship heading for us?: I ask as I catch hold of Laki's dorsal.

:I do not know, but its engines are getting louder.:

That's not good.

:I'm going topside to take a look,: Janni announces. She and her dolphin, Tosi, flash up to the surface.

:The cutter is headed toward us,: Janni declares a minute later, :but its crew may not have seen the dinghy yet. We've gotta get it inside that cove.:

Mariah contacts me. :if the rest of the pod pushes, they can make the little boat go faster.:

:Mariah, you're brilliant!:

I relay her suggestion to Janni, Thom, and Tobin.

:You trust the dolphins to get the dinghy to the cove and out of sight without us?: Janni asks. Tosi is towing her right next to me now, and I can see the doubt in Janni's expression.

:In a heartbeat. I know they can do this.:

Janni hesitates for a long moment before she says, :Tell them all to push the boat. Rohan, jump overboard now,: she adds. :We gotta lighten the load.:

The moment I let go of Laki's dorsal, she darts away with Tosi to join the others pushing the dinghy. Rohan jumps into the water, and the five of us swim after the dolphins as fast as we can, kicking hard.

Soon I hear the deep throb of the cutter's engines in the distance and kick even harder. The throbbing grows louder and louder, but I still can't see the ship when I glance back.

:we have reached the cove,: Densil finally announces.

:Can you pull the boat inside it now?: I ask him. :You've *got* to hide it from the people on the big ship.:

:the mouth of the cove is narrow, and we will take your brother's boat inside to a place where the people on the big ship will not see it,: he assures me.

I'm panting and my legs are burning by the time we reach the mouth of the cove. The bass roar of the cutter's engines fills my ears. We surface behind a rock spire covered with barnacles and peek around it. I clench my speargun tighter. The Marine Guard cutter is still speeding straight for us . . . but then it turns, and I relax my grip a little. The ship is definitely heading up the strait.

"Whew. That was *way* too close," Tobin says for all of us.

We swim inside the cove. I blink in surprise when I see the dolphins have already beached the dinghy for us.

Janni shakes her head and smiles at me for the first time all morning. "I have to admit, your dolphins are pretty amazing. I've been getting a little tired of hearing people say how cool it is that you can talk to them, but now I can see how useful that ability is on a mission."

I just have time to send Janni a quick smile in return before we're mobbed by happy dolphins. :Nice job, you guys,: I tell Mariah, Densil, and Sokya, and I broadcast feelings of gratitude to the rest of the pod.

:Please go feed and rest. I'll call if we need your help again,: I tell my dolphin friends after we give them rubs.

Sokya and Nika lead the rest out of the cove, showing off with a couple of spectacular leaps along the way.

"Let's really hide that dinghy now," Janni says, getting back to business.

We take off our travel fins and stride from the water, the small round pebbles of a shingle beach crunching under our feet. I breathe out the last of the water in my lungs and try to ignore how heavy and awkward I always feel now on land. Rohan, Tobin, and I hurry to check on James, and I'm relieved to see he's still breathing. As I untie the towlines, Janni searches for a good place to hide the boat. Eventually she chooses a spot behind a big boulder and a massive cedar tree, and Thom drags the dinghy up there all by himself.

Then he glances up at the sky. "If we turn over the dinghy and prop it up, it would give your bro some shelter. Looks like it might rain soon."

"That sounds like a great idea," I say.

Carefully, we lift James and settle him on the beach. I

bite my lip when I realize how hot his skin feels beneath my hands. Thom uses a couple of thick pieces of driftwood to prop up one end of the small boat. I stay right by James's side, hoping he'll wake soon.

"If I cover the dinghy with branches, it would be harder to see," Thom says to me.

"Nere and I will help you," Janni says shortly. I think she's irritated that Thom keeps looking to me for orders, but for four long, dangerous weeks, I was his commander, and we're both still getting used to someone else being in charge.

Reluctantly, I leave James to gather some branches. By the time we've finished covering the dinghy and settled James under it, I'm panting and dizzy. Our lungs aren't very efficient when we're out of the water, so Thom, Janni, Tobin, and I head back to the sea to reoxygenate properly. Rohan stays behind with James, but Tobin promises to come relieve him shortly. Janni and I check in with Roni, a young marine biologist who is one of the few telepaths on Dad's helper staff, and give her an update on our status.

For the rest of the afternoon, we take turns keeping an eye on James. When it's finally my turn to go up on the beach again, it's raining lightly. I check the strait for boats, but it's quiet for now. Beyond the strait to the north, tall hemlock and red cedar trees retreat in dark green waves to the rugged blue mountains beyond.

I duck under the edge of the dinghy, and I'm relieved to see James is dry and his color's a little better. Rohan and

Tobin covered him with a blanket from their first aid supplies and tied his IV bag above his head. I'm glad he's already getting fluids and antibiotics. I try to sit down quietly next to my big brother, but the shingle pebbles still rustle beneath me.

His gray eyes flutter open and he manages a smile despite his blistered lips. "Hi, sis," he says weakly. "I knew you and Mariah would find me."

"Actually, Sokya's the one who found you, and she's not ever going to let us forget that."

"Well, tell her thanks." He pulls a water bottle close with his good arm and takes a small sip.

"Dad's going to send a boat for you when it's dark. We'll have you set up in the topside infirmary in no time. I'm *so* happy you're finally here." But I can't help wondering *why* he's here. Because he looks too tired to talk, I decide not to ask him that just yet.

James sighs. "Remember, brat, I can hear most of your thoughts when you're sitting this close to me, whether I want to or not. The Marine Guard found the *Kestrel* and sank her, so I lost my home. I figured I might as well come north and see if I could give Dad a hand, and I wanted to find out if you'd made it okay. I crewed for a black-market fisherman, and he got me as far as San Francisco. Then I joined a band of young smugglers heading north, but the Marine Guard caught us and sank us just south of Vancouver Island."

"Is that when you got hurt?"

James shakes his head, but I see a shadow in his eyes. "It

was bad, Nere. They cut those kids apart with solar rifles as they struggled to swim in the cold water. They didn't manage to kill me because I dove deep and stayed down until they left."

"So your free diving saved you," I say, swallowing a sudden lump in my throat. I don't want to think about how close my big brother came to dying. Even before his failed Neptune transformation, James loved to dive long and deep without scuba gear, which wasn't the safest hobby. His free diving used to drive my parents crazy.

"Yeah, I guess it did." A smile touches his eyes briefly, and then it fades. "Nere, you should know that losing the *Kestrel* wasn't the only reason I came. It's getting worse down south. The weather just keeps getting hotter and dryer, and most of this spring's crops have already failed. This could be the start of the worst famine yet, and the Western Collective's been forcing thousands of young people to join its army. A day ago, I found out why."

He winces as he shifts his arm. "They just launched an all-out attack on Canada."

"But I thought the Canadians were our allies."

"I guess our fresh water supplies were running low, and the Western Collective wants lakes and rich farmland where it still rains once in a while."

"That must be why the strait's been so busy. We'll have to try even harder to avoid their ships." I wonder about the kids I knew back home. I didn't have any close friends except

Cam and Robry, but I wouldn't want anyone to be forced to fight for a government as corrupt or totalitarian as the Western Collective.

I try to keep my voice even as I ask, "Have you heard what happened to Cam? Some of his friends were smugglers."

James gives me a sympathetic glance. "I heard he survived the fight on the beach where they killed Gillian, and they sent him off to a work camp."

My throat clogs again at his mention of our mom's death, and I can't stand the thought of Cam imprisoned in one of those horrible places.

"Hey, at least he's still alive," James points out. "And I bet he stays alive. Cam's one smart, tough guy."

"Thanks," I manage to say, and then my gaze falls on his wounded arm. "So if the Marine Guard didn't shoot you, how did you pick up that gash?"

James's mouth tightens. "I had a little run-in with some thugs who were spying on Safety Harbor. I was hiking along the coast, and I stumbled across their camp while they were gone. I tried to steal the smallest of their boats, but one of the guys came back and shot me before I could focus my thoughts and control him."

I hope *none* of my friends are on shore right now. I duck under the rim of the dinghy to check. *Whew.* The beach is empty.

:You can't talk about being a controller where people can hear you!: I yell at him on a private send.

This is James's big secret, and it's one that could get him killed. His failed Neptune transformation strengthened his telepathy and gave him the ability to control other people's actions. But controllers played a terrible role in the Eugenics Wars that destroyed whole countries fifty years ago, and the nations of the world agreed to hunt controllers down and exterminate them.

"It's okay, Nere. I know no one is close enough to hear us talking. I'd hear their thoughts if they were," James replies aloud with a grimace.

"Did you find out who those men were?"

"They were just hired muscle. It's who sent them that scares me."

Something in his tone sends shivers down my back. "Who was it?"

"They were hired to spy on Safety Harbor by Ran Kuron."

chapter four

I STARE AT JAMES, my stomach churning like a pebble caught in the surf. The moment I hear the name Ran Kuron, I think of Dai, the mysterious boy who came with us on our journey from the southern sector. He fought bravely during our battles against sharks and Marine Guard divers, and we all believed he was on our side. But right before we reached Safety Harbor, we found out he was really a spy sent by Ran Kuron, a renegade scientist who left the Neptune Project.

"So what do you know about this Ran Kuron guy?" I ask James. It hurts too much to think about Dai right now.

"I hacked into Gillian's computer files one day and found out a lot about him," James admits. "He was one of the founding members of the Project and a genius at raising funds. He became obsessed with creating the perfect human-oid to rule the seas. He was even willing to try splicing genes from all sorts of marine life into his subjects, but Gillian and Dad and the rest of the scientists wanted to make sure we were as human as possible. Eventually they had a huge fight and kicked Kuron out of the Project."

"We ran into some of Kuron's kids just a few days from

Safety Harbor. One of them was this scary girl named Wasp who had poisonous tentacles on her fingers. And there was a boy in that group who had six arms."

"Kuron probably spliced some sea wasp and octopus genes into them."

I can't imagine having tentacles on my fingers that could kill people. "Did you find out why Kuron wanted them to watch us?"

"No. They were just supposed to report back to Kuron on when the topside staff enters and leaves the water and stuff like that. But it can't be good that he's so interested in Safety Harbor," James says grimly.

As I think about what he just told me, James's eyes flutter shut. Even though I'm full of questions about Ran Kuron, I let my brother slide back into sleep.

I'm left with too much time to wonder about Dai, the angry, abrupt boy who loves the sea as much as I do. We were friends, and for a while I'd thought maybe he wanted to be more than friends. My cheeks burn when I remember he even kissed me at my birthing day party, right before we found out he had betrayed us all. As I listen to the cold rain patter on the roof of James's makeshift shelter, I blink away tears I refuse to shed because of Dai.

Still, I can't help wondering if I'll ever see him again.

~ ~ ~

This far north in the summer, it takes *forever* for night to fall. We're all bone tired by the time a small gray inflatable zode from Safety Harbor arrives to pick up James around midnight.

"How's James doing?" my dad asks me the moment he jumps from the zode with two of his helper staff.

"That IV the guys gave him seemed to make a huge difference. He still has a fever, but his color is better. You should get a real medical report from Tobin and Rohan."

"I will, and when he's better and strong enough, we'll set James up in an old trapper cabin near our topside head-quarters. It's far enough away to give him some peace and quiet but close enough to stay safe, considering our new security concerns." Through Roni, I'd already told my dad and his helper staff about the Western Collective's invasion and Kuron's spies.

"I think he'll like having his own cabin." We both know James has always been a loner.

"You did a good job today, Nere-girl." Dad envelops me in one of his big, warm hugs, but I feel awkward with Janni and the rest watching us.

"Thanks, Dad," I mumble into his shoulder. After he lets go, I step back. He hurries up the beach and kneels at James's side. As I walk toward the water, my eyes prickle and my throat is tight. It's hard not to mind that James and Dad get to be together on land while I have to return to the sea.

During our return trip, we don't encounter any boats, and we reach Safety Harbor around three in the morning. I head up to the surface to say good night to Dad, and he tells us that we can sleep in and skip our morning classes, which is *awesome* news because I feel like I could sleep for a week.

I pause in front of my dorm cave to say good night to Thom and Tobin. :Hey, thanks for everything today.:

Tobin sends me a tired grin. :Rescuing your brother was definitely more interesting than hanging out around here.:

:Yeah, it was almost fun dodging the Marine Guard again,: Thom adds with one of his shy smiles.

:You guys sure have a weird idea of a good time.: Yawning, I turn away and head straight for my hammock.

~ ~ ~

The next morning, no small fish bother me, or if they do, I'm too soundly asleep to notice them. I get up just before lunch, my stomach rumbling. I'm hungry enough to eat an entire king salmon by myself. In the mess cave, I'm relieved to hear from the helper staff that James is stronger and his fever is almost gone.

Ree, Kalli, and the rest of our southern sector friends eat with Thom, Tobin, and me and demand to know all about our adventures yesterday. I think they're disappointed we went off without them.

:So that's why there are so many Sea Ranger sentries around today,: Kalli says after I tell them about the men Kuron hired to spy on us. :I wonder if your dad thinks Kuron or some of his freaky kids might actually try to attack us.:

:I hope not. I never want to see that Wasp girl again,: Ree admits, rubbing her arms. :She was too scary even for me.:

:I never want to see Dai again,: Lena says, tossing her head. :I still can't believe he was one of them, and he never told us.:

I catch Kalli and Ree sending Lena reproachful looks before I stare down at my food pouch, fighting to keep my face blank.

:I think we all have a few things we'd like to say to Dai,: Tobin says after a long, awkward moment.

I'm relieved when Kalli quickly changes the subject and asks everyone what their work assignments are this afternoon. Just thinking about Dai has made me lose my appetite, but I force myself to choke down a few bites of halibut. Then I go with the rest to check the screens by the cave entrance, and I feel happier when I discover that I'm supposed to help out with dolphin classes this afternoon. I can't wait to see if clever little Tisi has some new trick to show me. I'm actually smiling as I swim out to Dolphin Bay, but my smile fades when I pass two armed Sea Ranger sentries who are clearly on the lookout for trouble.

Seth, the head dolphin trainer, hurries over as soon as I arrive. A year or two older than me, he has shaggy blond hair, a wide smile, and a crooked nose, thanks to an overly playful dolphin who broke it a few years ago. Seth's fascinated by Mariah and is forever asking me questions to ask her.

:Boy, am I glad to see you,: Seth greets me. :We have more kids than we can handle this afternoon. I swear most of our new arrivals this past month have no dolphin-handling skills. I want you and Mariah to work with the youngest beginners.:

:That will make Mariah happy. She loves the younger ones.:

Actually, I don't mind working with younger ones, either. Younger kids aren't as full of themselves as some of the older ones, and they listen to me way better. Seth assigns us two little girls named Pansi and Tala. They tell me they're cousins, but they look like sisters with their big brown eyes and black hair.

Pacific white-sided dolphins aren't a large species of dolphin, but they can seem pretty big and strong if you haven't been around them before. I sense that both girls are scared of Mariah. I wish Bria was here with me today. She's totally comfortable around dolphins, and she's one of the few people beside Tobin and me who can actually hear Mariah's words in her mind. But she was assigned a self-defense class along with Robry in the Gymnasium this afternoon.

I take the girls off to a quiet spot near a small kelp forest where the dolphins love to play. There, beside tall columns of greenish brown kelp that sway gently with stray currents, I introduce Pansi and Tala to Mariah and Tisi. Little Tisi is in a playful mood. He succeeds in making them giggle when he shows off his favorite trick, swimming upside down. By the end of our lesson, both girls are giving Mariah the correct hand signals for fetching and finding, and Pansi is even brave enough to let Mariah tow her for a short distance.

After the session ends, Pansi and Tala thank Mariah and me, their eyes shining with excitement. I stay behind in the bay to play with the pod and check them for parasites. Suddenly I hear a frightened shriek in my mind. It sounds like Bria!

:Tobin, Nere, Wasp is here. She's making Robry and me go with them—: And then her words are cut off. It's as if a dampening cloud absorbed Bria's words.

:Bria!: I shout. :Bria, are you okay? Robry, are you all right?: I concentrate, straining my senses, but I can't pick up a reply.

Frantically, I reach out to Sokya and Densil. :I think Wasp is kidnapping Bria and Robry! They were out at the Gymnasium. Watch where she takes them.:

:we go!:

The dolphins arrow past me. I could ask them for a tow, but I know I'll just slow them down. Instead, I call Mariah, and moments later she and Tisi are by my side. She tows me after Sokya and Densil, and the rest of the pod swirls around us.

:Be careful,: I call to Densil. :Wasp has poisonous stingers on her fingers and her gang has powerful spearguns.:

As we fly through the sea, all I can think about is Bria and Robry. Why would Wasp take them? Are they all right? I keep calling to Robry, and since he's such a strong telepath, I should be able to hear him easily. Instead, there's just a strange, ominous emptiness.

We reach the Gymnasium a minute later, but there's no sign of Bria or Robry. Several Sea Rangers are clustered in a group talking angrily. Kalli and Tobin are floating nearby, Tobin's face pale and strained.

:What happened?: I ask the moment I let go of Mariah's dorsal.

:A Sea Ranger told us that kids on fast skimmers swooped across the perimeter,: Kalli replies. :They grabbed Bria and Robry as they were leaving the Gymnasium and darted away before anyone could stop them.:

:Then they forced them into a small sub and took off heading south,: Tobin says, his mental voice radiating pain and anger.

:I bet they were some of Kuron's mutates,: Kalli adds. :The Sea Rangers who saw them said they had weird swirling tattoos on their faces, like those kids who attacked us on our way here.:

:It was Kuron's kids all right,: Tobin says tightly. :Bria told us that Wasp was making them go with her, and then suddenly, I couldn't hear her anymore.:

I really hope Dai had nothing to do with this. I think he liked both Bria and Robry.

An angry, bitter mind touches mine. It's Wasp! :Nere Hanson, tell your daddy that if he wants your sweet little friends back alive, he has to send a bunch of you to Atlantea to get them. Ta-ta for now. Oh, and by the way, Dai says hi.:

Her casual mention of Dai makes me more furious. :Don't do this!: I shout at Wasp mentally. :Don't take them. They'll be so frightened.:

All I hear in reply is a long, nasty laugh that makes me want to strangle her, and then she breaks off contact.

Sokya streaks up to Tobin and me and bobs her head in agitation. :we could not stop them. the young ones were already in the sub, but my brother follows it. he talks with the little girl to make her less frightened. he will follow it and tell us where they go.:

:Thanks, Sokya. You guys are great,: Tobin tells her. His dolphin partner, Mali, hovers near him. She must be able to sense how upset Tobin is.

:I just don't understand,: Kalli says. :Why would Wasp take two little kids?:

:I don't understand why we can't hear Robry or Bria anymore,: I add. :They're both such strong telepaths that we should be able to communicate with them even if they're already four or five miles away.: I don't want to suggest in front of Tobin that I'm worried they might be unconscious.

:I wish I'd been with Bria,: he says, clenching his hands. :It's my job to watch out for her.:

:We thought everyone would be safe here with so many sentries around,: I say.

:Maybe we should head back to the home caves,: Kalli suggests with a sympathetic look at Tobin. :The helper staff might know more.:

Since it's clear we aren't going to find any answers here, we head back. When we reach the home caves, people are hurrying everywhere and dolphins from the Safety Harbor pod streak back and forth. I spot Thom and Penn hovering on the edges of a crowd gathering outside the arched entrance to the large cave that serves as the Rangers' headquarters. Easy-going Thom looks like he wants to break something in two.

:We're gonna do whatever it takes to get them back,: Thom tells Tobin.

My dad appears in the entrance to the Sea Rangers' cave and raises his hand to get our attention. The crowd of kids milling about quickly stills. Our friends gather around Tobin and me. I'm grateful for their support. They all love Bria and Robry almost as much as we do.

"A short time ago, four young people from Kuron's fortress crossed the bubble wall on skimmers," my father announces, "and kidnapped Robry Cruz and Bria Masterson. We'll be reviewing our security protocols to make sure this never happens again, but in the meantime, the Sea Rangers will conduct patrols constantly outside the perimeter."

My father pauses to scan the crowd, and his gaze finds Tobin and me. "My staff and I will start planning a rescue mission right away. Even though we want to go after Robry and Bria this very minute, we have to be patient. This mission will be conducted by the Sea Rangers, and they need a few days to plan carefully and make sure the mission's successful."

The moment Dad finishes with this announcement, my friends and I look at one another in dismay. I know they all want to be on that rescue mission as much as I do, but we aren't Sea Rangers.

Tobin reaches out and grips my arm. :Nere, you gotta do it,: he says, his eyes pleading. :You have to ask your father if we can go.:

chapter five

I DRAW IN A DEEP BREATH. Asking to join the mission won't be easy. I'm not sure Tobin understands how strained things are between Dad and me right now. I never thought that being Dr. Mark Hanson's daughter was complicated, but now that he's in charge of the entire Neptune colony, it kind of is. I feel like two hundred kids are always watching us and wondering if he's going to treat me like everyone else. But I promised Cam that I'd look after his little brother, so special treatment or not, I *have* to be part of this rescue mission.

Before Dad turns away, I swim up to him. Tobin's right beside me. Even through my dad's scuba mask, I can see the worry on his face.

Dad, we really need to talk to you, I key into a small compad on my wrist. My words will appear instantly on a screen inside his mask.

"I have to go topside to meet with our helper staff. We can talk at the surface."

My father heads for the shallow sea cave that leads to Safety Harbor's shore facilities. Tobin and I follow him, and we all surface together.

"Wasp contacted me," I tell Dad as soon as I breathe out the water in my lungs. "She said if we wanted to get Robry and Bria back, we need to send some kids after them to Atlantea. But what *is* Atlantea?"

"Kuron radioed us a message that said much the same thing. Atlantea's the grandiose name he's given his marine fortress," he explains, pushing his scuba mask up on his forehead.

"I don't understand. Why would they want Robry and Bria? Why do they want more of us to go after them?"

"We have some ideas about that," my father says soberly, "but I can't go into them with you now."

I swallow my rising frustration. As he heads for the ladder bolted into the cave wall, I dart in front of him. "Dad, wait. There's something else. I know we just got here, and none of us is officially a Sea Ranger yet, but my friends and I *need* to go on this mission."

My father opens his mouth to speak, but Tobin cuts him off. "Sir, it's going to take trust and teamwork to get Bria and Robry safely away from Kuron and his people. We work well together and we proved during our journey here that we can handle ourselves in tough situations."

"You said the rescue mission probably wouldn't launch for a few more days," I argue. "Couldn't someone find the time to give us the Sea Ranger test?"

"We could be Bria and Robry's best chance of getting back here alive," Tobin adds.

"*Please*, Dad," I say, holding his gaze for a long moment.

He sighs and places an arm around my shoulder. "Sweetling, the last thing I want is for you to be involved in this. I just got you and James back. But I know I'd feel the same way if I were you. I'll speak to Vival about it."

He drops his arm from my shoulder and swims for the ladder. "I'll make sure you get tested," he says as he slips off his dive fins, "but I can't promise Vival's going to pass you or make you Sea Rangers."

"Thanks," I say, letting go of a long breath.

"You can thank me by not getting hurt." My father sends me a stern look. "Vival's trials are hardly a picnic."

~ ~ ~

Janni swims over to our group at dinner. :Well, you got what you wanted,: she tells us all, but she's looking at me. :We'll be testing you tomorrow. Make sure you only bring equipment we specify for patrols. You can find the list on the computers in the dorm caves.:

I blink at the resentment I hear in her tone. :I thought you wanted us to join your Sea Rangers.:

:Yeah, but not right now. There are a million more important things my Rangers and I should be doing tomorrow besides testing you guys.: Janni turns and swims away before I can think of a retort.

:Whoa, that wasn't like Janni,: Kalli says, looking after

her curiously. :Usually she's really chill. I wonder what's bugging her?:

I don't really care what's bugging Janni. I'm too busy worrying about Robry and Bria and our tests tomorrow. My stomach's coiled so tightly, I can hardly eat, and I'm not the only one. Tobin's barely touched his food. Thom, however, shovels down his portions of halibut and seaweed like a machine. He even gets seconds.

:You guys gotta eat if you wanna do well tomorrow,: he scolds us, and I force myself to swallow several more bites.

After dinner, I'm glad to see Thom and Penn stay close to Tobin as he swims off to the boys' dorm cave, and I'm grateful for Lena's, Kalli's, and Ree's company as we head for ours. We look up the list of gear we're allowed to take on our Sea Ranger tests and pack our equipment carefully.

After I tug off my seasuit, I tie myself into my hammock. As I stare up at the dark rock overhead, I'm achingly aware of Bria's empty hammock next to mine.

:I hope our niña isn't too scared tonight,: Ree says softly. She had a little sister of her own who died in the last famine.

:I hope she's isn't, either.: And I hope Robry isn't too frightened.

~~~

After a long, restless night, my friends and I report to Janni and Vival promptly at 0800 hours the next morning. Vival carries herself like a soldier even when she's swimming in scuba gear.

"Good morning, Nere," Vival greets me coolly. "Are your team members ready for their Sea Ranger test?"

I hope so, ma'am, I key into my com-pad.

She looks irritated by my reply. I bite my lip. She was probably expecting a "Yes, ma'am" answer instead of an honest one.

"I'm going to be straight with your group," Vival says. "I have serious reservations about any of you going on this rescue because of your lack of formal training. The Sea Rangers we're currently considering have been preparing for a mission like this for months."

Don't we get any credit for having survived six weeks in the ocean on our own? Fighting back an angry reply, I try to focus on her words.

"I wasn't impressed during your training drills this past week," Vival is saying. "I hope you people do better today."

Ree's eyes flash, and I'm afraid she's about to lose it. I contact her on a private send. :Ice it, *chica*. Don't give Vival a chance to fail you before you even get started. We need you on this mission.:

Ree takes a deep breath. :Okay, boss,: she says after a long moment.

"Since the time we have to test you is limited," Vival announces, "we're not giving you our usual skills tests.

Instead, you are about to participate in an SPC, or Simulated Patrol Challenge. Our observers will evaluate your sea skills, and you will also be judged on how well you function as a team while following our protocols as you work through an emergency scenario. If you pass, you will be considered as candidates for the rescue mission."

As soon as she finishes speaking, four Sea Rangers arrive with tows. After we're blindfolded, I find myself holding on to the tow grips so tightly that my hands hurt. We just *have* to pass this challenge, for Bria's and Robry's sakes.

Lon, the Sea Ranger piloting my tow, drives us in so many circles, I totally lose my sense of direction. After he removes my blindfold, I look around and see we're floating on the edge of a large forest of greenish brown kelp.

I reach out to Mariah and the rest of the pod, who followed behind the tows.

:Mariah, where are we?:

:they've taken you to an inlet a mile north of the home caves.:

Vival motions us to gather around her again. "Here's your scenario: a Marine Guard boat found your patrol on sonar. Their divers have shot two of you. Rohan here is losing blood fast from a spear-dart wound in his thigh."

I'm glad Rohan's part of our test, but I'm guessing he'll be a tough judge of our performances.

"Dav is also too hurt to swim on his own." Dav is a

young blond British scientist who helps with undersea technology. Most of the older girls in the colony have huge crushes on him.

"Dav has a deep cut along his right arm and will run out of oxygen in thirty minutes. You can't let him surface, though, because he'll get the bends unless he decompresses properly."

My team and I exchange worried looks. This challenge is getting complicated.

"Two Marine Guard vessels are anchored at the mouth of this inlet. If their sonar operators detect someone trying to pass beneath their boats, they will launch a simulated depth charge. Our computers can register your location thanks to the sensors the Rangers will give you. Those sensors will start blinking yellow if you are close enough to the explosion to be seriously injured, and red if you're dead."

At her nod, Sea Rangers come around and clip sensors on our wrists.

"In ten minutes," she continues, "the boats will launch a dozen charges. When those charges hit the water, anyone still left in this inlet will be considered a fatality. Dav is a telepath, by the way, so he'll be able to listen in on your discussion."

Vival nods to Janni, who looks me in the eye as she speaks. :Your goal is to bring as many of you home safely as possible. Time begins now. Good luck.:

chapter six

I TAKE A DEEP breath and try to concentrate as Janni and Vival swim away. How can we possibly get ourselves *and* Dav and Rohan past the mock Marine Guard boats and their sonar in ten minutes?

:Everyone, mark the time,: I say. :Tobin and Lena, check our wounded and try to keep them stable. Anyone got an idea?:

Tobin meets my gaze, his expression worried. :It's an impossible challenge. The dolphins might be able to tow our healthy swimmers under the boats fast enough to avoid sonar detection, but the boat crews are going to sense us when we have to transport our wounded. Vival wants to see if we have the guts to sacrifice Rohan and Dav to save the rest of us.:

:In a real situation, we might, but we'd try to find other options first. So let's find some fast.:

:Their boats have to be close by,: Lena says, glancing up from Dav. :Maybe you could scan the crew's thoughts and see if *they're* worried about how we might get out of this inlet.:

:Since this is an emergency, I'm willing to listen in

on what they're thinking,: I say. Dav looks startled, but he makes no objections.

:We have to fool their sonar somehow,: Kalli says quickly. :Remember the way Mariah got the wild dolphins to confuse those smugglers chasing us back in San Francisco? Ask Sokya if any of the Safety Harbor pod is hunting near here.:

:That's a great idea,: I say and reach out to Sokya. :She says many dolphins hunt near here, and she's asking them to come help.:

Penn holds up a device that looks like a small radio. :We could try this. It's a sonar disrupter.:

:Tell us fast. What's this thing do?:

:Robry and I designed it to break up the sonar signature of Neptune kids and make us look like a school of fish. The small battery I brought should power it for maybe two minutes.:

:That's perfect.:

:But what if they think we're cheating?: Thom asks. :That's not on our official list of Sea Ranger equipment.:

We glance at our monitors, but Dav just acts like he's in pain, and Rohan pretends to be unconscious.

:It's a resource we have,: I decide, :and if this were a real emergency, we'd use it. But this could get us into serious trouble. Everyone okay with trying Penn's gadget?:

:I'd rather bend the rules than leave two of our people behind to die,: Tobin says, and the rest nod.

I glance at my watch. Only seven minutes left.

:Everyone, pair up with your dolphins and get ready to sprint out of here. I'm going to try to pick up something useful from those boat crews.:

I close my eyes and reach out with my senses. There are two helpers topside sitting in the two pretend Marine Guard vessels. I scan their minds, searching for any information that could help us. One of the sonar operators is fretting over her scope. As I listen to her thoughts, I realize her main concern *is* something we can exploit.

:Listen up,: I tell my group. :Topside, they're worried about a deep, narrow channel where there may be a blind spot in their sonar coverage, and they don't want us to find it.:

Penn frowns. :We can't risk searching for that channel. They'll sense us if we get too close to their boats, but Mariah can look for it when the other dolphins arrive.:

:Good idea. On my signal, Ree, Thom, and Kalli, sprint through that channel one at a time as fast as your dolphins can swim. When you're three hundred yards beyond the boats, hold up. We'll need everyone's help to get our wounded back to Safety Harbor.:

I reach out to Mariah and explain about the channel that might help us escape detection. :we will look for it when the other dolphins come,: she promises me.

I turn to Tobin. :Is Rohan stable enough to travel?:

:Not really, but he's dead if he stays here,: he replies.

:We need to get him back to sickbay as fast as possible. Same goes for Dav.:

:'Kay. Lena, you and Penn and your dolphins tow Dav out of here right after the others leave. Tobin and I'll follow you carrying Rohan. Penn, use your disrupter when it'll help the most.:

:Here come the dolphins!: Kalli cries as the first Safety Harbor dolphins arrive. They swim excitedly all around us.

:Sokya, ask them to circle under the boats.: I hope the helpers won't toss a depth charge the moment they see dozens of dolphins on their scopes. We're gambling that they'll think a wild pod just entered the inlet.

:Mariah, can you find that channel?:

:we have already found the deep way under the boats.:

:Show it to the others. Please tell them we must swim through it fast.:

:I will. this is fun!:

:All right, Ree and Halia, go. Kalli, you and Mona head out. Thom, you and Kona, go now.: I wave the teams off and check my watch. Blood thunders in my ears. Only four minutes until the boat crews lob their charges.

I swim quickly to Tobin to help him with Rohan. Mali is already waiting beside him, and Sokya speeds straight to my side to give me a tow. Penn and Lena and their dolphin partners are already pulling Dav toward the channel.

:We've gotta stay close together if this disrupter is going to hide us,: Penn warns me.

Our dolphins tow us down into the old stream channel. It's so narrow, deep, and twisting, I can see why the helpers were worried about their sonar coverage. But we're moving too slowly. I'm still scared they'll detect us topside.

:All right, we should be in sonar range,: Penn declares. :I'm turning on the disrupter . . . now.:

I glance at my watch. Only two minutes left.

:Swim faster,: I urge everyone.

As we pick up speed, Dav starts muttering that his arm hurts, but we ignore him. I glance at my sensor. If it lights up, I'm dead. One minute passes like a lifetime, and still my wrist sensor stays dark. We startle several wolf eels with bristling teeth hiding in the rocks as we flash past.

:How you doing there, Dav?: I ask him.

:My arm's killing me, and my air is running low,: he says shortly.

:You'll be back at Safety Harbor soon,: Tobin says. If we don't get blown up in the next thirty seconds.

:Mariah, are we past the boats yet?: I ask.

:you are beneath them now.:

I check my watch. One minute left.

:Sokya, we've got to sprint for it!: I tighten my grip on Sokya's dorsal. Our dolphins surge forward, and Dav starts moaning.

:we need to breathe soon,: Sokya warns me.

:I think we're almost clear.:

At last I see Kalli, Thom, and Ree ahead of us, and

they're all grinning. I glance at my watch. Ten and a half minutes have passed. My sensor is still dark. They must have tossed the virtual depth charges, but we were out of range when they hit the water.

:Thanks, Sokya. Go breathe, and then we've got to race back to Safety Harbor.:

:We did it!: my group starts cheering.

:Hey, we still have to get our two wounded back to Safety Harbor as fast as possible,: Tobin reminds us.

:And we have to get Dav oxygen while he decompresses,: Lena adds.

I send Mariah and Nika out to search for a current to speed our trip back. We carry Dav and Rohan as smoothly and quickly as we can, changing dolphins frequently so they can breathe and rest.

A half mile into our journey, Mariah finds a current that doubles our speed. I reach out and contact Roni and ask her to make sure medical help is waiting for us.

A group of Sea Ranger medics meets us at the bubble wall with a stretcher for Rohan and oxygen for Dav. Janni is with them.

:I don't know how you all got out in one piece,: she says ruefully, :but congratulations.:

I only nod in reply because we're still making sure Dav gets a regulator attached to a fresh oxygen tank as Rohan is transferred onto the stretcher.

When they are set, I let go a sigh of relief. :Nice work,

everyone,: I say, meeting the gaze of each of my friends, and I mean it. :Mariah, you and your family were amazing, as always.:

:did you do well on your test?:

:I think so.:

:I am glad.: Mariah brushes against me in farewell, and I see the rest of my team rubbing their dolphins before our friends rush off to feed and play.

My stomach tightens when I see Vival and my father swimming toward us. Are they going to give us our official test results right now?

"How did your entire group get past our boats?" Vival asks me. I blink at the coolness of her tone.

I choose my words carefully before I start keying them into my com-pad. I read your sonar operators' minds and found out about the deep channel. Our healthy patrol members took that route under your boats with their dolphins. When we were moving our wounded, Penn used a sonar disrupter to make us look like a school of fish. Safety Harbor dolphins also helped to disrupt our sonar signature.

"That disrupter wasn't on the list of your specified equipment," Vival points out. "And none of our other Rangers possesses your powerful telepathy or the ability to communicate with dolphins so specifically. Your team used resources unavailable to most Sea Rangers and broke the SPC rules."

"I disagree," Dav speaks up. "I thought Nere's team was bloody brilliant. These kids demonstrated terrific teamwork under pressure and remarkable ingenuity. Penn, I want to see that sonar disrupter you designed ASAP."

"The point of the drill wasn't for everyone to survive," Vival declares. "This was actually a test to see if this untrained group could follow our basic protocols, and in my opinion this patrol completely failed that aspect of the challenge."

My cheeks start to burn. I can feel my team's disbelief and anger building behind me. Before Ree can say anything that would get us into more trouble, I squeeze her arm. Then I swim forward from the others and square my shoulders.

It was my decision to use my telepathy to help us, and it was my decision to use Penn's disrupter. I'm responsible for how our SPC turned out.

Vival nods. "So noted. I also understand that my observers were impressed with your sea skills and your overall performance. We will discuss your results and inform you tomorrow at breakfast if you get to go on the mission. Nere, you and your team are dismissed."

I glance at my father. His gaze is sympathetic, but he doesn't say a word in our defense. I can't believe he's not going to stand up for us.

Gulping down my disappointment, I lead my friends away.

chapter seven

MY GROUP DOESN'T TALK much at dinner, since we feel like Vival hit us with a dozen depth charges. And after our difficult debriefing with her, I'm surprised when we're joined by Rohan and some of her Rangers who tested us today.

:We just wanted to say we thought you guys did a great job,: Rohan tells me, his expression earnest. :Bottom line— we'd all go on a mission with your team in a heartbeat.:

The Rangers want to know exactly how we fooled their sonar operators. Then they share stories of their own SPCs that didn't go so well. During one, a team managed to sink Vival's inflatable zode by mistake, and in another, a pair of lovesick killer whales blundered into the middle of a rescue drill. The Sea Rangers' stories are funny, and. I appreciate that Rohan and the others are trying to make us feel better about today, but I still feel like crying. I'm so scared we've lost our chance to go after Robry and Bria.

When dinner's over, the others head off to the rec cave to hang out. Tobin lingers with me by the entrance to the mess cave and studies me in his thoughtful way. :Today wasn't your fault, you know. We all wanted you to use your telepathy and Penn's disrupter.:

:I know that, but I thought if I took the blame, they still might let the rest of you go. We know Bria and Robry, we know each other, and we've fought our way out of some really tight spots in the past.:

:We do make a good team, and I don't think we were wrong to use your telepathy or one of Penn's inventions. Those are some of our strengths.:

:I can't believe Vival thinks we messed up today.:

:Go talk to your dad. He didn't look happy about what Vival said to us when we got back, and maybe you can get to him before he and the helper staff make their final decision. Bria and Robry could be running out of time.:

:But Janni said we're not supposed to go topside unless we're invited.:

Tobin sends me a rueful look. :Nere, the rest of us aren't supposed to bother the helper staff on their off hours, but we don't have family up there. You do.:

:Maybe I *should* talk to him, and I'd like to see James.:

Although Tobin's one of my best friends, I don't want to tell him how unsure I feel around my dad right now. As I swim through the cave entrance, though, I realize Tobin has made me feel a little better.

I look back. :Hey, Tobin, thanks.:

:Hey, you're welcome.: He sends me a smile that lights up his face, but when it fades, I see the worry he's trying to hide. At least I still have a father and a brother. Tobin's parents are both dead, and his only sister is being held in a fortress full of dangerous mutates. And Tobin is the one trying to make *me* feel better.

I reach out to Penn because the two of them are good friends. :Um, Penn, I think Tobin could use some company right now.:

:Maybe we'll go see the dolphins,: Penn replies promptly. :Being with Mali always seems to cheer him up.:

I head for the shallow cave that leads to the buildings topside where the helper staff work and live, but Densil contacts me before I reach it.

:I am back. the sub took the young ones to a huge building in the sea. I can show you where it is, but it is a bad place.:

:Thank you so much. How are Robry and Bria?:

:the young ones are very frightened and want to come home. do we go soon to get them back?:

My eyes prickle with tears. I *hate* to think of Robry and Bria being scared. :We'd better go soon,: I say, :or Tobin and I are going after them ourselves.:

:those people should not have taken them from our pod,: Densil says with great disapproval in his mental tone.

More determined than ever to talk to my dad, I kick for the cave and climb the metal ladder bolted into the rock wall.

Once I breathe out the last of the water in my lungs, I can smell pine trees and earth. I pause for a moment because

I miss smells. My sense of taste has become sharper since my Neptune transformation. I can actually taste different conditions in seawater, but I don't really smell them.

At the top of the ladder, a metal walkway leads to a low wooden shed containing racks of neatly hung scuba gear. Beyond the shed, I come to a small cluster of cabins built into a hillside.

My father told me that they tried to make sure no one from the Canadian government or the Western Collective could spot Safety Harbor from the water or air. The cabin rooftops are painted shades of green and gray to blend in with the surrounding rocks and trees. At night, the helper staff even uses blackout curtains.

I stop by sickbay to talk to James, but the medic on duty tells me that he's with my dad right now. As I walk quietly across the small clearing toward the tiny cabin that doubles as my dad's office and bedroom, I hear someone playing guitar.

I pause for a moment to listen. Live music is something else I rarely get to experience. The sea has its own music— the sound of dolphins whistling and sawing, the noisy crackle of shrimp, and the rattle of small pebbles shifted by currents. But the ocean is quieter than the surface world.

I move on and tap at Dad's door. There's a fluttery sensation in my stomach. How can I be apprehensive about seeing my own father? But so much has happened in the past two years since he left us. As much as I love him, I can't forget *he's* the reason I hardly ever get to smell pine trees or hear live music anymore.

The door opens, and my dad's face lights up at the sight of me. An instant later, I'm engulfed in a warm hug. He's always been a big hugger. Maybe he's still trying to make up for my mother, Gillian, who wasn't so good at hugs sometimes.

"Nere, I'm so glad you're here," he says after he steps back from me. "Come in and have a seat."

He glances around his messy cabin and rakes a hand through his hair. I would take a seat, but I'm not sure where. James is sitting in the one clear space on the bed, and dive equipment, boxes of supplies, and computer gear are heaped everywhere else. I spot a framed picture of my mother on his cluttered desk and smile sadly. My mother was always the neat freak in our family. She never would have let his stuff get this disorganized.

Dad sweeps some clothes off the end of his bed and motions to me to take a seat.

"But I'll get your bed all wet," I protest, because my hair and seasuit are still dripping.

"I'm not exactly worried about a little seawater around here." My father smiles quizzically as he hands me a towel, and James laughs.

I study my big brother. "You look a lot better," I say as I towel my hair, and it's true. He's still far too thin, but his color is normal again. He's wearing clean clothes, and his injured arm is in a sling. Someone even trimmed his wild, shaggy hair and beard.

"I feel a lot better," he admits, "except that there are too many people around here." I almost tell him I feel the same about the underwater part of the colony. But then I notice the crease in his forehead, which makes him look like he has a headache.

"I do have a headache," he says, and I try not to jump. I'm still not used to my brother's ability to hear everything I'm thinking. "I always get headaches when I'm around too many people for too long."

"We'll move you out to the cabin tomorrow," Dad says, "as long as you promise to take it easy."

"If you just get me out of here, I swear I'll be a good boy," James retorts, and I find myself grinning at him. I've missed my brother, sarcastic comments and all.

"I've missed you, too, little sis," he murmurs and makes space for me.

After I sit on the foot of the bed, Dad drags his desk chair closer and sits across from us. I hardly ever get to see his whole face now, since I usually just see it through a scuba mask, and I've missed hearing his voice directly, instead of through an earpiece. He looks tired tonight. The light on his desk reveals strands of gray in his brown hair and wrinkles and frown lines he didn't have two years ago. That's the last time I saw him before my transformation.

My parents faked his death in a sudden storm so he

could come north and start building Safety Harbor for the hundreds of Neptune kids they hoped would find their way here. But my parents didn't trust me with the truth, and a part of me is still furious at them both for that.

"So, how are you feeling about today?" he asks.

"Pretty frustrated. I thought my team did a great job, but I guess Vival felt differently."

"For what it's worth, I thought you and your friends did an excellent job, too, but the Sea Rangers is her program. Thanks to her military background, Vival's brought order and discipline to the Sea Rangers, and to all of Safety Harbor, for that matter. I'm grateful for her contributions."

"But I'm not sure she's right about all her Sea Ranger rules and regs." I stand and pace around his tiny cabin. "In the sea, you have to use everything you've got to survive. Penn, and Robry, too, are so smart that they're always going to come up with crazy ideas that don't fit with Vival's rules." My voice thickens when I say Robry's name. A part of me wants to go charging off this instant to get him back, no matter what my dad or Vival has to say about it.

"So you think we're getting a little too set in our ways here?"

"I just don't think my group should have gotten in trouble when we got the job done," I say shortly and sit down again.

"Much to my surprise, the kid's got a point," James drawls, and I make a face at him.

"But you did break her rules in terms of what you could

use during her test," Dad counters, "and Vival's got good reasons for instituting rules around here." He leans back in his chair and sighs. "It was chaotic up here during the first six months after we started the colony. I had kids arriving every day, equipped with lethal weapons like spearguns and dive knives, and I didn't have enough adults to supervise and train them properly. We lost a girl in the Gymnasium to a stray spear dart, and a boy died when a tidal current smashed him against a cliff."

He looks haunted by the memory of the kids he lost. "Since Vival took over the Sea Rangers and our survival training, we've had some kids hurt, but no one's died, and I'm sure that's thanks to her rules and regulations."

"So maybe you have to have some regs around here, and I'm sorry we broke them. But, Dad, we *really* need to go on this mission. My friends and I can do this better than anyone else because we know Bria and Robry, we work well as a team, and we can handle ourselves in a real fight."

"Nere, I hear what you're saying, but there's more to this mission than just rescuing your two friends. It's going to be a hundred times more dangerous than you realize. I just got you back, and I don't want you risking your life again. The three of us don't have much family left."

I hear the sadness in his words, and I look past him to the picture of my smiling mother on his desk. She appears so young and carefree in that photo—not at all like the distant, self-contained scientist I remember. After my transformation, she died blocking a shot from a solar rifle meant for me. I look away from her picture, my eyes blurring with tears.

Dad clears his throat. "I know how hard losing her must have been on you. She loved you so much, and she would have wanted you to know that."

Angrily, I swipe the tears away with my hand. I know she loved me, but sometimes I wonder how much I was an experiment to her and how much I was a daughter.

"I don't really want to talk about her right now," I say, my voice high and tight.

After a long, awkward moment, Dad changes the subject and starts asking me how I'm settling in. I follow his lead, but all I can really think about is whether or not he's going to let me and my friends try to get Robry and Bria back. As we talk for a little while longer, I grow short of breath and my lungs feel dry and itchy.

Finally, I rise to my feet. "I need to head back to the water now."

My father looks disappointed but stands at once. He checks his watch. "I have to meet with Vival and our helper staff in a few minutes anyway to make our final decisions about the rescue team. I promise I will share your concerns about all our rules here."

Then he pauses for a moment.

"You know, I was just thinking how much I miss hearing your voice." I guess that's kind of like how much I miss seeing his face.

As we look at each other, I bite my lip to keep from say-ing it. He's the reason he doesn't get to hear my voice much anymore, he and his Neptune Project.

Maybe he can tell what I'm thinking because he's the first to look away. I wonder if he's ever going to say he's sorry for what he and my mother did to me. I wonder if I'm ever going to completely forgive him.

"I'm so glad you came," he says instead as he opens the cabin door. "You're welcome here any time."

"I—I wasn't really sure about that. Janni made such a big deal about telling kids not to come up here and bug you guys."

"Yes, well, we had to get strict about enforcing that rule because all the girls coming to see Dav were driving us crazy." He smiles. "But the rule certainly doesn't apply to you."

"I'm glad to know that," I say, and Dad gives me another big hug.

"I'll walk you back to the ladder," James offers and gets to his feet. "I gotta get back to sickbay. Doc Iharu is about to come looking for me anyway."

We say good night to Dad and start across the clearing. "How are you really doing with so many people around?" I ask James.

"I can't wait to move out to that cabin," he admits. "There are only twenty helpers, but twenty people sure can generate a lot of psychic noise."

"Could you like living up here?"

"Yeah, I think I could. It's so pretty and wild; this area reminds me of the Channel Islands. Dad wants to get a team doing research on ocean acidification, and I'd like to help them out."

"I'm glad. I was really hoping you'd stay."

"Only now you may be the one leaving me behind. I don't like your going off to this Atlantea place any more than Dad does, but if they'd taken my friends, I'd feel the way you do."

"Thanks." It means a lot that he understands.

At the top of the ladder, James gives me an awkward hug. I'm panting hard now, and I'm so hot that I'm dying to plunge back into the cool sea.

"Good luck tomorrow, little sis," he says. "I hope they do choose you and your friends to go on the rescue mission."

I send him a grateful smile before I hurry down the ladder. At last the cold water washes over my legs, and then my body. I breathe in deeply, and the seawater rushes down into my dry lungs.

As I swim back toward the dorm caves, I decide I'm glad I went to see my dad. Even though it's complicated between us now, he was happy to see me and I was happy to see him. But I can't help wondering about what he said concerning the mission.

How could it possibly be a hundred times more dangerous than we expect?

chapter eight

THE NEXT MORNING, my friends and I head to breakfast together. Everyone looks even more tense than yesterday. After we go through the food line, my dad and Vival enter the mess cave, and I promptly lose what little appetite I had.

"We're here to announce our choices for the rescue mission to Kuron's fortress," Dad says.

Vival glances down at the computer pad in her hands. I hold my breath as I wait for her to read out the list. "Thom, Lena, Tobin, Penn, Kalli, Ree, Rohan, Janni, Seth, and Nere, please report to the briefing cave right after you've eaten," she announces crisply.

My friends and I smile and hug one another. But I can also see the nervousness in their smiles. Soon, we'll hear exactly how my father and his helpers plan for us to sneak into Kuron's Atlantea and bring Robry and Bria back home.

We head straight to the briefing cave after breakfast. I'm not surprised to see that my dad, Vival, and several helpers are already there. Janni looks just as anxious as the rest of us.

My father's expression is serious as he begins to speak.

"Rohan, Janni, and Seth, Vival has chosen you as candidates because you are some of our most responsible and experienced Sea Rangers."

Then he looks at my friends and me. "Nere, yesterday you and your team demonstrated your sea skills and resourcefulness. Before you commit to this mission, however, you need to know what you're getting into."

I feel my father's eyes on me as he speaks, and I can sense how much he doesn't want me to be a part of this.

"We wouldn't let you go at all, but there's more at stake here than two lives. It's time we told you about the full scope and purpose of the Neptune Project."

I shift uneasily. I thought its purpose was pretty straightforward.

"I know your Neptune mentors told you that we were trying to create a new species of human that could survive in the sea," my father continues. "In case humankind is doomed on land, we hoped our species could flourish in the oceans that cover more than five-sixths of our world. But we had an even more vital goal when we devised the Project."

He pauses to look at each of us in turn. "We came up with a plan to save life on the entire planet from global warming."

Kalli and I exchange startled glances before I focus on his words again.

"One scientist who joined the Project was a brilliant

young geneticist named Idaine Campbell. You all know the upper levels of the sea are filled with tiny one-celled plant life called phytoplankton that create oxygen and capture carbon dioxide throughout their life cycle. Idaine devised a kind of supercharged phytoplankton she called 'c-plankton' that could absorb a hundred times more carbon dioxide. When this c-plankton dies, it sinks and takes with it to the ocean floor all the carbon dioxide molecules it has absorbed in its lifetime. We planned to establish Neptune colonies around the world to grow and spread this c-plankton throughout the seas."

So you want us to turn the oceans into a massive carbon sink? Kalli keys into the computer, her face alight with enthusiasm.

"That's exactly what we hope to do. If we can sow enough of this c-plankton in our oceans, we could significantly reduce the amount of carbon dioxide in the atmosphere and finally start cooling our planet."

So what does this c-plankton have to do with getting my sister back? Tobin keys in, his impatience obvious.

"I'm getting there," my dad assures Tobin. "While working on the Project, Idaine met a charismatic marine geneticist named Ran Kuron. They fell in love and married. They even had children while working secretly on the Project, and then something went terribly wrong. Idaine's research vessel sank in a calm sea off the coast of Vancouver Island, and Kuron became more and more unstable after her death. He refused to give us the c-plankton cultures she'd developed. We also discovered that he'd sought out rich investors around the world and used their backing to break the most fundamental rules and ethics of our program."

I stare at my father's set face. I'm not sure I've ever sensed so much anger in him.

. "Our goal had always been to create humans who were superbly adapted to the sea, but still human in terms of their basic nature. Kuron became obsessed with creating the perfect species of humanoid to dominate the world under the waves. He began splicing genes from all sorts of sea creatures, including sharks and electric eels, into his human subjects, with little concern for their mental stability or happiness. Wasp and her gang are examples of his warped program."

I remember an old novel my teacher back home gave me to read. It was the story of a man who was determined to create life no matter what the consequences. He even loved the tormented monster that he made.

He sounds like a Dr. Frankenstein of the sea, I key quickly.

"That's a good analogy, although I think Dr. Frankenstein had a conscience and was a great deal saner than Ran Kuron is at this point," my father replies grimly.

Are Idaine's c-plankton cultures in his fortress? Kalli asks, her face intent.

"We think it's likely. Kuron seems obsessed with her

memory and determined to hold on to every bit of her research. We've tried to make him see what incredible value these cultures have for all life on the planet, but Kuron won't listen to us. He doesn't care what happens to the surface world because he's so determined to establish a new civilization under the waves, one that's completely under his control."

"That's why we're now willing to take some greater risks where Kuron is concerned," Vival says. "Millions are dying all around the world because of the scarcity of food and water caused by global warming. We can't afford to wait any longer. Your mission would be to infiltrate Atlantea, find your friends, and try to free them. But we also want some of you to locate those cultures, steal them, and bring them back to us."

My heart skips a beat. Densil told me this place is huge, I key quickly. We'll never find the cultures and get out without being caught.

"You're right," Vival says. "You will be caught, but that's also part of our plan."

My friends and I glance at one another uneasily. I wonder if we heard her right.

"You see, Kuron seems insane to us," Vival continues calmly, "but he has been consistent in his ultimate goal of creating the perfect human to survive in the sea. We believe he's come to realize the results of his own program are too wild and mentally unstable. That's why he's become so interested in our program again. He has demanded several times now that we send him some Neptune young people. Of course we refused, and now he's resorted to this."

So that's why he took Bria and Robry. He wants us to go after them so he can capture even more Neptune kids. Tobin looks like he's ready to hit someone.

And you want us to swim in there and say, "Hey, go ahead and take us prisoner"? Lena scowls as she keys her question into the computer.

"No, we want you to do your best to not get caught," Vival replies. "We want you to find Bria and Robry and send them back. But we need a team of four volunteers who will penetrate farther into the fortress, knowing full well they eventually *will* be caught. Their mission is to stay on; pretend that they are willing to join Kuron's group; and, when they can, steal the cultures."

This Kuron nut job isn't going to let us just swim out of there when we're ready, Thom points out.

"That's why Nere's dolphins are going to play a crucial part in this," Vival declares. "We need one of you with the ability to speak to Mariah and her family to be on that team. You can tell them when you are ready to escape, they will relay that information to us, and the Sea Rangers will mine the fortress supports and stage a diversionary attack to help you get away safely."

Tobin and I look at each other. We're the only two who can actually hear Mariah's words in our minds. Bria can, too, but I know if we manage to free her, Tobin and I will send her straight back to Safety Harbor.

What about those shredders we ran into on our last two patrols to the south? Janni asks. If Kuron has a hundred more of those monsters swimming around his fortress, it's really going to be tough for us to get away.

Exactly what are these shredders? Lena keys in before I can.

"Kuron appears to have spliced great white shark genes with human ones to create a powerful new mutate to guard his fortress," Dav replies soberly. "We won't lie to you. These shark mutates will make your mission even more dangerous. We're certain, though, that Kuron controls the shredders through an underwater radio frequency, and we've been developing a system to jam that communication. You'll be taking some of our jammers with you, but they're still prototypes."

Meaning you're not exactly sure if they'll work, Penn points out.

I don't care if those jammers work or not. I'm in, Tobin keys swiftly. When can we leave?

My father holds up a hand. "We plan to send you off first thing in the morning. Remember, we need four of you to stay on and try to steal the c-plankton. Don't volunteer for that job unless you have strong mental shields. We have reason to believe Kuron has some powerful telepaths working for him."

With a pang, I wonder if they're referring to Dai, who is one of the strongest telepaths I've ever encountered. I glance at my friends. Dad, could we have a few minutes to talk this over?

After a moment, he nods, and we all swim from the cave and float in a circle outside it.

:I think this Kuron guy and his shredders are a major threat to Safety Harbor. I'll volunteer to stay on. We have to find out what he's really up to,: Janni says earnestly.

:I'm in, too, for all of it,: Thom declares, his face serious. :I fought the Western Collective and saw a lot of friends die, but we never changed anything. We pull this off, we change everything for people back on land.:

:Yeah, it will help people on land, but we don't live on land anymore,: Penn points out. :Our future is in the sea now. Is this really our fight?:

:It totally is,: Kalli argues. :Phytoplankton, the foundation of the food chain, is dying as the oceans heat. The seas are also absorbing more carbon dioxide and becoming more acidic, and that's killing corals and shellfish.:

:A whole bunch of life down here will die if global warming isn't reversed soon,: Seth adds soberly. :That's why I'm volunteering to be one of the four who stays.:

:Me, too,: Rohan adds.

:The gangs I ran with back home,: Ree says, her

expression pensive, :we were always fighting just to live. There was never enough food and never enough water. It all goes back to this planet burning up. Those *loco* kids at Atlantea scare me, too, but we gotta try to steal that c-plankton stuff. I'm in.:

Closing my eyes, I think of the scorching days I endured down south and all the species of plants and animals that have disappeared from there. Because I already love this green, rugged coast, I don't want it to die, too. I also know my telepathy could be a big help on this mission. Telepaths are great at finding things that people want to keep hidden, things like secret c-plankton cultures.

But I'm not sure I'm brave enough to face Dai or Wasp again, much less to try to save the world. I just want Bria and Robry back safe with us.

I open my eyes when Tobin speaks up. :I'm going to volunteer to be one of the four as well,: he says, his gaze never leaving my face. :I can talk to the dolphins, too, so there's no reason for both of us to stay on there.:

I am sure of one thing. I don't want Tobin to become a prisoner in Kuron's fortress, surrounded by Wasp and the rest of those angry mutates.

:You *can't* be one of the four volunteers,: I blurt, :because I'm also volunteering.: I decide on the spot. :And they don't need both of us to talk to the dolphins.:

Tobin has a stubborn set to his jaw that tells me he's

already made up his mind. Desperately, I search for a way to convince him he shouldn't volunteer.

:Bria will need you when we get her back to Safety Harbor. You can't leave her on her own. You're all the family she has.:

:I wouldn't be leaving her on her own. I know you'll look after her. She already feels like you're her big sister.: He turns and looks at the others. :But if something happens to me, you guys will look after Bria, too, right?:

:You know we will,: Lena promises him, and the rest nod.

:That settles it, then,: Tobin says. :We'll tell the doc and Vival that eight of us volunteer, and they can decide which four should stay on to steal the c-plankton cultures.:

We return to the briefing cave, and my father and the helper staff promise they'll tell us after lunch which four of us they've chosen.

The chicken part of me really hopes they don't pick me to try to steal the c-plankton. Rescuing Robry and Bria is scary enough. Staying on with those freaky kids, the shredders, and the twisted man who created them is even worse.

~ ~ ~

We spend the rest of that morning poring over charts of our route to Atlantea and Nootka Sound, where Kuron's fortress is located. We also study photographs the helper staff took of the surface fortifications of Atlantea, which bristle with formidable laser-gun emplacements. Penn spends a great deal of time with Dav looking at the jammers and figuring out how they're supposed to work.

After lunch, Vival and my father call us back to the briefing cave. I try not to look too scared when they name me along with Thom, Kalli, and Janni as part of the team to steal the c-plankton. Tobin, Ree, and Rohan are alternates in case some of us get hurt or killed. Tobin does *not* look happy that I was picked instead of him.

"Janni, you'll be in charge of the team as you travel to Atlantea. Nere, we're placing you in charge of the insertion team," my father says. "We hope you'll have a chance to use your telepathy to search Kuron's mind and find out where he's keeping the c-plankton."

As I look at my worried dad, I realize my strong telepathy is probably why he had to agree to my selection even though he *really* doesn't want me to go on this mission.

We spend the rest of that day packing our travel gear and training Sokya to carry the probe we'll use to scout the fortress.

After dinner, I swim to the perimeter and surface. Looking at the craggy, forbidding coast of Vancouver Island, I picture sweet Bria and smart, funny Robry clearly in my mind. Atlantea lies on the far side of the island, so I know they are beyond my telepathic range. Still, I call out to them,

:You guys have gotta hold on just a little while longer. We're coming to get you!:

The next morning, our rescue team gathers by the bubble wall with our travel gear just as the sea starts to lighten.

chapter nine

JANNI AND ROHAN carefully inspect our gear and spearguns. After they finish, my father's helper staff hands out spear darts tipped with powerful explosive charges, or "boomers," as everyone at Safety Harbor calls them.

:In case shredders or large sharks attack us, each of you will be issued one of these today,: Janni tells us soberly, nodding toward the boomers. :I know you've been practicing with mock-ups, so remember to be careful as you carry these. If you trigger a boomer by accident, it could blow off your head or your hand.:

I watch as Janni slips her own boomer cautiously back into her quiver. I really hope we don't run into shredders today. Those mutates sound so dangerous, I wonder if the boomers could truly help against them.

Vival, Dav, and my father wish us good luck, and then Janni leads us through the bubble wall. After we cross it, Mariah and her family swim excited circles around us. Four dolphins from the Safety Harbor pod join us as well. Soon we settle into our travel formation with Janni swimming point, Seth bringing up the rear, and our dolphins swimming protectively around us.

Although we're constantly on the lookout for danger, I can't help smiling when we come across a group of playful sea lions diving, flipping, and twisting through a nearby kelp bed. A curious pod of black-and-white Dall's porpoises, which look like small killer whales, keep pace with us for a time, and once we even hear a pod of real orcas squealing and calling to one another in the distance.

As we swim, Janni explains Sea Ranger procedures for dealing with various threats, from sharks to Marine Guard vessels. Clearly she sees this time as a chance to further our training. She even talks to us about Sea Ranger protocols for hunting. I'd be more irritated with her, but I'm starting to understand that Janni wants to keep us safe, and her lectures do help to keep my mind off Bria and Robry, and where we're going.

We're three hours out from Safety Harbor and making good time when the dolphins start whistling and clicking in alarm.

:What is it?: I ask Sokya. She's scouting the waters to the south of us.

:there are many shark people coming.:

A shiver races down my backbone. :Can you send me a visual?:

Halia, who is with Sokya and can't communicate in human words, sends me a vivid picture instead. I try not to panic as I absorb her image of several strange shark mutates cutting swiftly through the sea. They look like strong teen guys with elongated shark faces and sharp teeth.

:I think the dolphins just spotted several shredders,: I tell Janni quickly. :And they're headed right for us!:

Janni doesn't hesitate. :Signal your dolphins that you need a tow, and load your boomers. We have to be able to react quickly. Stay in tight formation as we keep heading south.:

:We're still going on? Shouldn't we try to hide from these things?: Lena asks exactly what I'm thinking.

:Our job is to get to Atlantea as quickly as possible,: Janni snaps. :Last time we saw these shredders, we kept calm and pretty much ignored them, and after they checked us out, they left us alone.:

Tobin and I exchange looks of disbelief. Right now we're in open water with only sandy bottom beneath us.

:But, Janni,: I blurt, :we just passed an underwater canyon that could give us some protection if these mutates do decide to attack us.:

:I'm the leader of this mission, and I say we stand a better chance if we keep going,: Janni retorts. :Your job is to follow my orders, whether or not you're the doc's daughter.:

Is that what's been bothering her? I don't have time to deal with her issues now. Instead, I call Sokya to tow me, and I tell her that the rest need tows, too.

:Mariah, we're going to try to slip past those shark

mutates, but no matter what happens, you and Tisi hang back.: Mariah's like a mother to me, and her language abilities are so valuable, I never risk her life in a fight if I can avoid it.

:be careful. they feel very wrong to us,: she warns me.

:We will be.: I hope I can keep that promise.

Our dolphins quickly find their human partners while three from the Safety Harbor pod come to tow Seth, Janni, and Rohan. I take hold of Sokya's dorsal. She surges forward, her powerful tail propelling us both through the sea. My heart is thudding against my ribs as our brave dolphins pull us toward the approaching shredders.

:There they are!: Janni says, pointing to the southeast. :I'm going to lead us around them. Have your spearguns ready just in case the shredders do attack, and Penn, get ready to turn on your jammer if we need it.:

At first all I can see are six dark shapes kicking swiftly through the water. As they draw closer, I shudder. Their bodies appear human, but their faces are impossibly long and pointed. They swim with their mouths partly open, the way sharks do. A big school of Pacific cod darts away from them in a silver flash.

When the shredders get closer, I see they have at least two rows of sharp, pointed teeth in their lower jaws. Their eyes are a flat, dark slate, with little sign of feeling, like bull sharks and great whites.

I feel Sokya's fear rising, just like my own. I give her a quick rub, then grip my speargun tighter and get ready to fire.

But the shredders don't attack us. Instead, they swim right past our team. At first I think they are going to ignore us completely, and then they turn and start circling around our group.

:Should we turn on the jammers now?: Penn asks Janni tightly, his hand hovering over the small square device clipped to his utility belt.

:Not unless they charge us. This is like what happened last time. They just watched us and we watched them,: Janni says, her mental tone cool. She might seem calm, but these mutates have me completely freaked. :They didn't attack us that day, but they did tear apart one of our dolphins when it got curious and swam too close.:

:You've told the dolphins to stay away from them?: Seth asks me anxiously.

:Oh yeah,: I reply. :My dolphins want nothing to do with these things.: It's eerie to watch the shredders swim in perfect unison, just the way schools of small fish do.

:Hey, Nere, check that out.: Kalli points to a shiny shape in the distance. There's a small triangular-shaped sub hovering to the south of us.

:That's probably the same sub they used to snatch Robry and Bria,: Tobin says, his face flushing.

:I bet someone in that sub is controlling them.: Penn jerks his head at the shredders. :Do you want to try and get a read on whoever's driving that thing?: he asks me.

:Good idea.: I close my eyes and extend my senses, but I'm overwhelmed by an intense, gnawing hunger close by. I open my eyes and stare at the shredders circling us.

:Those shredders are starving,: I tell the others as goose bumps chill my skin. :It's like all they can feel is hunger. They desperately want to eat us, but something's stopping them.:

:Or someone,: Penn says with another glance at the sub.

I close my eyes again and push past the waves of hunger coming from the shredders. Farther away I touch another mind, one that's dark and angry. There's a man in the sub, and he's completely focused on the shredders. He feels possessive toward them and eager to see how they perform.

Then I sense a different mind, one I've encountered before.

:I think Wasp is with that sub,: I warn everyone.

Seconds later, the shredders halt their circling and charge straight at us.

:Penn, hit your jammer!: Janni cries, but she doesn't have time to press the button on her own. She's too busy shooting the lead shredder in the head. Her boomer explodes with an orange flash, and the shredder veers off, its head partly blown away. Then a second shredder is on her. She tries to hold it off with her empty speargun. The creature reaches out and slashes her shoulder with its sharp, curved talons.

I lunge forward and shoot the shredder in the face. My boomer blows a hole between its eyes, but it keeps coming, trying to rip us apart. Desperately I shove it away with my empty speargun. The shredder claws my forearm, but the mutate's strength is finally fading. The creature falls away from us, twitching and seizing. A third one streaks downward and begins to tear at it.

Our entire group fights the remaining shredders now. The dolphins help where they can, ramming the shredders with their hard beaks. Intently focused, Thom fires at a mutate charging Ree. Kalli shoots at a shredder trying to get at Lena. Kalli's boomer tears a hole in its side. The wounded creature breaks off its attack and dives to feed on the crippled shredders below us.

I see one of the monsters has latched on to Seth's thigh, and I reload my speargun with a regular dart as fast as I can. The shredder shakes Seth the way a great white shakes a seal. His loyal dolphins keep ramming the shredder's ribs. I can't get a clean shot—the dolphins are in the way! At last the mutate breaks off the attack. Penn finishes it with a shot through its gills. Twisting and lashing around in a dark cloud of its own blood, the shredder sinks into the midnight depths beneath us.

Now there are only two shredders left swimming. Both

are wounded, but they still devour the dying ones. After Thom and Ree kill them by firing spear darts through their heads, they drift down beyond the limits of our vision toward the black floor of the strait.

I glance at the sub, gulping when I spot a second group of eight shredders passing it and closing on us fast. We'll never be able to fight off this second wave! I reach out with my mind, scanning them for any weakness. Once again, I'm overwhelmed by their searing hunger. A desperate idea comes to me.

:Sokya, take Nika and drive that school of cod to the east of us into the shredders. The fish might distract them.:

:we go,: Sokya says, and our two fastest dolphins streak away.

:Eight more shredders heading our way!: I warn our group. :Mariah, keep an eye out for real sharks, too.:

I glance toward Janni for orders. Clearly she's struggling to stay conscious. Tobin's already working on her shoulder and Rohan is bandaging a nasty bite wound in Seth's thigh.

:You take command,: Janni says faintly. :I'm useless now.:

:'Kay,: I say, fighting panic. We're out of boomers, we don't have time to race back to that canyon, and the jammers appear to be worthless.

:Let's circle up around Janni and Seth,: I tell the others, :and reload our spearguns.:

My blood thunders in my ears as I watch the shredders

drive through the sea. They swim impossibly quickly, their legs kicking with machinelike efficiency. Where's Sokya?

The lead shredder is so close now that I can see its dead gray eyes. Trying to keep my trembling hands steady, I raise my speargun and aim for its head. I can't afford to miss. But even if I manage to kill this one, seven more will be on us in seconds.

Taking a deep breath, I squeeze the trigger. The speargun recoils in my hands as my dart pierces the lead shredder's eye. The creature stops, but the others keep charging!

I raise my empty speargun, hoping to fend off the next shredder rushing toward me. It's so close that I can see a third row of jagged teeth in its lower jaw. Suddenly, Densil rams it so hard, he knocks the mutate away from me. Before the creature can twist about to attack either of us, a school of silver cod darts through the shredders, desperate to escape the dolphins chasing them. The starving mutates break their perfect formation. They chase the cod in every direction, frantically gobbling them down.

Ree coolly picks off a shredder. I reload and wait for my chance. A frenzied shredder flashes past me, gulping one cod as it chases another. I send a spear dart through the gills at its neck.

Another shredder veers toward us, intent on devouring three fish that race ahead of it. Thom's beside me with his speargun loaded. :This guy's yours,: I say.

Thom fires, and his dart buries itself in the shredder's belly. Two more shredders stop charging us to tear apart the one Thom wounded. Tobin takes out the first, and Lena shoots the second.

The last two shredders start back toward the sub as if someone called them off us. But seconds later, they break formation and dive down to feed on their dying companions. Kalli, Penn, and Thom finish them off.

I feel the fury of the man inside the sub. Cold dread washes over me as the sub speeds toward us. What if it's armed with torpedoes?

But the sub veers away and heads south, and I release a deep breath. Our dolphins come to find their human partners. I think they're as shaken as we are. Mariah, Tisi, Densil, and Sokya crowd around me, and I rub their flukes.

:Densil, you just saved my life, and Sokya, you were wonderful. You and Nika saved everyone.:

:I am glad you killed those things,: Sokya says as she tilts to stare at the shredders sinking into the shadowy depths. :they are even worse than the big sharks.: For once, Sokya's mental tone is subdued.

:We have to hand over Seth and Janni to medics from Safety Harbor as quickly as possible,: Tobin tells me. :They're both too badly injured to continue on to Atlantea.:

:Is anyone else hurt?:

:Just you.: He nods toward my forearm. The cuts burn

like crazy, but I'm relieved to see they're shallow. Lena comes over and helps me wrap a pressure bandage around them.

:Mariah, keep an eye out for that sub, and for more shredders and sharks.:

Shortly, we're racing back to meet a medical team from Safety Harbor. We swim in a close formation, keeping an eye out for trouble. I don't want to think about the precious travel time we're losing.

:Just how many of those shredder monsters do you guess Kuron has?: Lena asks me the question I think we're all worrying about right now.

:I don't know. If he has lots of them guarding Atlantea, it's going to be a whole lot harder getting in there,: I admit grimly.

:Maybe we can still sneak into the fortress, but how are we going to get away if he can send a hundred more shredders after us?: Kalli asks. :Those jammers were useless.:

:I've been thinking about the jammers, and I don't think they are useless,: Penn speaks up. :Janni never turned hers on, and once mine was on, the shredders stayed away from me. Nere said the shredders were starving, and they acted like it. I think we can count on their drive to feed to override everything else.:

:They did do more damage to one another than we did to them,: Tobin points out. :The moment one of them was wounded, the others turned on it, and whoever was in that sub couldn't stop them.:

:So if we have the jammers and we wound enough shredders to get them to turn on one another, and we have help from the Sea Rangers, maybe we can manage to get away after we find the c-plankton,: Thom says.

:If that fortress is full of those shredders, we really have to get our *niños* away from there, and we still have to try to steal that c-plankton,: Ree tells us. :I vote we go on.:

:I agree we should keep going, too,: I say, and Tobin sends me a grateful look.

But will the rest want to come? I wouldn't blame them for turning back. My throat goes tight as one after the other, each of my old friends from the southern sector votes to continue with our mission. Rohan does as well, and he even volunteers to take Janni's place on the team that stays at Atlantea to search for the c-plankton.

Soon we meet up with the medical team from Safety Harbor. I stay near Janni as the medics transfer her carefully into a stretcher strapped on the back of a big tow. Her eyes flutter open and her gaze meets mine. :You told your dolphins to distract the shredders with the fish, didn't you?:

I nod.

:Quick thinking. Sorry I've been so snarky. Guess I didn't like the way people kept talking about your long trip here and your being Doc's daughter. I'd go on a mission with you any day.: She sends me a weak smile, and then the medics close in around her.

:Is she going to be okay?: I ask Rohan.

:Yeah, I think both she and Seth are going to make it,: he reassures me. After passing us a new round of boomers, the medics speed away on their tows. As I watch them disappear into the green sea, a part of me *really* wishes I were going back to Safety Harbor, too.

chapter ten

WE EAT A QUICK meal from our seapacks, and then we start off again for Atlantea. We're a quiet bunch as we travel. I think each of us is coming to terms with our terrifying fight this morning.

:I wonder what we'll actually find inside Atlantea,: I say to Rohan, who's swimming point. I know he's spent a lot of time reading the reports sent back by Dad's observer team.

:Originally, Kuron had hundreds of scientists, guards, and technicians working for him,: Rohan replies, :but now a much smaller staff of twenty or so keeps the fortress running.:

:I'd like to know why all those others left,: Kalli says uneasily.

:Me, too,: Rohan admits. :So, can you tell me more about this Dai character who traveled with you guys?: he asks me.

I don't know where to start. A part of me freezes up when anyone says Dai's name.

:He was the best fighter of all of us.: I'm grateful when Kalli replies for me. :He's fast and strong, and he can out-shoot Nere or Robry with a speargun. Oh, and most girls would think he's gorgeous, if they're into the distant, temperamental type.:

I bite my lip. Being around Dai was like trying to surf a rogue wave. He could be funny one moment and sarcastic the next. He tried to act like he didn't care about anything, but sometimes I think he was so sarcastic because he cared too much. But I never dreamed, during all those weeks he traveled with us, that he could be lying about who he was. Now I wonder if I knew Dai at all.

:He probably wouldn't want to admit it,: Kalli is saying thoughtfully, :but I think he really liked Bria. He kept them from hurting her the first time we ran into Wasp and crew.:

:Do you know anything about his family?: Rohan asks me.

:He claimed he was raised by his father, a marine biologist, and spent most of his childhood on research vessels. Because his father was so excited about the Neptune Project, he put Dai through the transformation when he was only ten.:

:He had to start living on his own in the sea when he was ten?: Rohan looks shocked.

:I think that's why he's so impatient sometimes,: Kalli says. :He got too used to being independent and doing things his own way.:

Even though Dai could be abrupt and irritable, I still really liked him. I thought he understood what it was like to be different. Thanks to my scientist parents and my weak eyes and lungs, that's what I've been most of my life. Dai and I both love the sea, and he seemed to care about me. But then I found out he wasn't one of us at all, and I realized how wrong I'd been. And now we're headed straight for his home.

I think Kalli senses how much I don't want to talk about Dai anymore, and I'm relieved when she changes the subject.

Late in the afternoon, the dolphins start sawing and clicking in alarm. Rohan signals us to stop swimming, and we ready our spearguns. I'm terrified we've run into more shredders, but it turns out the dolphins just want to warn us about a *huge* silvery white lion's mane jellyfish drifting sedately below the surface. Its bell-shaped hood is easily six feet wide.

:Whoa, the tentacles on this sucker have gotta be longer than a whale,: Thom says as the dolphins lead us around it.

:A few stings from a lion's mane wouldn't be fatal, but supposedly they burn like crazy,: Kalli tells us.

We stop for the night and string our hammocks in a large cave the Sea Rangers often use when they're patrolling this area. Before we sleep, Tobin insists on checking my shredder cuts.

:You don't want to risk them getting infected,: he points out when I try to put him off.

:I bet you're going to use something that hurts.: I look with suspicion at his med kit.

:You really need to toughen up, Hanson,: he teases while he unwraps my bandage. Working fast, he gently applies an antibiotic ointment and soon has my arm neatly bandaged.

:Those cuts are already starting to close. I don't think they are going to scar,: he tells me, his green eyes earnest.

:Thanks for patching me up,: I say. I do appreciate Tobin's concern, but right now I'm a lot more worried about being eaten by a shredder than being scarred by one.

~ ~ ~

As we start off early the next morning, I ask the dolphins to watch even more carefully for shredders and small submarines. During the afternoon, we have to split up several times and hide from boat traffic. The dolphins spot one shredder patrol, but they don't spot us.

That night, the best shelter the dolphins can find us is a cramped sea cave only four miles from Kuron's fortress. I hang my hammock close to the cave's entrance because I hate dark, close places.

:All right, you know the plan,: Rohan tells us when we finish eating. :We'll leave here at one a.m. That should put us at the fortress around two, when we hope most of Kuron's staff will be sound asleep. Nere, try to contact Robry now.:

I nod and swim to the mouth of the cave. I look out into the dark sea. There's a full moon tonight topside, which makes the water a little lighter, even at this depth. Some silvery Pacific perch drift by, looking like a school of ghost fish.

Robry is such a strong telepath, there's a chance he can hear me. I take a deep breath, close my eyes, and reach out with my telepathy, broadcasting as strongly as I can.

:Robry, can you hear me? Are you all right?:

After a moment, I feel Robry's mind stir, and I feel his surprise. :Nere, where are you? Your touch is so strong, you must be close.:

:We are close. We're coming to rescue you. Where are they keeping you?:

:Nere, don't. Kuron's people will catch you for sure!:

:Not if we can surprise them.:

Suddenly, a strong, restless mind I haven't felt in weeks links with mine. :Nere, Robry's right,: Dai says. :I swear I won't tell them you're here, but *don't* come inside Atlantea. Promise me you won't.:

I've never heard Dai sound so desperate.

:I swear I'll find a way to bring Bria and Robry out to you— No, Wasp, don't!:

All at once, my link with Dai's mind is broken, but not before I sense he's in searing pain. Then there's only a strange, muffled silence.

:Dai? Dai? Are you all right?: But something or someone is blocking my ability to reach him. I reach out to Robry. Now I can't link with his mind, either.

Tobin's there beside me. :Nere, what is it?:

:Dai contacted me, and then I'm pretty sure Wasp stung him, and n-now I can't hear Dai or Robry. This weird psychic interference came between us. It's just like what happened when they took Robry and Bria.:

Tobin touches my shoulder briefly. :I'm sure Dai's okay. He's pretty tough.:

I hope Tobin's right, but sea wasp venom can be lethal. As the others gather around, I try to keep it together and tell them what just happened.

:At least we know both Robry and Bria are still alive,: Kalli points out.

:Should we continue with the mission now that Kuron's people know we're here?: Rohan asks.

:I'm not sure they do know,: I reply. :Just Dai knows about us right now.:

:Won't he tell the others?: Lena asks.

:Dai swore he wouldn't tell the rest and that he'd try to bring Bria and Robry out to us, but then I think Wasp stung him.:

Sea wasps are among the most poisonous creatures in the ocean, and I'm afraid Dai could be dying. But I can't believe that strange, twisted girl would want to kill him.

:I know he was spying on us,: Kalli says, :but I still think he liked Robry, and he cared about Bria. He stopped them from hurting her before, and I bet he didn't want them to take her this time. Maybe he won't tell the others.:

:This is your call, Nere,: Rohan says. :I understand you knew Dai better than anyone.:

But I didn't know him, I feel like yelling at everyone. Clearly I didn't know him at all.

I try to focus on our mental exchange moments ago. Although Dai's concern for Bria and Robry felt so real, can I really trust anything he said? Even if Dai was lying, we still have to get inside that fortress to find the c-plankton cultures.

:I think we have to go ahead with the plan,: I say finally.

:Then it's time we got some rest,: Rohan declares.

While Penn stands watch, we tie ourselves into our hammocks. I can only pretend to sleep. The walls of the cave seem like they're closing in, and it's hard for me to breathe. I keep trying to reach out to Robry and Dai. Their ongoing silence feels ominous. I twist and fidget in my hammock as the endless minutes crawl by.

I'm jealous that Thom, who slung his hammock next to mine, is already sound asleep. I glance over and see Tobin is wide awake, too, and staring into the dark. He sends me an encouraging smile. I do my best to return it, but I'm afraid my effort's pretty weak.

It's a relief when Rohan officially wakes us at one a.m. After we pack up our gear, we leave the cave and kick through the black sea, beginning the final stretch of our journey to Atlantea.

chapter eleven

ONCE AGAIN, six of our dolphins swim in a tight formation around us. The rest range ahead watching for shredders, Wasp's gang, or submersible vessels. My stomach is winding itself into knots. I glance at Lena swimming right next to me. Her face is white, but she looks determined.

I reach out, trying to contact Robry, but he doesn't reply. I'm still afraid that something terrible has happened to him. A quarter mile from the fortress, the dark sea starts growing brighter.

:That brightness is coming from the underwater lights on the fortress supports,: Rohan tells us, his mental tone amazingly steady. I'm so scared, my teeth are chattering. I glance around constantly for shredders.

:Call your dolphin partners in,: Rohan orders. :We'll cover this last stretch quickly to avoid being detected on sonar. Nere, is the water still clear between here and Atlantea?:

:The way is clear for now,: I say after checking with Densil.

I call Sokya back from her scouting. She moves up beside me without any of her usual tricks, while the rest of the dolphins find their towing partners. I think she senses how terrified I am.

:Let's go,: Rohan says, and I finally hear strain in his own mental tone.

Rohan leads off, his dolphin, Luca, pulling him quickly and steadily. The sea ahead of us soon turns to a pale, milky green as we draw closer to Kuron's underwater lights. I can't help feeling exposed as the water brightens all around us.

A black mass appears ahead. It's one of the metal structural supports for the fortress. Powerful lights along it point out into the sea. That support is so gigantic, I finally begin to grasp the massive scale of Atlantea.

Rohan leads us straight to a rib of rock protruding from the ocean floor thirty feet from the support's square cement foundation. We dive behind the rib and send away most of the dolphins. Sokya and Densil remain, keeping a lookout for danger.

From his seapack, Penn pulls out a small probe he nicknamed "Spyfish." A tiny video camera is hidden in its mouth. He switches on the camera and sends the probe swimming in a circle to make sure it responds correctly to his commands. From ten feet away, Spyfish looks remarkably like a real rockfish.

:See if you can contact your little sister,: I hear Rohan say to Tobin.

:I already have. She's awake and waiting for us. She

says they're keeping her on the southwestern side of the fortress.: Which is a stroke of luck for us, because we were planning to sneak into Atlantea through its southwestern entry bay.

:Have you reached Robry again?: Rohan asks me.

:No.: I don't understand why we can hear Bria but we can't hear Robry. I'm afraid if I say any more, I'll fall apart.

Ree squeezes my shoulder. :I know he's okay, and you're going to see him soon,: she says.

:Thanks.: I can't manage a smile. My face is too stiff with fear.

:Okay, Spyfish is up and working,: Penn tells Rohan.

:We're ready for a dolphin to deliver the probe.: Rohan nods to me.

The day before we left, Sokya practiced carrying a mock-up of Spyfish. It's her job to deliver it to the closest entry bay. I ask her to come fetch the probe, and she gently grasps Spyfish between her teeth. I bite my lip as Densil leads her away. My dolphin friends look so small compared to the looming dark gray structure above them. *Please don't let them run into any shredders.*

:Way to go, Sokya. Spyfish is now inside,: Penn declares moments later. He begins deftly controlling the probe with a tiny joystick. :Let's go see what's happening inside the big house tonight.:

He and Rohan gaze at the small screen on the controller.

:Things are quiet. Nothing's moving inside the entry bay,: Penn reports.

:Send the probe down the corridor to the right,: Rohan orders, :and head for that deck access that leads to the second level. Stay near the roof of the corridor in case someone comes by.:

:You got it, boss,: Penn says absently. :Hey, here comes a patrol of five shredders. Looks like Kuron's using them like watchdogs. Rohan, mark the time. We'll see how long it takes those shredders to make a whole circuit.:

While the little probe swims its way to a deck access, the opening that leads to the next level of the fortress, I keep trying to call Robry.

A lifetime later, Penn says, :Spyfish has reached the deck access, and here comes that shredder patrol again.:

:So a patrol of five shredders appears to make a circuit of the corridors every five minutes,: Rohan reports to the rest of us. :This group is heading northeast, or clockwise. The lead shredder has a camera attached to its shoulder, and that camera is pointed forward.:

:Which means whoever's watching that feed can see ahead of the shredders but not behind them,: Kalli says with satisfaction.

:Okay, send Spyfish on up to the next level,: Rohan tells Penn.

:Whoa, here comes another team of shredders, heading

around counterclockwise on this level,: Penn says. :Looks like they're synched to pass the patrol below every two and a half minutes.:

:The timing's going to be tight,: Rohan declares. :That shredder patrol should be crossing the entry bay in another three minutes. We're going to wait right outside and enter thirty seconds after they swim past. That should give us just under four minutes to reach the deck access to the next level.:

Penn shrugs on his seapack but keeps the probe control in his hand. We call our dolphins, and seconds later, we're flying up and over the rock rib. We ride on the left side of our dolphins, away from the security cameras mounted on the fortress supports. The dolphins swim closely together to help hide us, but I still feel terribly exposed as we cross the open, well-lit area.

:I sure hope whoever's supposed to be watching those cameras is asleep right now,: Lena says.

Rohan leads us upward until we are skimming along just beneath Atlantea. Its dark gray metal exterior is so new, little sea growth has had a chance to gain a foothold on it yet. Rohan stops twenty feet away from a large rectangular opening that glows with greenish light. The fortress seems to extend forever beyond it into the darkness.

I let go of Sokya's fin. :Thanks for taking the probe, and thanks for bringing me here.:

:be careful in there,: Sokya says as she looks at me with unusual seriousness. :my brother is right. this is a bad place.:

:You and Densil be careful while you wait. I may be inside here several days before I can leave again.:

:we will be careful,: Densil promises me. If a dolphin can look worried, he does. I give them both a final rub, and then they flash away from me. All at once I feel very alone.

Ree extends a small mirror on a collapsible pole to see into the entry bay.

:Here they come. The shredder patrol is passing over the bay . . . right now.:

:Everyone get ready to move fast.: Rohan looks at his dive watch, counting off the seconds.

:Okay, let's go,: he says.

Rohan passes Ree and leads us up into the bay. Trembling, I follow behind them. I wonder if I'll ever leave Atlantea again.

chapter twelve

I GRIP MY SPEARGUN tightly and ignore the blood pounding in my ears as we swim up into the entry bay. I expect a wave of shredders to ambush us, but the large, open chamber is empty. It's illuminated with a diffused light that's just right for our eyes. Two long gray corridors lead off the bay in opposite directions. Several powerful-looking tows and skimmers are moored along one side. An intimidating array of harpoons and spearguns hang on the wall above the skimmers.

:Whoa, those babies look like fun,: Thom says wistfully, gazing at the skimmers.

:If you could steal a couple of those, you could get away faster,: Tobin says to me.

:So could you guys, tonight.:

:Good point,: Penn says as we kick our way as quickly as we can down the gray corridor. With its solid floor and thick metal bulkheads, the corridor almost looks like a passageway on a ship.

I'm aware that we're passing open doorways to workshops and storage bays that appear almost frighteningly clean and orderly. We stop just before a large metal rectangular access that leads to the level above us, and it's lit with the same pale, diffused light.

I check my watch. We covered the distance in less than a minute. Penn grabs Spyfish and tucks it into his seapack.

:All right, the next patrol should be passing in sixty-five seconds,: Rohan says.

Ree uses her mirror to watch the level above us. My heart thuds against my ribs. What if the second-level shredder patrol is late? What if we're still here when the first-level patrol arrives?

We'd be in for a nasty fight without dolphins to help us. I reach back to my quiver to make sure I still have my boomer.

:Hey, Nere,: Penn says, :I'm going to hide a jammer for you guys behind this bulkhead.:

:Thanks, Penn,: I say, hoping my mental voice sounds steadier than I feel.

:The second-level patrol is right on time. Get ready to move,: Rohan warns everyone.

Penn hides the jammer and darts back to join us. Thirty seconds after the shredders pass the access, we swim up through it to the second level. We head the same direction the shredders went. As we sprint down a long gray hall, I read the numbers on the doors.

:Bria says she's in Sleeping Compartment 214,: Tobin tells us. :They lock her in there every night.:

We kick our way down the long, stark hallway, searching frantically for the right door.

:Here's 214,: Rohan finally calls out and tries the handle.

:It's definitely locked,: he declares. :Thom, you're up.:

Thom reaches into his seapack, takes out a small explosive device, and attaches it right above the door lock. Thom's our demo expert, since he knows all about explosives from when he was a guerrilla fighter.

:Bria, you need to move back into a corner, on the same wall as the door,: I hear Tobin tell her. :We're going to use a charge to blow the lock.:

:Okay,: she says. :We're out of the way now.:

We? There's someone else in there with her? Before I can ask Bria what she means, Thom sets the charge.

:Everyone, move back,: Thom warns us. :This sucker's gonna fire in ten seconds.:

We all dive away from the door. I glance at my watch. The shredder patrol will be back here in less than three minutes.

There's a flash of light, a dull thud, and Thom goes to check his handiwork.

:Think I got it,: he says and shoves against the door. It swings open easily. We let Tobin go through first, but I want to be second.

Bria is there, her hazel eyes wide with excitement. I'm relieved to see her bright smile. Tobin grabs her in a big hug. Still wondering about the "we" Bria mentioned, I glance around the small room uneasily. Hoping to pick up a stray thought, I listen hard but don't sense anyone besides Tobin and Bria in the chamber.

I hug Bria, too. :Sweetling, I'm so happy to see you, but didn't you say there was someone else in here?:

:Just Shadow,: Bria says. :You don't need to worry about her, though. She wanted you to come.:

A girl materializes out of a shadowy corner. She has large, dark eyes and very pale skin. Her long black hair, moved by stray currents, twines about her face. I raise my speargun to cover her.

:I'm not going to stop you from taking Bria,: the girl says.

I stare at her suspiciously. :So . . . do you know where they're keeping Robry? We've come for him, too.:

She hesitates. :You'll never be able to reach him without getting caught. His room is too far inside the fortress. You should just take the little girl and go.:

I study her for a long moment. Should we trust her? I try to read her thoughts, but she has strong mental shields. :We can't possibly leave Robry,: I say at last.

:You really do care about him, too, don't you?: The black-haired girl eyes me curiously. She has a small octopus shaped like a flower tattooed on her right cheek.

:We all do,: I say. :He's a part of our team.:

A wistful expression crosses her face, but it's so fleeting, I think maybe I imagined it. I keep trying to probe her mind. She's definitely hiding something, but I also sense she cares about Bria.

:Let's make sure Bria gets away safely before you go

after Robry.: The girl crosses to the door, but Rohan is blocking her way.

:The next shredder patrol is due here in two minutes,: Rohan says.

:We'll never get to the deck access in time,: I reply.

:We'll close the door and hope the shredders don't notice the hole,: Rohan decides. :Everyone inside Bria's room now!:

Our rescue team piles in, and Lena pulls the door shut. A large round portal sits along the outside wall and a hammock hangs in the corner. The small chamber is light gray, and the metal floor is a darker shade. I'm startled by a beautiful picture, painted on the inside wall, of a dolphin surrounded by flowing lines. It seems so out of place in the otherwise bare room.

Considering what Shadow just said about reaching Robry, I wonder if it's time for our groups to separate.

:Ree, our squads should probably split up soon,: I purposely broadcast on a public send. :Shadow says they are keeping Robry deeper in the fortress. You, Penn, Tobin, and Lena head back out with Bria. The rest of us will go look for Robry. Hold up outside the fortress, and we'll let you know if you should wait for us.:

Ree's gaze flicks to Shadow and back to me. :All right,: she says after a brief pause.

:Then we should probably say good-bye now,: Shadow says to Bria.

:Thank you for everything, Shadow.: Bria swims across the room and wraps her arms around the older girl. :I'll never forget you.:

I'm surprised when Shadow hugs her back. :Take care of yourself, little fish,: Shadow tells her with a sad smile. Then she stiffens, an accusing look on her face. :Someone in here is bleeding.:

:Crud, it's me,: Lena says, staring down at her hand. :I guess I cut myself on the door just now.:

:Get that bandaged fast,: Shadow says flatly. :The mutates you call shredders are hypersensitive to the scent of blood. They're even worse than real sharks.:

Tobin is already moving toward Lena and reaching for his med kit.

:Ree, Thom, help me hold this door shut,: Rohan orders, :in case the shredders do sense Lena's blood. Everyone else, stay quiet. The shredder patrol should pass by any second now.:

He leans over and watches through the hole torn by Thom's explosive. I hold my breath.

:They are passing us . . . they're past us, and they didn't hesitate,: he reports. :I think we're good.:

I'm not the only one in the room who sighs with relief. Tobin's already finished putting a small pressure bandage on Lena's hand.

:Okay, we'll see you to the deck access, and then we'll go find Robry,: I tell Rohan.

Thom opens the damaged door and we start down the corridor, swimming swiftly. After fifty feet, Ree yells from the rear, :Those shredders turned around. They're heading our way fast!:

:Load your boomers,: Rohan snaps.

:They must have smelled blood after we opened the door,: Kalli cries.

:Penn, hit your jammer now,: I order him.

:You got it,: he says, hitting a button on the jammer he has strapped on his belt. I look down the corridor, my throat tight. The shredders keep coming. The scent of blood must be too tempting.

:Nere and Ree, form a front line with me,: Rohan says coolly.

:I will protect Bria,: Shadow offers to Tobin as she moves in front of Bria.

I glance at her as I raise my speargun. Shadow doesn't look very dangerous floating there with no visible weapon.

:They won't get past me,: she promises.

Her confidence convinces me, but I can't blame Tobin when he takes up a position right beside Shadow.

:Pick your targets,: Rohan says as the shredders close the distance with frightening speed.

:I'll take the one on the left,: I say. :Ree, you take center; Rohan, you take the right.:

We fire at the same time. Three of our boomers strike

the shredders' heads. The darts explode with a flash and a dull thud, slowing the creatures' onward rush. The two shredders behind them keep coming.

Ree, Rohan, and I dive to the side to give the others a clear field of fire, but the two unharmed shredders are on us. Thom and Kalli fire next. They hit the charging shredders on their torsos, but these mutates wear body armor that appears to limit the boomers' impact. Frantically, I reload my speargun.

One shredder stops and twists around, distracted by its wounded companions. It starts tearing at the closest, jaws chomping convulsively. The other heads straight for Lena. She fires at his head, but the shredder is moving so quickly that she misses.

:Lena, watch out!: Thom cries.

He lunges between Lena and the charging shredder, ramming his empty speargun into the shredder's mouth—right up to his hand. The shredder clamps its teeth around Thom's wrist and shakes its head. Before I can fire, Lena darts past Thom and drives her dive knife deep into the shredder's eye. The mutate finally stops moving.

I twist around. Its jaw partly blown away, one of the shredders is still attacking. It lunges at Rohan and claws his arm. Before I can shoot it, Ree moves in close and fires a dart deep into its brain.

All at once, the whole ugly fight is over, and mangled

shredders sink to the floor. Lena pries open the jaw of the shredder that attacked Thom. Gingerly he pulls his bleeding wrist from its mouth.

Tobin is next to Thom in a heartbeat, checking out his wound.

:Whew, I was afraid that mutate nicked your artery, but you lucked out. I think it still did a number on some of your ligaments, though,: Tobin says, shaking his head as he bandages Thom's wrist.

:Thank you *so* much,: Lena says to Thom, her face still white with shock. :In another moment, I think that monster would have torn me to pieces.:

:You showed that sucker, though,: Thom smiles at her through his pain.

:I'm afraid you're too hurt to keep going on with us,: I tell Thom. :You've got to head back with the others now.:

:Rohan's too hurt to continue, also,: Kalli says as she bandages his torn arm.

:Then I'll stay and help you search for . . . Robry,: Ree says with a quick glance at Shadow.

:I will, too. Ree and I are the only alternates left,: Tobin declares.

:But Bria needs you,: I can't help protesting. I know she'd be devastated if something happened to her big brother.

:I want him to stay and look out for you,: Bria tells me, looking pale but determined.

:How are you going to get past the shredders on the lower level with three hurt people?: Kalli asks Penn.

:That won't be hard,: Shadow says coolly. :The shredders are always starving. We'll distract them with a nice snack.:

I'm startled when she grabs the leg of a badly mangled shredder, pulls the creature toward the deck access, and leaves it near the opening.

:All of you,: Shadow tells us, :get on the far side and stay absolutely still. The shredders on the lower level will sense the blood from this one soon. When they charge up here and start feeding on it, you can slip past them.:

:Won't someone notice they've turned on one another?: Penn asks.

Shadow shrugs. :It's possible, and then they'll send more shredders after you. But you might get lucky. When you reach the entry bay, take some of the skimmers.:

:Why are you helping us?: I ask, poised to use my telepathy to probe her mind as she answers me.

:I like Bria, and I want her safely away from here,: Shadow says, a fierce light in her eyes. :Once he knows she's escaped, Kuron's going to send some of us after her on our fastest skimmers. You'll never stay ahead of them just using your dolphins, especially with some of you injured.:

Once again, I sense she's hiding something, but her concern for Bria feels real.

:The lower shredder patrol should be passing by here in about a minute,: Lena reminds us.

Rohan meets my gaze. :I say we go for it. The way shredders react to blood, I don't know how we'll get past them without a fight.:

:'Kay,: I say. :Everyone, let's get to the far side of that deck access—fast.:

Leaving the dead shredders behind us, we sprint over to the other side.

:Let's put Bria and the wounded behind us,: Ree suggests. :Who has boomers left?:

Tobin and Penn raise their hands.

:You're our front line,: I say. :Have your spearguns ready. Penn, how long until they pass beneath us?:

:Fifteen seconds.:

If we have another fight with the shredders, I doubt we'll all survive this time.

chapter thirteen

I GLANCE AT my dive watch. Fifteen seconds takes forever to tick down. My stomach clenches tighter. Will the shredders below us sense the blood on our deck? I see a flicker of movement. My breath catches.

:Shredders are passing beneath us now,: Ree reports, watching her mirror. :They aren't stopping . . . uh, now they are. Get ready.: She yanks her mirror probe back. :Here they come!:

Seconds later, the first shredder flashes up through the deck access, swimming so fast it's a blur. I aim my speargun, terrified the shredder will scent Rohan's and Thom's wounds and turn on us. But the mutate never looks our way. Instead, it heads straight for the shredder Shadow left and tears at its body in great, gulping bites.

Four others follow, and within moments, they are wolfing down their dead.

:Nere, we've gotta go *now*,: Lena says. I force myself to look away from the shredders' feeding frenzy.

:Good luck,: Rohan says, his expression somber, then he ducks down through the deck access. Thom starts to follow him, but I sense how much he hates leaving us.

:I'm so sorry,: he says, gesturing to his injured wrist.

:We know. Take good care of him.: I nod to Lena.

:Take care of yourself, too,: Lena says fiercely, and then she's gone.

Bria hugs me next. :I knew you'd come for me,: she says. :Look after my brother.:

:I'll do my best,: I promise her. My throat's so tight, I'm glad I don't have to speak to Bria aloud. She embraces Tobin quickly and follows the others.

:Nere, you're smart and stubborn,: Penn says. :*Think your way out of this place.*: Then he's gone, too, with a flick of his fins.

I feel so alone again, but I know Ree, Kalli, and Tobin will help me complete our mission. I draw in a deep breath, hoping I don't look as scared as I feel. Shadow is watching us all, her face impassive.

:Shadow, can you take us to the cell where they're holding Robry?: Though I'm still not sure why Shadow's helping us, she's the best chance we have of finding Robry and getting him away from here.

:Yes,: she replies and swims quickly down the corridor away from the feasting shredders. She moves with a strange, rippling grace.

:Are you sure Robry's all right?: I ask. :I lost contact with him hours ago.:

:I can promise you he's still alive. But are you sure you

want to do this?: She looks back at us. :If Kuron catches you, he won't let you go, *ever.*:

I glance at my team. Their faces look tight but determined as they swim after me. This is what we came to do. I still hope we can find a way to free Robry before we let ourselves get captured.

:I'm sure,: I reply as firmly as I can.

Shadow turns left down another long gray corridor, then turns left again. I feel swallowed up as we head deeper into this cold maze of a place.

At last, Shadow slows when she comes to a large door.

:You'll find Robry in there.: She floats beside it, still studying us.

I realize why Shadow's stare is odd. She never seems to blink.

I test the door handle. It's locked, so I nod to Kalli, our backup demo expert. She reaches for a charge in her seapack. While Kalli sets the explosive, I try to reach Robry a final time.

:Robry, we're here. We're about to blow the door. Are you all right?:

I still hear only silence. How could Robry be so close, and I can't hear a whisper of his thoughts? Even if he were asleep, my mental call should have blasted him awake. Is he unconscious? Shadow only promised us that he was still alive.

I extend my senses outward, desperately trying to figure out if someone else is with Robry. Again, I pick up only blankness. I glance at Shadow. I have a terrible feeling we shouldn't have let her lead us here.

:This is set to fire,: Kalli says, and we all shift back from the door.

:You guys ready?: I ask.

Their expressions are still tense, but Tobin, Kalli, and Ree nod and raise their loaded spearguns.

:Tobin, you shove the door open. I'll go in first,: I say.

He nods, his freckles standing out against his white skin.

The charge blows with a flash and a dull thud. Tobin pushes the door with his shoulder and I lunge through, speargun raised.

I'm surprised to find we're in some sort of large, well-lit room full of control panels and computer screens. When I spot Robry, relief floods me. He's alive and looks okay, but a tall, muscular boy with stark white hair and cold charcoal gray eyes has him in a headlock. Fear and anger burn my insides when I see that boy has clawlike nails on his hands.

I draw in a breath when I realize Dai's there, too. His arms are pinned behind him by a huge, grinning kid with a wide face and black-and-white hair. A red welt stands out on Dai's pale cheek like a brand. His dark eyes blaze with anger.

:Welcome to our home.: A familiar, cold mind touches mine, and Wasp swims toward us. She's even more dramatic-looking than I remembered. Thin and pale, Wasp wears her black hair cropped short. High cheekbones and slanting amber eyes give her a catlike look, and her lips are startlingly red against her white skin.

:Oh, would you like to be able to talk to Robry and your darling Dai again?: she asks, her eyes glittering with malicious excitement. :I guess I can let that happen now.:

Wasp smiles, and suddenly Dai's words are beating at my mind.

:Nere, why didn't you stay away?: he shouts at me. :I was going to find some way to bring Robry and Bria back to you.:

He's angry with me?

:You don't look like you can help anyone right now,: I fling back at him. :And how can we believe anything you say after the way you lied to us?:

:You should have believed me on this. I kept trying to warn you not to come here.:

:I just heard your one warn—:

:Oh, I'm so sorry about that,: Wasp says, breaking in on our conversation, :but you see, I'm a special sort of telepath.: She smiles coolly. :I can listen in and block the transmissions of even the most powerful telepaths whenever I want. It drives Dai crazy, which is why I love to block him as often as I can.:

So that's why I couldn't hear Dai or Robry. While Wasp is speaking, I desperately try to size up the odds against us. The two boys hold Dai and Robry, and a blond girl sits at a control panel off to our right. Near Wasp is the boy with six arms who shot ink in Thom's eyes the night these kids attacked us on our journey to Safety Harbor. That boy has a round, serious face and watches us carefully out of unblinking eyes that remind me of Shadow's. None of them appear to have spearguns.

:We don't want to hurt anyone, but we're taking Robry with us,: I tell them all.

:Oh really?: Wasp looks bored. :Just how do you plan to accomplish that?:

:For starters, that boy with the white hair is going to let go of Robry, and if he doesn't, we'll shoot him.:

:I can hit him, easy,: Ree says. The white-haired kid stares at her, his eyes cold and emotionless.

:That isn't such a good idea,: Wasp says smoothly. :Whitey has plenty of great white genes. And Shamu here, or Sham for short:—she nods to the boy holding Dai—:has a lot of orca spliced into him.:

Sham glares at us. He has a thick neck, blunt features, and massive shoulders. He's bigger than Whitey, but somehow Whitey and his distant stare scare me more.

:I'm afraid our boys always go a little crazy around the scent of blood,: Wasp continues airily. :We can never be sure whom they'll attack when they get worked up. But since Robry and Dai are closest, I'd guess they'd probably tear a few chunks out of them first.:

With a shiver, I can't help remembering how the shredders tore one another apart just a few minutes ago.

:Is this true?: I ask Dai, hoping he'll be honest about *this*, anyway.

:Yeah,: Dai admits. :If you shoot Whitey, a lot of people in here are going to end up hurt.:

I lower my speargun, my heart dropping like an anchor. We'd planned to be caught, but I had *so* wanted to get Robry out of here first. I reach out to contact Rohan. Wasp may be able to overhear me, but I have to take the risk.

:Rohan, leave now. There's no way we can get Robry to you.:

:Roger that. Good luck, Nere,: Rohan replies.

I glance around the big control room. Is there another way out? The only exit appears to be the door behind us. I'm not giving up on freeing Robry, but for now that seems impossible.

:We aren't the least bit surprised to see you,: Wasp taunts. :Our sonar buoys picked up your patrol five miles out. We had so much fun watching you trying to sneak up on—:

:Um, Wasp,: the blond girl peering at one of the consoles interrupts her, :those Neptune kids just stole four of our fastest skimmers.:

:Well, send Rad and Mako after them,: Wasp says impatiently.

:Rad says they can't get any of the other skimmers or tows to power up. Somehow the Neptune kids must have disabled them all.:

:I gotta admit, Penn does good work,: Ree says with a grin.

:If they took my skimmer, I'm going to tear them apart.: Whitey's mental voice is like a growl.

:The bossman isn't going to be happy about Bria getting away with the rest of those kids.: The girl at the sonar scope shakes her head. She has short blond hair and a thin face. I think she may be the one who emitted flashes of light that blinded and confused us the night we first fought them. Only, that night I mistook her for a boy.

:Sunny, he's not going to care. We have *her* now.: Wasp jerks her head toward me. :Her father will probably exchange a dozen Neptune kids to get her back.:

:He'd never do that,: I declare.

Tobin reaches out and squeezes my wrist, hard. :Actually, I think he might. Dr. Hanson was really happy when Nere showed up at Safety Harbor a few weeks ago.:

He shoots me a sideways glance, and then I get it. If they think my father might bargain for me, they're more likely to keep me alive. I'm glad someone on my team is thinking more clearly than I am.

:Shadow, stop skulking around back there,: Wasp says crossly. :Come out where I can see you.:

Shadow appears in front of a nearby support pillar. I had no idea she'd been hovering there. I gasp when I see her skin shift from dark gray back to its normal pale color.

:She must have some squid or octopus genes that give her camouflage abilities,: Kalli guesses.

Shadow swims slowly past us toward Wasp. Her expression is as impassive as ever, but I can feel anger and resentment radiating from her.

Tobin and I exchange looks. Not everyone around here is happy with Wasp. I sense a sudden commotion behind us. Two grinning boys hover in the doorway, and both of them are armed with lethal-looking spearguns.

chapter fourteen

:RAD, YOU TWO are supposed to be chasing down those Neptune kids,: Wasp says angrily as the boys enter the control room.

:Kinda hard to do after they put all our skimmers out of commission.: The first boy shrugs as he swims around us.

When I see he has a lightning bolt tattoo zigzagging down his right cheek, I realize Rad's the kid who shocked Dai and knocked him unconscious the night Wasp and her gang attacked us. He's not nearly as big or muscular as the boys holding Dai, and he has short brown hair and coffee-colored eyes. Maybe it's just because he's smiling, but he doesn't seem quite as frightening as the other kids.

:Besides, we didn't want to miss all the fun here,: the second boy adds. He darts around us so quickly that I blink in surprise. Even Dai can't move that fast. The kid fidgets with the grip on his speargun as he peers at us curiously out of wide gray eyes. He looks a year or two younger than the others, with silver streaks in his shaggy brown hair and some kind of round flower tattooed on his right cheekbone.

:Hey, they sent three girls,: he says in surprise.

:Well, yeah, they're girls. Sharks alive, I'm glad you

can tell the difference, Mako,: the first boy says, shaking his head.

Despite their light mental tone, the two boys have spread out and are keeping their spearguns carefully trained on us.

:Since you're here, Rad, why don't you do something useful like take away their spearguns,: Wasp says, looking tired. :Mako, keep them covered.:

:You heard the boss girl. I guess we have to take your weapons now.: Rad moves closer to us.

He reaches for Ree's speargun. There's a blur of movement, and then she has him in a headlock, a dive knife at his throat.

:No one takes my weapon away from me,: she says with a wild look on her face.

Sometimes I forget the rough gang world Ree came from. She drags Rad back toward us, and we close ranks around our new hostage. The blond girl looks worried, and the boy with the speargun raises it to his shoulder. Instantly, tension is thick in the room. Only Wasp looks nonchalant.

:Um, Ree, let's not lose it here,: I tell her on a private send. :*They're* supposed to capture *us*, remember?:

:Hey, that was one sweet move,: Rad says, looking surprisingly unconcerned about the knife Ree is holding to his throat. :Would you show it to me sometime?:

:I'll show you how to cut your tongue out, *idiota*,: Ree says.

:Stop messing around, guys,: Wasp orders them. :Rad, just fry her.:

:You really want to let go of me, my *chica*,: Rad says to Ree.

:I'm not your anything,: Ree snarls.

:Ree, you need to let go of him before he shocks you,: Dai speaks up. :Rad has a lot of electric eel spliced into him.:

:I take my orders from Nere,: Ree retorts.

:I think you'd better let him go,: I say.

Smoldering, Ree lowers her knife. Rad turns to face her and smiles widely.

:*Gracias*, pretty *señorita*.: Rad nods. :And now, if I could have your speargun, *por favor*, and your knife, too.:

Wordlessly, Ree gives them to him.

:You can try that same move if you want,: Rad says hopefully as he approaches Kalli.

:I'll pass,: Kalli says with a scornful look as she hands him both her speargun and dive knife. :You didn't warn us that we'd land in the middle of some girl-crazy boys,: she says to me.

:That possibility hadn't really occurred to me,: I admit, feeling a little dazed.

:Guess it's your turn now,: Mako says to me. Then he glances over his shoulder at Dai. :Hey, Ice, this is Nere, right? I don't get why you're so gone on her. She's just okay-looking.:

:Shut up, Mako,: Dai says.

:I guess I like her eyes. They're like the color of a clear sky, and her yellow hair's kind of pretty.: Mako tilts his head and stares at me, looking younger than ever. He reaches toward one of my braids. Tobin grabs Mako's wrist before he can touch me.

Faster than thought, Mako bares his pointed teeth and lunges forward to bite Tobin's arm. I just have time to block him with my speargun.

:Mako, BACK OFF,: Dai roars.

Mako jerks back from us as if he's been struck.

:Ice, I'm sorry . . . I'm sorry . . . I'm sorry . . .: Mako moans, the muscles around his right eye twitching. :I did something wrong again, didn't I?:

:Mako, you can't go around biting people,: Dai says with a sigh.

:But he touched me. I don't like when people touch me.:

:You were about to touch her.:

:I just wanted to feel her braid.:

:Cut it out, you guys,: Wasp barks. :Mako, Rad, take Nere's and Tobin's weapons *now*.:

Tobin stiffens when Wasp uses his name.

:Oh yes, Dai and Bria told us all about her wonderful big brother,· Wasp taunts him. :I've *so* been looking forward to seeing you again and finding out if you're as good a medic as Dai said, or as brave and smart as Bria claims. The fact you're here does make me wonder about the *smart* part.:

The fact Dai told her anything about Tobin makes me furious.

:So you did join our group to spy on us,: I accuse Dai, but he won't look at me. I try not to notice that the red brand on his cheek looks painful. Did Wasp sting him there? Numbly, I hand over my speargun and dive knives to Mako. He smiles at me shyly, but I don't smile back.

:It was all a setup, right from the start, wasn't it?: Kalli says, shaking her head as she studies Dai. :I can't believe we trusted you.:

:We thought you were one of us. We fought together, and then you broke our trust. You are worse than a coyote,: Ree says and starts yelling at him in Spanish.

:Dai didn't have any choice,: Shadow interrupts with such quiet authority that Ree shuts up. Shadow addresses our whole group, but she's looking at me. :Kuron never gives us any choices. You'll learn that soon enough.: The hopeless look in her eyes fills me with dread.

:Well, I hate to break up this party, but I've had enough fun for tonight,: Wasp declares with a yawn. :Sham, you can let Ice go. I'm pretty sure he won't do anything stupid now. Whitey, you can let Robry loose, too.:

I can't help looking at Dai again. Sham lets go of his arms, but he still doesn't make a move toward me.

:Dai, don't you have anything to say to us?: I ask him.

He meets my gaze at last. His face is set, but his eyes are stormy.

:Nere, I'm so sor—: he starts to say, but then it's like his next word is cut off, muffled so completely that I can't hear it at all.

Wasp smiles at him. :I don't think it's a good idea for the two of you to talk right now.:

Murder in his face, Dai starts for her. Looking unconcerned, Wasp raises her ungloved hand. She's floating close enough to us that I can see the small, clear tentacles sprouting from her fingers. Sham grabs Dai's arms again.

:Ice, you already got stung by her once tonight,: Sham tells him. :She gets you another time and you'll end up in the infirmary for sure.:

:Shadow, you and Rad show our new *friends* to their quarters,: Wasp orders them, and sends us a final cold smile that makes it very clear she doesn't feel the least bit friendly toward us.

Rad starts out the door first, and Robry darts to my side. My team looks to me. After a moment, I nod. We were supposed to become prisoners. Now we are going to find out what that really entails in this horrible, cold place.

~~~

I don't look at Dai again. Instead, I square my shoulders and follow Rad through the door, and Tobin, Ree, Robry, and Kalli follow me.

:Nice job you did on our door, by the way,: Rad says to

me as he starts swimming down the corridor. :And you did a sweet job of blowing up those sharkheads, but I guess that means we'll need to keep your packs overnight and make sure you don't have anything else in them that goes bang.:

I can't think of anything to say in reply, but that doesn't seem to faze Rad as he leads us through a maze of gray corridors. Shadow doesn't say a word, but I'm very aware of her quiet presence as she follows behind us.

:Are you okay?: I ask Robry as we swim along.

:Yeah. Dai, Ocho, and Shadow looked out for Bria and me, but you gotta be *really* careful around Whitey, Mako, and Sham. And Wasp is nasty pretty much all of the time.:

:I'm so sorry we didn't get you out of here with Bria.:

:I'm glad she got away,: Robry says, looking fierce. :This place was harder on her than it is on me. There's so much primo tech around here, it's amazing exploring it. But I'm sorry they caught you, too.:

:I promise we'll find a way to get us all out of here.: Until I learn which of these kids are the strongest telepaths, I decide not to risk telling Robry about the c-plankton yet.

:I know this place is pretty scary, but it's not all bad,: I overhear Rad say to Ree. :Our skimmers are way cool. Ocho and me'll get them running again, and maybe we'll take you on a ride tomorrow.:

All he gets from Ree is a scathing look in reply. Tobin

stays right beside me as we swim deeper and deeper into the fortress. I'm trying to keep track of the turns we've taken, but already I'm completely lost.

:Here's our first stop,: Rad announces. :Nere, this is where you'll be staying.:

He's floating in front of a door with a big deadbolt above the handle. A plaque reads SLEEPING COMPARTMENT 255, which doesn't exactly sound warm or welcoming.

Rad pulls the door open and gestures to the room beyond. My stomach twists. I hope it's not too small. If I go into a small space and I can't get out, I panic. *You were dumb enough to volunteer for this, remember?*

Knowing they're all watching me, I lift my chin and swim forward into the room. It reminds me of Bria's chamber, with a hammock slung in one corner and a large porthole looking out into the sea. I'm *super* relieved that I'll be able to see outside.

Rad follows me into the room and shows me how to lower and brighten the lights. Then he opens the door to a small bathroom and sea toilet. He even demonstrates how to activate the computer at a workstation built into one side of the room.

:So, yeah, that's about it, 'cept I'd better take your pack now,: Rad finishes awkwardly. Without a word, I hand it to him.

:Thanks. Well, g'night, Nere,: he says and swims from

the room. I look past him and meet the worried gazes of my friends, and then the door closes them off from me. With a thud, the bolt outside slides home.

I'm now officially a prisoner.

Taking a deep breath, I tell myself that the room isn't too small. So what if I can't get out? They'll probably let me out in the morning. I hope.

I swim to the window, trying to fight my uneasiness over being shut in. Thanks to the bright lights on the fortress supports, I can see forty feet out into the milky-green sea. A school of lingcod swims near the supports, attracted by the light, but there's no sign of the dolphins.

:Densil?:

:we are near. you are well?:

His mental touch makes me feel a little better. :I'm okay,: I reply, and it's true. At least I didn't get torn apart by shredders. But my thoughts are whirling like a waterspout. I tell him good night, and then strip off my travel fins and sink down into the hammock.

I stare at the cold steel beams above my head, but in my mind all I can see is Dai back in that control room. It's *so* unfair. He looked even more amazing than I remembered, with his long black hair caught back in braids, his strong cheekbones, and his dark eyes.

Clearly those rough boys cared enough about Dai to keep him from being stung by Wasp again. No matter how much

I wish it weren't true, he really *is* one of them. Since he left us, I'd been hoping there'd been some terrible mistake, but now I know there wasn't.

Dai, how could you have lied to me? How could you have lied to all of us?

I turn my face into the side of the hammock and burst into tears.

~~~

I wake to someone pounding on the door. For a moment, I wonder why I'm lying in a hammock in a stark gray room with steel beams over my head instead of black cave rock. All at once, I remember where I am. Cold fear floods through me. I glance at the door and reach for my speargun. Then it hits me that I don't have it anymore.

The door bolt slides back. I slip from my hammock and glance frantically around. There's *nothing* I can use as a weapon.

The blond skinny girl pokes her head in my room.

:Hi, I'm Sunny,: she says with a guarded smile. Her bright blue eyes and turned-up nose make her look a lot less frightening than Sham or Whitey, and my panic eases a little.

:Hi,: I reply cautiously. :I'm Nere, but you probably know that already.:

:Yeah. Ice told us all about you. Sorry to wake you up,

but you wanna be on time for meals around here, and breakfast will be up in ten minutes.:

:Okay,: I say. I don't want to know, for the moment anyway, what happens to people who are late for meals.

I follow Sunny out the door. Kalli and Robry are waiting in the corridor. I peer past them uneasily, searching up and down the hallway.

:Um, do we need to worry about running into any shredders?: I ask as I swim after Sunny.

:Nah, they only patrol the corridors after nine at night. You don't want to be outside your room without permission then, or the sharkheads will tear you to pieces.:

The matter-of-fact way she talks about the shredders creeps me out. :Why didn't we run into them when we were with you guys last night?:

:Partitions are built into these corridors that can drop down and close the sharkheads out of certain areas. We contact the keeper staff and let them know where we're going, and they keep the sharkheads away from us.:

:I hope those keepers never make any mistakes,: Kalli says.

:Once in a while they do, and then it gets interesting,: Sunny replies, and this time I sense anger in her.

:Hey, your tattoo's cool. Does it mean something?: I ask, looking at the sun design with spiraling lines on her right cheek. We need to find out all we can about our captors if we're going to locate the c-plankton and escape from here.

:I've always loved the sun and I'm bioluminescent,: Sunny replies and holds out her hand. It begins to glow so brightly, I have to squint to keep looking at it.

:That's *so* amazing,: Kalli says, and seconds later, the light Sunny's generating winks out.

:I'd rather be able to shock people like Rad can,: Sunny admits. :You'll figure out pretty quickly that around here, it's nice to be able to protect yourself.:

The bleakness in her tone gives me another shiver. I realize she's studying me just as carefully as I'm studying her.

A few minutes later, Sunny leads us into a large room with a long oval table. :We call this room the mess hall,: she tells us. :You'll see why in a few minutes.:

I gulp when I see Whitey, Sham, and Mako horsing around at the far end of the room. Even as I watch, Sham slams Mako into a wall, but Mako doesn't seem to mind too much. He just darts away and then jumps right back into the wild wrestling match.

Sham and Whitey look even stronger and tougher than they did last night. Now I see Sham has the outline of a killer whale tattooed on his right cheek in the midst of curling lines that extend up to his hair. Whitey has the swirling outlines of dozens of triangular shark teeth and fins tattooed on his. I wonder if Whitey's buzzed flattop is naturally that white, and if Sham dyed the dramatic light streaks in his black hair.

:Does everybody eat at the same time?: I ask Sunny. I notice she's staying well away from Whitey and the rest.

:The bossman likes us to eat together at meals. He says it's more civilized,: Sunny says with a shrug.

:But there's nothing civilized about the way *they* eat.: Shadow seems to appear out of nowhere again and jerks her head toward the boys.

:How does she do that?: Kalli asks me in a private send. :I'd swear she wasn't in this room a moment ago. Somehow her skin and her seasuit must change color.:

Before I can answer Kalli, Ree appears with Rad beside her.

:*Dios* save me from this idiot,: she fumes. :He swam into my room and woke me up with a shock from an electric eel.:

:I thought you'd like Sparky,: Rad says, looking like a scolded puppy. :He's just a little eel and he's, like, one of the coolest pets we have around here.:

:Don't come in my room again unless I say so, and don't you dare bring anything else alive, *comprendes?*:

Rad nods quickly.

A diver enters the room carrying a large Chinook salmon. From the big stream of bubbles leaving his regulator, I can tell he's breathing hard as he swims carefully around Sham and Whitey. I reach out to touch the diver's mind. He's scared and angry, and he *hates* all of us.

Startled, I try to look at his face through his scuba mask, but the diver's too busy watching the three boys to glance our way. He barely has a chance to shove the salmon on the table before the boys tear the fish to pieces with their hands and teeth. The diver flashes back the way he came, his legs kicking swiftly.

Sham and Whitey have long, pointed fingernails that remind me of the shredders' claws. Whitey bites off a huge piece of salmon, shiny gray skin and all, and gulps it down in a single swallow just the way sharks do.

:I think I just lost my appetite,: Kalli says faintly.

I know I just lost mine.

chapter fifteen

:**YOU'LL GET** used to them after a while,: Shadow says with a shrug, catching me staring at the feeding frenzy at the end of our breakfast table. :And in the meantime, welcome to our *mess* hall.:

The diver returns carrying a box full of square white containers and places it on our end of the table.

I look into his scuba mask as he backs away. He has a livid scar over his right eye and his face is tight with dislike as he glances at Kalli and me. *The boss better get these new freaks collared up soon, or I'm quitting,* he's thinking bitterly.

I bite my lip as the man swims away. He just looked at me the same way my old classmates did. Most of the kids at my school thought I was weird because of my weak eyes and lungs, and I *hated* the looks they gave me. And what did the man mean about the boss getting us "collared up" soon?

After a moment, I follow Sunny's example and pick up one of the white containers. It's filled with a raw fillet of fish and a bowl of wakame mash that look a lot like a meal back at Safety Harbor. A pang of homesickness hits me.

:I wish we were back in our own mess cave,: Kalli says, glancing at me across the table.

:I do, too.: I didn't think I'd been there long enough to miss it, but now I realize I felt at home at Safety Harbor. There the helper staff actually liked us, and I felt safe.

I've just started in on the mash when Tobin appears in the doorway followed by Wasp. I'm relieved to see she's wearing her gloves.

:Are you all right?: I ask Tobin on a private send, even though I know Wasp is probably listening.

:I'm okay. You?:

:Okay.:

Dai shows up last, followed by the boy with the round face and six arms. That guy looks sleepy and doesn't say anything, but he does fist-bump Rad with all six of his hands. Dai has shadows under his eyes, and the welt on his cheek still appears sore and red. He doesn't even look at me as he takes a place halfway down the table.

:So, Ocho, what are we supposed to do with them today?: Rad asks the boy with six arms.

I try not to stare, but it's just so freaky when he uses two hands to open his breakfast and a third to scratch his ear.

:The bossman wants them to take some computer tests in the school room,: Ocho replies. I try to focus on his face instead of his arms. I see he has a series of eights tattooed on his right cheek, and his short, light brown hair is so thick, it almost looks like he's wearing a rug.

:I got two more of the skimmers working again,: Rad says. :Maybe we could take the newbies outside later.:

:Nope. The bossman's orders were clear. They can't leave the fortress unless they're collared.:

:What do you mean?: Tobin asks sharply.

Shadow pulls down the neck of her seasuit. A black metal band about an inch wide circles her neck. :This is a collar, and, trust me, you don't want to wear one,: she says, loathing in her tone.

:Why not?: Kalli's brave enough to ask.

:Because they're the main way the bossman punishes us,: Shadow replies resentfully.

:How do they work?:

:We get shocked every time we do something against the rules or something the bossman doesn't like.: Sunny answers Kalli this time. :The bigger the infraction, the bigger the shock.:

:But that's incredibly cruel,: I protest.

:Hey, everyone, you hear that?: Whitey smiles coldly, baring strange triangular teeth. :The Neptune princess here thinks we're all incredibly cruel.:

:No, I think these collars are cruel,: I shoot back. :Do you all have to wear them?:

:Everyone but Ice,: Mako chimes in.

I'm not going to ask a single question about Dai. I don't even want to think about him right now, but Ocho says, :The bossman has his own ways of making Ice do what he wants.:

It's the first time Ocho's looked at me directly. His eyes

are as black and unblinking as Shadow's, but I think I see a kindness in his gaze that reminds me of Tobin.

:We're not going to collar them,: Dai says. He doesn't glance up from his food, but suddenly, all of Kuron's kids are looking at him.

:That isn't fair. If we gotta wear 'em, they should have to wear them, too,: Sham blusters.

:And the bossman is going to be furious if we don't collar them.: Wasp almost seems happy at the prospect. I'm starting to wonder if this girl's brain is wired wrong.

:Fine.: Dai glances up from his food. :Tell him I said not to.:

:On your head, bro,: Whitey says with a shrug.

Nobody says much after that, and I'm puzzled by the tension in the room.

:Dai?: I reach out to him on a private send, but instead of touching his mind, I encounter the same strange muffled emptiness I'm starting to recognize as Wasp's telepathic barrier.

When she sends me a triumphant smile, I know she's blocking us. Seething, I stifle an urge to hit her.

After breakfast, we follow Wasp to the "school room," which is really just a big computer lab with more than thirty terminals. The plasma screens and workstations are all primo tech for sure.

Wasp calls up some sort of testing program on our screens and says we have to work through several levels today. Kuron's kids take their places at computer stations, too. Dai chooses one across the room, and Mako picks the one next to his.

:So, what are you guys doing on the computers this morning?: I ask Rad because he's next to me, and he seems a little less scary than some of the others.

:The bossman wants us to develop our 'natural intellectual gifts,' as he calls them,: Rad replies readily.

:Like you have any, sparkhead.: Ocho rolls his eyes at Rad.

:Hey, at least I don't have to spend an hour each week cutting my thirty fingernails,: Rad zings Ocho before he turns back to me. :We all studied math, English, and science until we reached a basic level together, and then about a year ago, we were allowed to start studying stuff we liked.:

:Like what?:

:Like Ocho, Shadow, and Ice are our resident brainiacs,: Rad replies, :and they study everything from philosophy to foreign languages and physics. Ice is nuts about deep-water marine biology, Shadow and Ocho love music, Sunny's into art, and I really like engineering and electronics. Ocho and me are always building and inventing stuff.:

:What are those guys into?: I jerk my head toward Whitey and Sham.

:Well, they haven't graduated from the basic program yet, but they're both seriously into military weaponry.:

:How about Mako?:

Mako jumps at the mention of his name, but he's too shy to look at me.

Shadow glances up from her computer, and her cool expression warms a little. :Mako's crazy about plants. He has a big greenhouse up on the first dry deck. He can stay out of the water longer than the rest of us, so he's been able to make it amazing.:

:I'd like to see it sometime,: I say. I miss green, growing things.

:Really?: Mako's face lights up and he finally meets my gaze. :Maybe I can show it to you later.:

For the first time all morning, Dai looks at me. He frowns and shakes his head. Is he trying to warn me not to go to Mako's greenhouse? Right now I *really* don't care what Dai wants or thinks.

:Sounds great,: I say, and Dai scowls at me before he focuses on his computer screen again.

:Nere, you'd better stop talking, or you'll never finish the first four levels of this test program before lunch,: Wasp says coldly. :Then you just might not get anything to eat.:

I could think of worse punishments, but I shove that thought away before Wasp can read it. After I answer two math problems, I reach out to my friends on a private send.

:Robry, what do you think these tests are for?:

:I'm guessing they're intelligence and aptitude tests.:

:Do you think we should do our best on them?: Ree asks.

:You can always try to answer incorrectly and look even more stupid than you obviously are,: Wasp interrupts us, :but if the bossman finds out, he won't be happy.:

:Didn't anyone tell you it's rude to listen in on private conversations?: Ree frowns at Wasp. :You're really starting to get on my nerves, *chica*.:

:How dare you speak to me that way?: Wasp spins away from her computer and starts toward Ree, tugging off one of her gloves.

Before I can react, Rad darts in front of Ree and crosses his arms. :Hey, chill,: he says to Wasp. :It's Ree's first day and she doesn't know how things work around here.:

:I can teach her right now,: Wasp snarls and raises her right hand. Small pale tentacles wave on her fingertips.

Rad uncrosses his arms. :You try to sting her, and I'll give you such a jolt, your hair will curl.: His tone is light, but his face is deadly serious.

:Is this the way it's going to be?: Wasp asks him, a furious glint in her strange amber eyes.

:The bossman doesn't want them hurt,: Rad replies steadily. :That's the way it's going to be.:

After a long moment, Wasp lowers her hand. :I'm not going to forget this, either of you,: she says like a curse. She turns away and storms out of the lab.

I let go of my pent-up breath.

:Whew,: Ree says to Rad. :Guess I owe you one.:

:Nah,: Rad replies. :You don't owe me nothin', but you don't want to cross Wasp again. She can make you crab bait in about one minute with those stingers on her fingers.:

Moments later, Sham starts pounding on his keyboard.

:I don't give a squid what two x plus fifteen equals!: His mental shout is so strong that it makes my head ring. :Why does anyone with half a brain care what x equals?:

:Cool it, bro.: Whitey speaks up for the first time. His mental tone is cold and distant. :A keeper's gonna zap you for sure.:

:The keepers can freakin' well zap me if they want to. I'm not doing any more of these dumb algebra problems.:

As Sham raises his hand to pound the keyboard again, his whole body convulses for a long, terrible moment. Sick to my stomach, I glance at my friends. They look as horrified as I feel.

:Whitey warned you,: Rad says, shaking his head.

I reach out to scan Sham's thoughts. He's furious he got zapped, but he's more embarrassed that he doesn't understand his math problems. I almost feel sorry for him until he growls at Rad, :Keep your mouth shut, sparkhead, or I'll rip your head off.:

I shiver as I retreat hastily from Sham's angry mind. I think he meant that threat.

:Touch me,: Rad retorts, :and I'll fry your eyeballs out of their—:

:Everyone, the bossman's back,: Wasp says, interrupting Rad. I twist about to see she's hovering by the door, looking way too eager. :He wants to see us all, right *now*, in his private conference room.:

I swallow hard and glance at Dai. He meets my gaze, his eyes unreadable.

:Are we going to be okay?: I ask him swiftly. We're about to meet a man so twisted that he spliced sea wasp stingers and electric eel genes into these kids before they were born. He created dozens of those terrible shredder creatures. And my father believes he's crazy.

:Nere, just remember, he does want you here—: Dai starts to say, and then his next thought disappears before I can read it. Dai sends Wasp a furious look.

Is my team going to be all right? I mouth the words as clearly as I can at Dai.

I don't know, I think he replies, which isn't exactly reassuring.

Dai stays right beside me, though, as Wasp leads us through a maze of long corridors lined with doors. I know I should be looking for labs where Kuron might be storing the c-plankton, but we swim too fast, and I'm too frightened.

Instead, I touch the minds of Kuron's kids. Most of them dread seeing the bossman again. I can't read Wasp's specific thoughts, but she's the only one who seems to be looking forward to this meeting, which *definitely* doesn't make me feel any better.

At last, Wasp kicks upward to a deck access in the ceiling of Deck Four, the highest of the submerged decks, which means we're about to surface.

:Why are we leaving the water?: I ask Sunny.

:The bossman likes to talk to us face-to-face.:

:It's easier on him than it is on us, for sure,: Ocho says glumly.

One by one, we climb out and stand on the dry deck, but I'm surprised that Whitey and Sham seem to have trouble heaving themselves upright. They look huge and awkward out of the water. Dai climbs out last. His face appears more distant and cold than I've ever seen it. Now I understand why they call him Ice.

:Hang in there, bro,: Whitey says, clasping his shoulder briefly. :Maybe he won't want to talk to us for long.:

I look around carefully. We've surfaced in the corner of a stark white conference room. At its center is a large white table with a dozen black chairs surrounding it. A tall, handsome, black-haired man stands before a wide plasma screen, and I can't look away from him.

He looks just like an older version of Dai.

chapter sixteen

I LOOK FROM DAI TO KURON and back again while white-hot anger flares inside me. Kuron is more tan than Dai, but the resemblance between them is too strong to be a coincidence.

:*Dios mío*, he's your dad, isn't he?: Ree breathes, staring at Dai.

:I guess there's another little detail Dai forgot to tell us about himself,: Kalli drawls.

"Are you speaking to one another?" the man asks in a deep voice, looking irritated. "Wasp, block them, please. It's rude to leave someone out of the conversation. On the dry decks, you are to use your real speaking voices."

I stare at Dai, willing him to look at me, while my thoughts tumble and spin in a painful whirl. His father is the man who had Bria and Robry kidnapped *and* the same man who created the shredders that almost tore us apart. I can't believe that after all the dangers we survived together, Dai never told me the truth, that his father was once a part of the Neptune Project just like my own dad. I wonder if Dai feels the least bit sorry for hiding so much from all of us. When Dai finally glances my way, the misery in his eyes doesn't make me feel any better.

"I read your new paper on deep-water corals," Kuron is saying to Dai with a proud smile. "Your research was thorough and your conclusions brilliant."

"Thank you, sir." I sense he's surprised, but pleased, by his father's praise. This is the first time I've ever heard Dai's voice. It's deeper than I expected, and I'm startled to see his chest is already rising and falling rapidly. Clearly he's having problems getting enough oxygen, which is weird because he's only been out of the water for a minute or two. It's even weirder that his father doesn't seem to notice how uncomfortable his son is.

"So you must be Maria, Kallisandra, and Tobin," Kuron says as he strolls closer and studies each of my team in turn. He's wearing a simple black suit with a high collar. His gleaming black hair is cut short and styled carefully. He looks more like a successful businessman than a scientist.

"You look surprised that I know your names. You shouldn't be. I've had access to the Neptune files since the beginning, and I know all about you. Welcome to Atlantea."

I square my shoulders and force myself to meet Kuron's gaze when he stops in front of me. His eyes are a dark, velvety brown, just like Dai's. According to Dad, this guy's insane. So far he doesn't appear crazy, but there is something really frightening about how intense he is.

"And you must be Nere Hanson." He smiles at me, revealing perfect white teeth. "I know your parents well. I was sorry to hear about your mother," he adds, his smile fading. "She was a brilliant mind. Your father is hardly in her league. He demonstrates it every day with his stubborn refusal to join forces with me as I build a new order under the waves. I'm glad you're here."

All at once, he frowns and reaches out to touch my neck. Tobin starts for my side, but Ocho grabs his arms and holds him back.

"She's not collared yet." The sudden rage in Kuron makes me flinch. Now I have no doubt that he was in the sub when the shredders attacked us. I've sensed his fury before. Kuron looks away from me to stare at Wasp and Dai. "I left express orders that they should all be collared the moment they were captured." He bites out the words. I see the others pale.

"We would have collared them, but Dai didn't want us to," Wasp says in a high, girlish voice.

"You don't need to collar them," Dai says, panting hard now, but he still meets his father's gaze. "We'll keep a close eye on them. They won't escape."

"You'll keep a close eye on them, will you?" Kuron snarls. "The way you all kept an eye on Bria? Ordinarily I'd trust my son's word, but when it comes to this Hanson girl, Wasp tells me I shouldn't trust you at all."

"You can . . . trust me on this. . . ." Dai gets out between pants. "And Wasp won't let me speak to Nere. She blocks us all the time."

"Is this true?" Kuron turns on Wasp, looking angrier than ever.

Her pale skin turns even paler. "I don't block them *all* the time."

"I know Ice has been trying to talk to Nere, but Wasp w-won't let him," Mako speaks up bravely, his eye twitching nonstop.

Wasp shoots him an evil look.

Kuron turns back to me, and instantly his angry expression disappears. "I want our new friends to feel welcome and happy here," he says with a gracious smile, almost as if his furious outburst a moment ago never took place. "I want Nere and my son to be able to talk to each other all they wish, and I want our Neptune guests collared within the next hour. This meeting is over."

Kuron strides out the closest door. I stare after him, totally creeped out.

I glance back at Dai. He's staggering toward the water, but his eyes roll back in his head and he collapses before he can reach it. Whitey and Sham quickly drag him the rest of the way. His lips are actually turning blue.

:W-what's wrong with him?: I ask Shadow as the other boys throw Dai back into the water. They jump in and make sure his head stays below the surface.

:His lungs don't work as well as ours do in the air. They have too many gill filaments, which is why Dai is so fast and strong in the water.:

Shadow raises her fathomless eyes to me. :So basically he almost suffocates every time his father wants to talk to him up here.:

Shuddering, I slip back into the water. Kuron's kids cluster around Dai. His chest continues to heave as his lungs fight to reoxygenate his body.

:I'm fine now,: he tells the rest and waves them away irritably.

:We love you, too, big guy,: Ocho tells him with a grin, but I can tell they're all relieved as Dai's color improves and he begins to breathe more normally.

:Come on, we gotta take them to the lab and get them collared,: Whitey says.

:I wouldn't miss this show for the world,: Wasp adds with one of her awful smiles.

Wasp and Whitey lead off, and my team and I have no choice but to follow. We swim close together. From their tight expressions, my friends are clearly as scared as I am.

:Should we try to fight them?: Ree asks us on a private send. I'm miserably aware that Wasp's probably eavesdropping on everything we're saying.

:I don't think so. There are nine of them and five of us,: Tobin replies. :I have a bad feeling that either Whitey or Sham alone could tear us apart if they wanted to.:

:We don't have any choice,: I decide. :We have to go along with this and hope we can figure out a way to disable the collars later.:

Wasp halts in front of a door clearly marked CORREC-TIONAL EQUIPMENT.

:Your bossman's sure got a way with words.: Tobin shakes his head.

:He does, doesn't he?: Wasp sounds proud of the man who created her.

Whitey opens the door and waves us inside. My arms and legs feel shaky as I force myself to swim forward first. The dim lighting inside automatically brightens, and I'm relieved that nothing looks like it's meant to inflict punishment. Instead, the room contains one large worktable, two computer stations, and several white cabinets full of drawers and cupboards.

:Do I want to know what's inside all those?: Ree asks nervously, looking at those cabinets.

:No,: Sunny answers without her usual smile.

Wasp heads straight for the table, yanks open a drawer, and pulls out five collars just like the ones Kuron's kids wear.

:Ochy, make sure all of these collars work properly.:

Ocho sends us an apologetic look as he heads for one of the computer stations. :If I don't do this, Wasp will call the keeper staff to do it, and they'll be angry that they have to suit up in scuba gear. Bad things happen when the keepers are angry.:

:And since I know you're considering it:—Wasp sends us a sharp glance—:disabling this computer won't do you any good after your collars are turned on. Routine commands to our collars are sent from a locked control room high on the top dry deck. Once your collar's on, you won't be able to take it off again. Okay, Rad, you're up.:

Rad swims forward and picks up two of the five collars.

:Ochy, send them a test volt,: Wasp orders.

:But isn't that going to hurt him?: Ree protests.

:Nah.: Rad sends her a cocky grin. :Because I can generate electrical currents, the lower voltage from these won't hurt me. A zap from them feels more like a little tickle.: A second later, he adds, :Yeah, these are working,: and picks up the last three.

:So, do the collars work on you?: Kalli asked curiously.

:My collar works all right.: Rad grimaces. :The keepers just have to give me a much bigger jolt. These three are working, too,: he tells Ocho.

Rad puts the collars back on the table, and we all stare at them.

:Who wants to be first?: Wasp asks with spiteful enthusiasm.

:I'll help Nere with hers.: Dai picks up a collar and swims over to me. I notice him glance at Rad and give a tiny nod.

:You lunkhead—you shocked me!: Wasp cries shrilly a second later. She starts after Rad, but he's already halfway across the lab. Moments later, he's through the door and out of her reach. She hovers in the hallway outside shouting angrily after Rad.

All of a sudden, I can hear Dai's voice in my head. I realize he's speaking to me on a private send while Wasp is too distracted to eavesdrop on us.

:Nere, I'm so sorry about everything. I swear I'll find a way to help you and the others escape.:

:Why didn't you tell us the truth about who you were?:

:At first, I didn't care about lying to you. I just cared about making my father happy. Later, after I got to know you, I was afraid you'd look at me the way you're looking at me now.:

He reaches out and gently places the collar around my neck. It feels cold and heavy.

:I wish you'd never come here,: he says.

:I wish I hadn't, either.:

:There's no point in putting this off.: He takes a deep breath and then pushes the two ends of the collar together. I hear it clasp with an ominous click. I think I feel Dai touch my braid briefly, and then he retreats behind the table.

:Um, Ree, do you want any help?: Sunny asks after a long, awkward moment.

:I'll do my own,: she says stonily. She picks up a collar, slides it around her neck, and presses the heavy clasp shut. Tobin, Robry, and Kalli do the same.

:We have to test them now. You know that's the deal,: Wasp says as she swims back into the room and heads for the computer.

:We're not letting you anywhere near these controls.: Dai cuts her off and Ocho shifts until they're floating side by side. I'm surprised by the loathing in Dai's tone. He seems to hate Wasp even more than the others do.

:Fine,: Wasp says with a toss of her head. :Just make sure you run a proper test on them, or I'll tell the bossman.:

:We have to zap you now,: Ocho warns us. :I'm going to send the lowest voltage I can.:

:Do we have to raise our hands or something to show we can feel it?: Ree asks. I'm impressed she can talk. I'm so scared, I don't trust my mental voice.

Wasp snickers. :That won't be necessary.:

Moments later, I understand what she means. I jump when the collar sends a burning jolt that leaves my whole body tingling and quivering.

Then my friends jump, one after the other, and Whitey, Sham, and Wasp burst out laughing. My team and I stare at one another. Already I *hate* the thing around my neck. I want to tear it off, and I'm all jittery waiting for the next shock.

:They appear to be working just fine,: Wasp says with satisfaction. :And by the way, if you try to leave the fortress without the keepers sending your collar the proper signal, you'll receive a lethal dose of electricity. You know, I just realized I'm starving. I'm off to lunch.:

She sends us an airy wave and swims from the room. Dai, Shadow, and Sunny stay with us while the rest of Kuron's kids follow her.

:I'm starting to despise that girl,: Kalli says, looking after Wasp.

:Take a number and get in line,: Ree says.

:So who controls the collars when the bossman's gone?: Tobin asks Sunny.

I notice we're all trying not to look at Dai. I guess I'm not the only one still coming to terms with the fact that Kuron is his dad.

:The keepers stand in for the bossman when he's away,: Sunny replies. :If they catch us going someplace we shouldn't or they think we're about to break something they're going to have to fix, they'll definitely zap us.:

:So they're watching us right now?: Tobin asks, glancing around the lab.

:Cameras are hidden in every room of this fortress, and the keepers watch us constantly on a bank of monitors in their control room. The bossman has a set of monitors in his own rooms, too,: Shadow replies coolly, but once again, I can feel the hatred in her mind when she mentions Kuron.

I glance at my friends. They appear as freaked as I feel

over the news that we're being watched constantly by keepers who can shock us whenever they wish.

:We'd better go to lunch,: Sunny says, and heads for the
door. As I swim after her, I can't help expecting my collar
to go off.

:Nere, we can all talk now,: Dai says, moving up beside
me as we kick our way down the long corridors. :Wasp
knows my dad will punish her if she interferes with us.:

Just looking at his familiar face makes me ache inside.
His mental tone is so earnest, I almost burst into tears.

:I really don't feel like talking to you right now,: I say
instead, his father's collar pressing hard and cold against my
neck.

:Look, I really meant it when I promised I was going to
find some way to help you guys escape.:

:Do you honestly think we're going to believe a word
you say after this?: Kalli asks him, her eyes flashing.

:No, I guess not,: he says. :You guys always trusted
each other more than you trusted me. Some things never
change.: He looks away from both of us, his mouth twisted
in a bitter smile.

None of us says another word until we reach the mess
hall. There I find the only way I can choke down a few bites
is by focusing on my food. Whenever I look up and see Dai,
I think of the insane man I just met and how much it hurts
that Dai didn't tell me the truth about himself.

chapter seventeen

WE EAT AT THE FAR END of the table from Sham, Mako, and Whitey. Once again they rip apart a big salmon after a keeper leaves it on the table. Little bits of torn salmon float through the water toward us, and Kalli waves them away from her in disgust.

:So, what happens now?: Tobin asks Ocho when we finish eating.

:Now we get a break for two hours before we have to go back to the school room.:

:What are we supposed to do during the break?: Ree asks Rad. I notice she's been friendlier toward him since this morning.

:Pretty much whatever we want,: he replies with a smile. :You wanna see our skimmers?:

:Sure,: I reply before Ree can turn him down. :We might as well see how those skimmers operate,: I tell her on a private scnd. :Maybe we can use them when it's our turn to get out of here.:

Rad leaves the mess hall, talking excitedly to Ree about their skimmers.

:If I didn't know better,: I say to Tobin, :I'd think he's crushing on Ree.:

:Makes sense.: Tobin shrugs. :How many new girls do you think he gets to meet living in a fortress in the sea?:

:I guess not many,: I reply.

Rad leads us to the same entry bay where we snuck in. Looking around the huge space, I can't help thinking about the rest of our team. Hopefully they got back to Safety Harbor okay.

I freeze when I spot a keeper watching our every movement through a wide window in the interior wall of the bay.

:Looks like we have company,: I warn my friends. One by one I see them register the fact that there's a keeper staring at us.

:He makes me feel like I'm some sort of animal in a zoo,: Kalli mutters angrily, and I know exactly what she means.

Rad, though, seems oblivious to the keeper and proudly shows us his skimmer, which looks like a short surfboard with a low, V-shaped windshield. He lies down on it and steers with handlebar controls. Built into the bottom of the skimmer is a powerful torpedo-shaped engine and propeller. Grinning, Rad sends the skimmer flying around the entry bay.

:That's gotta be a great ride,: Tobin says, looking envious.

:Oh, yeah,: Ree sighs.

Sham, Whitey, and Mako arrive in the bay and go straight to the window and com-keyboard beneath it to ask the keeper for permission to leave. After they fire up their skimmers, they race off, laughing and yelling. When Rad goes to the same com-keyboard, I hover behind him. I want to get a closer look at that keeper.

A guy with a shaved head and tattoos all over his muscular forearms, he appears bored and irritated as he sends a command to Rad's collar. Following the other kids out of the entry bay on his skimmer, Rad leaves the rest of us just floating there.

:They don't seem too worried about us escaping,: Ree comments.

:Now that we have these collars on, they know we aren't going anywhere. Besides, the keepers could catch us in about a minute on these things,: Tobin replies, wandering over to examine the remaining skimmers. :Looks like someone's already installed a thick cable with a lock on this one. I guess they weren't too happy about our team making off with four of their skimmers last night.:

:What kind of lock is it?: I ask.

:You need a code to open it. We'll have to get ahold of that code if we want to steal some of these.:

:It would be a lot easier if we could get these kids to help us,: I say. :Have you noticed that some of them don't seem to like each other very much?:

:Oh, yeah. Shadow hates Wasp,: Kalli says.

:I'm pretty sure Rad hates Sham's guts,: I add, remembering their exchange in the computer lab this morning.

:Mako, Whitey, and Sham all give me the shivers,: Kalli says, rubbing her arms.

:You mean the shark crew?: Tobin looks up from the skimmer.

:Yeah, well, the shark and orca crew, I guess,: Kalli replies. :I think Wasp said Sham had orca spliced into him. Those guys are crazy.:

:But the other kids aren't too bad,: Robry says. :They've been looking out for me.:

:I guess Shadow and Sunny aren't as scary as the other kids,: Kalli says. :Rad drives me nuts, but he seems okay.:

:Ocho may be okay, too,: I say, thinking of the kindness I saw in his eyes at breakfast. Octopuses are fierce protectors of their family, and I'm guessing that both Shadow and Ocho have plenty of octopus genes in them. :We should try to get to know those kids better. We sure could use their help to find those c-plankton cultures in this huge place.: Quickly I fill Robry in on our real mission.

:Don't you think these kids will be too loyal to Kuron to help us?: Ree asks.

:Maybe not. They hate him worse than anyone, and I can't blame them,: Tobin says.

:His collars are horrible,: I say, fingering the cold metal band around my neck.

:Yeah, and how are we gonna escape if we get fried the second we go outside without those creeps' permission?: Ree asks, jerking her head toward the keeper.

:No matter what Wasp said, the central computer system here must control the collars,: Kalli says thoughtfully.

:If we can hack into that system and disable it,: Robry adds with a gleam in his eyes, :we could escape even if we are wearing these.:

:In the meantime, I think we need to be careful around all the keepers,: I say, and I warn the others about the hatred I sensed in the diver at breakfast this morning.

:So our job for now is to find out more about our collars, these kids, and the computer system. Most importantly, we look for likely places Kuron might keep the c-plankton,: Tobin sums up for us.

Rad reappears and parks his skimmer.

:I'm gonna hang out here for the rest of break: he says casually. :You guys wanna come see our gym?:

:Sure,: I reply. We might as well spend our free time learning the layout of the fortress and getting to know at least one of Kuron's kids better.

Rad takes us down the lowest deck, and on the way, I keep an eye out for any labs that look like a promising spot to store c-plankton. He shows us into a large chamber that really is a gymnasium, complete with exercise machines cleverly designed to function underwater. Ocho and Shadow are already there, working out. Once again, I find myself staring at Ocho as he lifts weights with all six of his arms at once.

:The bossman is into us staying fit mentally and physically,: Rad explains as he shows us around the gym. Wearing weighted vests, we can run on a treadmill that rises up and down or bounce on a trampoline. There's a balance beam and rings, and even a trapeze. Rad coaxes us inside a big, round device he calls the "Bounce Our Brains to Mush," or BOBM for short, which turns out to be a spherical trampoline. Then he proceeds to perform a series of spectacular flips and twists in slow motion.

Tobin talks me into trying the BOBM with him, and it's *way* cool. We can always do somersaults in the water, but the BOBM gives us extra speed as we bounce off its sides or ceiling. I grin after I pull off a double flip.

After an hour or so, Shadow and Ocho leave the gym together. Soon I hear haunting music that sounds like underwater church bells, but it's hard to tell where it's coming from. I notice my friends are glancing around curiously.

:What's that music?: I ask Rad.

:That's just Shadow and Ocho practicing,: he replies.

:They're really good,: Tobin says. :Do you think we could watch them play?:

:I guess,: Rad says. :They're always bugging the rest of us to come to their concerts. Shadow writes their stuff, and Ocho's constantly trying to find ways to make new sounds underwater.:

Rad leads us down the corridor to a large room that appears to be filled with piles of undersea junk. Hoses and weird long metal tubes that look like organ pipes cover the walls. Near the center, Shadow plays some sort of keyboard, her long black hair twining around her. Ocho's six hands hold hammers of different sizes. He strikes metal tubes, bars, pots, and bowls hanging down from a complex, twisting network of cables and metal supports that surround him. Both Ocho and Shadow seem lost in the music they're creating.

As we follow Rad into the room, the sound grows more intense. Deep bells, tinkling chimes, and muffled whistles seem to echo and vibrate inside my head. Their music is incredibly beautiful, but it's sad, too, and makes me miss my family.

Abruptly, Shadow seems to sense our presence and looks up from the keyboard. She stops playing, and then Ocho stops playing, too. They both stare at us.

:What are you doing here?: Shadow asks after an awkward pause.

:We just wanted to listen,: Tobin says quickly. :Is it okay if we stick around for a while?:

Ocho and Shadow exchange a long look.

:If you want,: he says with a shrug.

They start playing again, and I think they're continuing the piece they were playing before, the one that makes me think of people and things I miss, like our snug little cottage back home overlooking the sea.

We can't really make noise when we clap, so we smile and cheer mentally instead when they finish the piece. Ocho and

Shadow look surprised but pleased by our mental applause.

:Did you like it?: Shadow asks us shyly. :We call that one 'Lost.':

:It was amazing,: Tobin answers for all of us. :I've never heard anything like it. But what's that instrument you're playing?:

:It's our water organ. It creates sound by forcing water through all these pipes and hoses,: Shadow explains.

:And I'm playing my Omniphone.: Ocho pats his creation. :I call it that because it includes pieces of just about everything I've found that I can hit to make sound.:

I smile. Ocho does have a crazy variety of objects tied on his Omniphone, including metal spoons and forks.

:What you just played felt so much more intense than music on land,: Kalli says wonderingly. :I could hear your music inside my head.:

:That's because you're used to sound traveling through air and making your eardrums vibrate,: Robry says, his eyes sparkling as he examines Shadow's keyboard and the elaborate network of hoses leading to it.

Ocho nods. :Squirt here is right. Down here, water conveys the sounds we hear and touches our ear and skull bones directly.:

:Do you guys want to hear something else?: Shadow asks.

We all nod enthusiastically.

:Yeah, but play something more up. That last one was a downer,: Rad adds.

Shadow and Ocho launch into a song that's dramatic and angry, with deep rumbling vibrations, metallic clashing, and drumrolls. It reminds me of a stormy sea crashing on the shore.

Reluctantly, we all head back to the school room when they finish their second piece. We have to spend the rest of the afternoon on the computers, but I keep thinking about Shadow and Ocho and their music. The anger and sadness in their pieces still gives me goose bumps. Before I came here, it never really occurred to me that Kuron's kids might not be happy.

Just when I can't bear to stare at my screen a minute longer, Ocho tells us that we have one free hour until dinner.

:This schedule stuff is starting to get to me,: Ree grumbles.

:Let's head out on our own and get going on our search,: I say because Rad, our usual guide, is totally absorbed in some sort of combat game he's playing on the computer.

We split up into two teams. Kalli, Robry, and Ree head one way down the corridor outside the school room, and Tobin and I head another. Every door we pass has a number on a colored plaque.

:Do you ever get the sense that this place is obsessively well-organized?: Tobin asks after he glances at a plaque that reads, DECK THREE: FIRE PROTECTION EQUIPMENT.

:Oh yeah. I definitely get the impression Kuron is a serious neat freak,: I say after glancing into a storage room full of perfectly coiled hoses and cables.

:Wasp mentioned that he often goes off to meet with his investors,: Tobin says. :Must've taken a bundle to build this place and keep it running.:

Before I can ask Tobin more about what Wasp told him, we pass an open door marked ART STUDIO. I look in and see Sunny's already there, chiseling away on a large stone sculpture of a dolphin. Afraid to disturb her, I start to retreat, but she looks up and sees me.

:Hey, it's okay,: she says with a smile. :You guys can come in if you want.:

:Thanks,: Tobin says, and we both enter her studio. Along one side is a floor-to-ceiling window that looks out onto the sea.

:Wow, this is really good,: I say after I circle her sculpture.

:Thanks,: Sunny says, her cheeks turning pink.

:Did you do all these, too?: I ask, looking at beautiful drawings of seals, dolphins, and killer whales that cover the interior walls. She nods, and I realize she must have drawn the dolphin in Bria's room, too. Familiar spiraling lines also surround many of the dolphin images. :Based on these, I'm guessing that you designed everyone's tattoos, too.:

:Yeah.:

:So why'd you guys decide to get tattoos?:

:We wanted to belong to a group,: she says, her smile fading. :We did them right after Rad and Ocho finally managed to hack into the main computer system, and we found out a little too much about our birth mothers.:

:Like what?: Tobin asks curiously.

:Only a few of us remember our mothers.: Sunny returns to her chiseling. I'm pretty sure she's whacking her chisel with the mallet a lot harder than she was before. :We were dying to know how we came to be with the bossman. Everyone had different theories. Mako and Sham were sure he'd stolen us. I thought maybe he'd tricked my mother into giving me up. But when the guys broke into our files, they found the legal contracts our birth mothers had signed with the bossman.:

She looks up from her sculpture briefly. :Basically, our mothers sold us to him before we were ever born. After we found that out, most of us stopped dreaming about trying to find our real families and decided to build a family of our own. Ocho and Shadow came up with the idea of tattoos to show we're closer than family.:

Although Sunny says these words matter-of-factly, I sense her pain and disappointment.

:So why don't Dai and Wasp have tattoos?: Tobin asks.

:Wasp said she didn't need to be a part of any family,: Sunny says with a shrug, :and the bossman wouldn't let Ice get one.:

I wander over to inspect a big mirror on the interior wall. :This is huge. Do you dance, too?:

:Nah, I'm too much of a klutz. That's actually a two-way mirror. The bossman brings investors to watch me work. He likes to boast about the fact that I'm artistic. I don't like being shown off, but at least he gets me all the art sup-plies I ask for,: she concludes practically. :Plus, I'd rather investors watch me through that thing than the keepers.:

:Guess I'd feel the same way,: I say, rubbing my arms. I can't help wondering if there's someone on the other side of the mirror watching us right now. :Thank you so much for letting us see your studio.:

:You're welcome to come back anytime,: she says, and I think she really means it.

:I just might.: I smile at her.

Tobin and I head out the door and return to our search.

:I'm not sure I would have turned out that nice if I'd been raised the way she was,: Tobin says after a while.

:Me neither.:

Soon the corridor we've been following ends abruptly at a huge window. I jump when a gray shadow glides past on the other side of the glass. We swim closer, and I realize we're looking into a giant five-story tank full of shredders.

:There're so many of them,: I say, shivers going down my back.

Watching the shredders circle the tank endlessly, I

become mesmerized. If they notice us, they give no sign of it. Their arms, with clawlike hands, drift at their sides while their strong legs power them smoothly through the water. Even though their bodies appear mostly human, their elongated heads, cold gray eyes, and bristling teeth are all shark.

No wonder Kuron's kids call them "sharkheads."

:They never stop swimming, do they?: Tobin looks as mesmerized as I am.

:I guess they're like real sharks, and they have to keep moving to survive. Or maybe they're looking for food,: I say, remembering the hunger of the first shredders we encountered. When I look away from the tank, I notice one of the surveillance cameras swivels to focus on us.

:How human are they? Can you tell when you read their minds?:

I raise my hand and touch the glass, concentrating on a shredder passing by the window. Its mind feels alien and strange.

Moments later, a burning, vibrating pain shoots up my arm and fills my body. I try to pull my hand away from the glass, but I can't. Instead I jerk and twist helplessly as more waves of pain vibrate through me.

:Nere? Crud, they must be shocking you. She gets the message!: Tobin waves and yells at a nearby com-screen, even though he knows the keepers can't hear his thoughts.

Abruptly, the pain stops and I curl into a ball, every

nerve in my body jangling and tingling. Still, out of the corner of my eye, I can see a keeper on the screen. It's the guy with the red scar above his eye. And he's laughing at me.

:We gotta get you away from this tank.: Tobin grabs my arm and tows me down the corridor. My mouth tastes like iron. I must have bitten my tongue.

Tobin stops when he's towed me well away from the tank. :Let me see your hand,: he says, and I hold it out to him. I'm embarrassed that it's shaking. He takes it between his own and inspects it carefully. His touch is firm and warm, and gradually my shaking eases.

:It's a little red,: he declares, :but I think it's fine. How d'you feel?:

:Mostly just mad now. The tank must have some sort of security system built into it, and I think that keeper deliberately shocked me with it.:

:I'm starting to hate those guys as much as they hate us.:

:I hate this entire place,: I say with a shudder as I glance at a nearby camera.

:Let's head back. It's almost time for dinner anyway. What'd you sense about the shredders' minds?: Tobin asks me as we head for the mess hall.

I wonder if he's trying to distract me from what just happened. I'd almost rather think about deadly shark mutates than keepers who laugh when they hurt us.

:The shredders don't have language,: I reply to Tobin's

question, :not like us. I think they just feel, and what they're feeling now is hunger. They're angry, too. That emotion is distant and ice cold, not like the way we'd feel it, but it's strong just the same.:

:No wonder they tear other creatures apart,: Tobin says.

:How many do you think there were in that tank?: I meet Tobin's steady gaze.

:At least a hundred.:

So Kuron could send a hundred hungry shredders after us when we try to escape. That's not news I look forward to telling the rest of our team.

chapter eighteen

WHEN WE REACH the mess hall, Dai and Wasp aren't there, which is fine by me. This time when the shark crew attacks their food, I follow Sunny and Shadow's example and look away, trying to concentrate on talking to the kids closest to me. I'm still jumpy from being shocked, and it's hard not to stare at the two cameras in the room that constantly track us.

I notice that the shark crew rarely speaks to the rest of Kuron's kids, and vice versa. It's like there're two separate cliques here.

After we finish eating, the shark crew heads out, except for Mako. He lingers after the rest, sending me sideways glances, the muscles twitching around his right eye again. Quickly I fill in my team on what we saw and what happened at the shredder tank.

:I'd like to give those keepers a big zap,: Ree says angrily when I finish.

:Yeah, me too,: I admit, thinking of the guy who laughed after he shocked me.

:So, you wanna come see my greenhouse now?: Mako sidles closer and finally meets my gaze.

:Maybe,: I reply, thinking fast. He looks so hopeful that I'm torn. Mako reminds me of Robry and the way he can get excited and eager about things. But I can't forget the moment Mako almost bit Tobin.

Tobin contacts me on a private send. :I don't think it's a good idea. Dai didn't want you to go with Mako, and he must have had a reason. It might have something to do with the kid almost taking my arm off when I touched him.:

:So I'll make sure I don't touch him,: I argue. :If we ever want to get out of here, we need to start making allies.:

:Mako's not a good ally for anyone. There's something really wrong with him.:

:I promise I'll be careful.:

:Here's a better idea,: Tobin says, looking obstinate. :Hey, Mako, would it be okay if I came along, too? I'd really like to see your plants.:

Mako jumps when Tobin speaks to him. Then he looks from Tobin to me, never quite meeting our eyes, his tic more noticeable than ever.

:I just want to take her,: Mako says and starts pulling at his hair.

:That's okay,: I say. :Maybe Tobin can come next time. I'd love to go see your greenhouse right now.:

Tobin scowls at me. :Contact me if you have any problems,: he says on another private send, :and I'll get Shadow to take me there.:

:I'll be fine,: I tell Tobin. I hope I'm right.

As Mako leads me toward the landward side of the fortress, I'm careful to keep my distance from him. He swims so quickly, I have problems reading all the door plaques we pass, but I do see one labeled MARINE CHEMISTRY LAB, which looks promising. After he takes me up to a dry-deck access, I climb out of the water and look around cautiously.

Dry Deck One looks remarkably like the submerged ones, with long gray corridors that seem to stretch forever. It's very clean and new, and the lighting here is low enough that I don't have to squint. Once again, we don't see anyone, but I do notice a surveillance camera that pivots silently as we pass it.

:Um, Mako, are you sure it's okay we're up here?: I ask him as I glance back at that camera. I *really* don't want to get shocked by the keepers again.

:Oh yeah. I bring Shadow up here all the time.: Mako is almost running as he leads me down the corridor. He stops at a door and throws it open, and I'm engulfed in a wave of warmth and humidity. The damp air is full of the smell of rich dirt and green, growing things. I glance around in amazement. Mako has managed to raise a jungle of plants under grow lights.

He plunges into his greenhouse, walking under small palm trees and humming happily to himself.

I follow him more slowly, taking the time to peer at tiny

purple violets and lush plants I've only seen in pictures. Burying my nose in the soft petals of a pale pink rose, I inhale its sweet scent. Next I come to a small fountain flowing into a pool with mosses and dozens of soft green ferns growing along its edges. The water's trickling seems happy compared to the endless, ominous silence of Atlantea.

I'm gazing at a lavender orchid with beautiful gold spots when Mako approaches me shyly.

"Do you like my greenhouse?" he asks, his big gray eyes alight with eagerness.

"I love it. Mako, this place is really beautiful."

"Thanks," he says. For the first time, he meets my gaze for more than a few moments, and his tic has disappeared.

"Where did all these plants come from?"

"The bossman brings me back specimens from places he's traveled. Sometimes they die, but I've gotten better at looking them up and figuring out what they need to be happy here."

As Mako surveys his plants, his expression becomes determined. "Someday I want to see all the places these plants came from."

"But those red cedars and hemlocks grow on shore just a half mile from here," I say, gesturing to some young trees that look like a miniature grove from our coastline.

"I know, but I've only seen them from the water. I've never been able to walk under them, touch them, or smell them. I haven't ever lived on land."

"Mako, how long have you been with the bossman?"

"For as long as I can remember. We used to live in a smaller lab, and then we came here when I turned nine." That fits with what Sunny told us earlier.

"Did you know your parents?"

Mako's expression turns wistful, and he looks away, plucking a dead blossom from a plant. "Not really. But sometimes in my dreams I see this woman with long brown hair the same color as mine. We live someplace green, surrounded by plants like these. When I'm with her, I feel happy." Mako sends me a sideways look. "I think maybe she was my mother. I wonder all the time if she's still alive, and if the bossman knows where she is."

"Have you ever asked him?"

Mako's mouth twists. "I asked him once, and he shocked me so hard, he knocked me out. I've never asked about my mother again."

"Who looked after you in the lab?"

"Keepers watched us. Some were nicer than others," he says, his right eye starting to twitch again.

"What do you mean?"

"Just that some were nice, and some were mean to us," he says, and he starts pulling at his hair. "Can I tell you about my plants now? I'd really like to tell you about my plants."

"Sure," I say quickly, remembering Tobin's worries about Mako.

"This is one of my favorites," he says, pointing to an ugly, scraggly cactus. "It's called a Night-blooming Cereus. Once a year it produces these beautiful, big white blossoms, but they only last for a few hours."

He tells me about the moment he came to the greenhouse at just the right time to see his cactus bloom, and the sweet scent it produced. He liked both so much, he had Sunny tattoo a cereus blossom on his cheek. As he talks, I'm relieved to see him stop yanking at his hair. His tic soon disappears again, too.

He shows me other plants he's made thrive here. As he talks, I realize Mako loves them all.

But after twenty minutes or so, I start to pant, and the heat is making me dizzy. "Mako, I'm sorry, but I need to head back to the water soon. Don't you?"

"Nah, I can stay out longer than anyone else. But I'll come and make sure you get back to your room okay. Ice'd kill me if I let something happen to you. You always gotta be back inside there by nine anyway."

"Sunny told us the sharkhead patrols start up then. She also told us that once in a while the keepers make mistakes with the partitions."

"I think they do it when they're mad at us," Mako says, his eye starting to twitch again. "Whitey and Sham, they break a lot of stuff, and the keepers don't like having to fix things. Or if one of those guys gives the keepers a tough time at a meal, then suddenly the partitions don't work so good."

"Mako," I say, my stomach clenching, "what really happens if the partitions don't work so well?"

"I'm so fast, I can outswim the sharkheads easy, but the other kids, they gotta stay and fight 'em."

"Do they always win?"

"No, they don't always win," he says, and the pain I hear in his voice makes me want to cry for him. He crosses his arms and begins to rock silently.

I clear my throat. "I'm so sorry I made you sad, but I have to go back now. I'm sure I can find my way. You stay with your plants."

Mako doesn't reply. Doubting he's even heard me, I leave and shut his greenhouse's door quietly. The cold lens of the camera tracks me again as I stride down the long hall and dive back into the cool water.

I've just made it to the first corridor intersection when I hear Mako call my name and see him racing after me. He cuts through the water as fast as a real mako shark, which are like the racehorses of the sea.

I feel bad when he catches up and I see that his face is twitching again. We don't say much as we work our way back through the maze of gray hallways to my room, and we pass the marine chemistry lab I saw earlier. I'll definitely have to come back this way as soon as I can to check it out.

Mako opens my door for me and then floats beside it looking uncomfortable. I think I could have found my way back on my own, but I'm grateful for Mako's company.

:Thanks again for letting me see your plants.:

:You're welcome. Nere, please d-don't be too mad at Ice,: Mako says in a rush. :He didn't have any choice about lying to you guys, and I think he really likes you.:

I stare at Mako, my thoughts all tangled up like an abandoned fishing net. Does Dai really like me? He sure hasn't acted like it since I got here, and I'm not sure if I like him anymore. How can I like someone I'm not even certain I know?

Then Mako closes the door, and the outside bolt slides home.

I'm locked in again.

I have to think about something else besides how small and tight my room feels all of a sudden. Taking deep breaths, I swim over to the window and stare out into the artificially lit sea. Mentally, I reach out to Dai. Once again, I feel only muffled blankness, so Wasp is still blocking us.

I sigh, gazing at the milky-green ocean. I would have liked to ask Dai some questions about his friend Mako. As angry as I am with Dai, I still miss him.

chapter nineteen

THE FEEL OF THE cold collar around my neck keeps me awake for hours, the heavy weight of it pressing on me. I feel more closed in and trapped than ever. I keep telling myself that the collar is only supposed to zap me if I break the rules, but I can't help expecting it to shock me again.

It seems like I've *just* fallen asleep when Shadow knocks on my door to take me to breakfast.

:You okay?: she asks. Her face is as still as always, but I see sympathy in her unblinking eyes.

:Yeah.:

:You'll get used to it in time,: she says, her gaze flicking from my face to my collar. :And if you're careful, they'll hardly ever zap you.:

I think she's trying to make me feel better, but her words don't really help.

At breakfast, Sham, Mako, and Whitey wrestle and mess around like nothing happened last night, but the other kids don't say much. I sense they're sorry we have to wear collars now, too.

For some reason, our breakfast is late. After a while, the

boys get tired of their wrestling. My heart falls when I see Sham straighten up from pinning Mako, and his gaze focuses on Tobin.

:That collar looks real pretty on you, Tobin,: Sham says, his eyes gleaming. More and more I can see the killer whale in Sham. Orcas get bored easily, and they hunt in packs.

:Don't even go there, Sham,: Shadow says, swimming closer to Tobin.

:Hey, guys, check this out.: Sham grins at the other boys. :Shadow has a new friend.:

:I hope I have several new friends,: she replies evenly.

I glance at Shadow, surprised by her words.

:Well, I say Tobin's worse than a spineless jelly if he lets a girl do his talking for him,: Sham taunts him.

:She doesn't have to talk for me,: Tobin replies. :What's on your mind?:

Sham lunges over the table and floats with his face three inches from Tobin's, big round teeth bared in a ferocious smile. :Let's talk about how much I hate your face.:

Tobin doesn't flinch, but his skin pales. :That's not exactly the first thing I wanted to talk about,: he replies, his mental voice amazingly steady, :but we can go there if you really want to.:

:Oh, yeah, I really want to,: Sham mimics nastily. :I also wanna show you how much we don't like you here messing with our pod.:

Kalli, Ree, and I exchange panicked glances. What are we going to do if he goes after Tobin? Sham is HUGE!

There's a blur of motion, and Dai's at the table. He grabs Sham around the waist and throws him across the room. Before Sham can launch himself at Dai, Whitey grabs his arms.

:Lay off Tobin,: Dai says, his face deadly serious. :Lay off all the newbies.:

:Or what?: Sham looks furious enough to tear Dai apart.

:Or . . . I'll have to challenge you to a Power Match again.:

Sham looks stunned for a second, and then throws his head back and laughs. For some reason, the rest of Kuron's kids think this is hilarious, and they all crack up, too. Whitey lets go of Sham's arms. I glance at Sunny and Shadow, reassured to see even they are smiling. Whitey and Mako raise their fists and start chanting, :Power Match, Power Match, Power Match!:

:Bro, you're crazy.: Sham shakes his head. :I almost broke your arm last time.:

:I challenge you to a Power Match right now,: Dai says with a stubborn look I know only too well.

:It's your arm,: Sham says with a toothy grin.

:Whitey, ref us?: Dai asks.

:Oh, yeah.: Whitey's mouth lifts in a real smile.

:Ocho, you'd better tell the keepers to hold up breakfast for another few minutes,: Dai tells him.

:You got it,: Ocho says and swims to a nearby com-station. A keeper, one I've never seen before, appears on the screen.

I'm startled to see Dai and Sham both lie on the table, their legs spread wide. They reach for each other's right hand, and I finally understand. A "Power Match" is just an arm wrestling match. But Dai looks so small compared to Sham's huge bulk.

:Is he going to break Dai's arm?: I ask Sunny.

:Probably not.:

Sunny's reply doesn't really reassure me.

Whitey gives them the signal to start. Sham's muscles bunch, and Dai's arm is slammed backward. Whitey lies alongside both guys so he can call the moment the back of Dai's hand touches the table. At first, the match looks like it's going to be over in three seconds, but somehow Sham can't force Dai's arm down the last few inches. His broad face contorts with effort, the muscles strain in his massive arm and shoulder, and Sham still can't pin Dai's hand.

Kuron's kids gather around the two boys, yelling and shouting, making a psychic din so loud my head pounds. Sunny, Rad, Mako, and Ocho all root for Dai, and Wasp roots for Sham along with Whitey.

:You know Dai's doing this just to keep Sham from hurting Tobin,: Shadow says, giving me a serious look.

:I figured as much.:

:He does care about you. He cares about all of you.:

:Then he shouldn't have lied to us about who he was.:

:You would have done what he did, if you faced his choices,: Shadow persists. :You and Dai are more alike than you realize. He leads us reluctantly, just as you lead your friends.:

:I never would have lied to people I cared about, not the way he did.:

:He had no other option.:

:Mako told me that, too, and I still don't believe it,: I say. :Anyway, I don't really want to talk about Dai right now.:

But when I see Dai's wrist begin to bend at a painful angle, I can't help asking Shadow, :Will the keepers stop this before Dai gets hurt?:

:Since Sham and Dai aren't going to hurt anyone except each other, the keepers probably won't do anything,: she says, resentment back in her tone.

I glance at the com-screen. Two keepers are watching us now, and they're grinning over the Power Match, but not in a nice way. One guy is holding a fist full of money in his hand, and my stomach lurches when I realize they're betting on the outcome.

Angrily, I turn away from the screen and focus on the match. Sham's face is as red as a boiled lobster now. Dai's is cool and focused, but he is breathing harder and his arm is starting to shake. An endless minute later, Dai's hand finally hits the table. Whitey calls the match, much to my relief. Sham grins and grabs Dai in a rough hug, and then turns away to receive slaps and punches of congratulations from Whitey, Mako, and Ocho. Dai receives just as many, even though he lost.

:You gotta give Ice credit. He is one stubborn sucker,: I overhear Sham say to Whitey.

:I can't believe Dai held on as long as he did,: Kalli says to Rad.

:And Sham's even stronger than Whitey,: Rad says, shaking his head.

Dai's challenge has completely changed the atmosphere. A keeper finally arrives with breakfast, and both groups talk easily as they eat. Dai jokes with everyone, but he doesn't use his right arm to eat, and I know he's right-handed.

:We've gotta head to school now,: Ocho says when we finish breakfast.

:But we've got permission to take you outside after lunch today,: Rad says. :The bossman wants each of you to have your own skimmer. We'll teach you how to ride them.:

In the computer lab, we face another round of tests, but this time my questions are mostly about marine biology and oceanography. When I get an answer wrong, the program takes me to a lesson that teaches me the correct answer. As I work, I wonder if Robry could use the computer to generate a list of labs we should search. We need a plan for finding the c-plankton in this huge place. I'm also very aware that Dai uses only his left hand to type.

We come face-to-face as we file out of the school room to head to lunch.

:Is your wrist going to be okay?: I can't help blurting.

:Worrying about me again?: Dai lifts an eyebrow at me.

My cheeks burn. :Yeah, that was dumb. I forgot you have a bunch of really sweet friends like Wasp to look after you.:

:Actually, some of us do look after one another,: he says. :I did strain my wrist, but I heal quickly. It feels better already.: There's almost a smile in his eyes as he looks at me.

:Thanks for keeping Sham away from Tobin.:

:You're welcome,: Dai says, his gaze turning cool. :I know you like him.:

:I like everyone on my team,: I reply, and I don't speak to Dai again during lunch.

Even though I'm annoyed with him, I am relieved and grateful to Dai that Sham doesn't try to pick another fight with Tobin. After we finish eating and the others file out of the mess hall, I pull Robry and Tobin aside.

:Could you stay,: I ask Robry, :and hit the computer to look for a map of the fortress? We need to make a list of labs to narrow our search for the c-plankton, and then we can check them off after we've searched them.:

:Sure.: Robry nods. :And I'll look for a way to disable these collars. But I'm gonna miss driving one of those skimmers.:

:I bet you'll get another shot.: I smile at Robry.

:I'll stay with him,: Tobin offers. :After my run-in with Sham, we should probably avoid being alone around here whenever we can.:

:Thanks, guys, and good luck.:

I hurry after the others to the entry bay. We watch as, one by one, Kuron's kids communicate with a surly keeper, making sure their collars are reset to allow them to go outside. Then our own are reset as well.

:Today we can range five miles from base,: Ocho tells us.

:What happens if we go farther than five miles?: Ree asks.

:You'll get one warning zap, and then you'd better turn around,: he says so gravely that I doubt any of us will go beyond that five-mile limit.

:What if we don't want to get that warning shock?: Kalli asks.

:The skimmers have directional systems that will let you know exactly how far away you are from Atlantea,: Rad replies this time. :So if you pay attention, you don't have to worry about getting zapped.:

:What are those guys going to do?: I ask, watching Whitey, Sham, Mako, Wasp, and Ocho as they take powerful spearguns down from racks.

:They're going hunting again,: Shadow says.

:But Ocho doesn't seem the type to like killing things,: I say.

:He's not, but he likes to look out for Wasp,: Sunny replies.

:She doesn't seem like she needs *anyone* looking out for her.:

:I know, but Ocho's had a crush on Wasp ever since they were little.:

I stare at Sunny. :Does she like him back?:

Sunny looks at me like I'm crazy. :Nah, can't you tell? She's way gone on Dai. That's why she hates your guts. Well, she hates just about everyone anyway, but that's why she hates your guts in particular.:

:Um, thanks for letting me know . . . I think,: I say.

:Nere.: Shadow contacts me on a private send the moment the other group speeds off. :Sometimes Sham and Whitey hunt dolphins. Bria told me about your dolphin, the one that followed her here. If any more of your pod are near—:

I ignore the rest of Shadow's send and close my eyes, reaching out to Sokya and Densil before it's too late.

chapter twenty

:**SOKYA, DENSIL,** stay far away from here until tonight.: I send an urgent call to my friends. :Some of the kids here are going hunting, and they kill dolphins.:

:we will stay away,: Densil assures me. The weakness of his mental touch tells me that he's nowhere near us right now.

I open my eyes again. I probably just made it *way* too clear to Shadow that some of our pod is still in the area. :Thanks for the warning,: I say stiffly.

:You're welcome, Nere Hanson. Some of us would never hurt dolphins,: she says, giving me one of her long, unblinking looks, and then she glides away to her own skimmer.

I look after Shadow. I'm still not sure we should trust any of these kids, but I'm definitely grateful for her warning.

With great enthusiasm, Rad and Sunny start teaching us how to drive our new skimmers. The controls are simple. Twist the grips backward, the skimmers go faster. Shove the right grip forward, the skimmers turn to the left, and vice versa.

Soon we're outside the fortress, making careful loops around its network of massive metal supports and startling the hundreds of fish that hide inside them. Well, *I'm* making careful loops. In about a minute, Ree and Kalli take their

skimmers up to full speed and fly over and around the supports like dolphins with orcas on their tails.

Dai, I'm irritated to see, is quietly following me, so I crank
up the speed, and soon I'm driving as fast as the others.

The skimmers are really cool. But I still think it's a bigger rush to be pulled by a dolphin. Pointing my skimmer
away from the fortress, I head off to study the terrain around
Atlantea. We might need to know some good places to hide
during our escape.

Ton, the big Pacific white-sided dolphin who accompa-
nied Dai on our journey, appears and keeps pace beside my
skimmer. I wave and smile, trying to project how happy I
am to see him again. Even though Ton doesn't understand
human speech, he flips his head at me and performs a very
nice barrel roll around my skimmer.

Shortly after Ton joins us, Dai brings his skimmer up
even with mine. :Nere, we need to talk.:

:Yeah,: I admit with a sigh. A part of me never wants to
talk to Dai again, but I know I have to. While Wasp is off
hunting with the shark crew, this is a chance for Dai and
me to finally have a conversation without her listening in.

I park my skimmer on an open patch of sand and Dai
does the same.

:So, talk.: I swim up to Dai, cross my arms, and glare
at him.

Dai watches me for a long moment, his expression wary.

:Look, my dad wanted to find out what you Neptune kids were like, how smart you were, and how quickly you would adapt to the ocean. So he sent me down the coast to find a group of you to spy on, and that's what I did. I was just following his orders.:

:But you did more than that,: I say, struggling to keep my mental voice calm. :You helped us and you fought with us. We thought you were a part of our team. Then we found out you weren't really part of the Neptune Project, *and* your friends took Bria and Robry.:

Dai tugs on the end of one of his braids. :I was working on a way to get Bria and Robry back to you. You've got to believe me.:

:How can I believe anything you say now? It was all a big lie, everything you said to us—and me.:

:But it wasn't *all* a lie, Nere. I never wanted to hurt you and I never meant for any of you to risk your lives or your freedom by coming here.:

:Then you should have told us the truth.:

:I wanted to. I almost did the night after we first ran into Wasp, but then you guys acted like Wasp and the rest of my friends were complete freaks.:

:Well, yeah. About one minute after we ran into them, they threatened to kill us, and then they wanted to eat one of our dolphins. That's not exactly normal.:

:We haven't exactly been raised in a normal environment.

But you and your friends showed me there's a different way we could live. I wanted to come back here and show the others we could be different.:

:Good luck with that,: I murmur, picturing the way Whitey, Mako, and Sham tore into their breakfast this morning and how close Sham came to tearing Tobin apart. I wonder if we should tell him why we're really here. I'm starting to trust Shadow and Ocho, but I just don't know if I can trust Dai ever again.

:So, I get it. You can forgive and trust everyone else but me,: Dai says.

I draw in a breath. Dai's a strong hereditary telepath like me. Unless I shield carefully, he can pick up my thoughts just the way Wasp can.

:You know how I feel about you reading my mind. This discussion is over,: I say tightly and swim over to my skimmer.

Dai darts in front of it and grips my handlebars to keep me from driving away. :No, it isn't, not yet. There's one more thing. If Mako asks you to go anywhere with him alone, you've got to say no.:

:I don't understand why you're so worried about him. He seems really sweet.:

:I'm not sure any of us would call Mako sweet, and he's not the most stable kid.:

:So he's wound a little tightly. I'm sure he'd never hurt me.:

:Nere, you don't really know anything about any of us.

Mako's best friend, Kimi, was killed two years ago when the keepers 'accidentally' turned the sharkheads loose on us, and her death got to him. He blames himself because he used his speed to get away and didn't stay to help Kimi fight them off. He's been getting more anxious and weird since then. He injured a keeper so badly nine months ago that they had to amputate the guy's arm. Right now Mako's on serious probation.:

:Mako bit off someone's arm? Y-you're not saying this just to scare me?:

:Why do you think there are only nine of us left in this great big fortress?:

:I d-don't know.: From Dai's bleak expression, I have a hunch I don't want to hear what he's going to say next.

:We're all that's left. There were more than fifty of us when we were little.:

:What happened to the others?:

:Let's just say my father is a big believer in natural selection.:

:I don't understand.:

:My father left us without much supervision when we were younger, and over time, we killed one another off. Most of us didn't really mean to hurt anyone, but kids like Mako have so much shark spliced into them that they can't control themselves.:

:Didn't your father know what was happening?:

:He was off doing research and raising money. What I

told you about myself is mostly true. Part of the time he kept me with him as he sailed around the world, and the rest I spent with the other kids at a large research facility in the Philippines. When I turned twelve, this place was finished, and he and I came to live here. That's when Shadow and Ocho asked me to talk to him. I made my father see we needed more supervision, or he wouldn't have any subjects left in his big experiment.:

Dai pauses and tugs on one of his braids again. :But I'm not sure I should have said anything to him.:

:Why?:

:Because his solution, the collars and the security cameras, was almost worse than the problem.:

:But you had to do something.:

:Now I'm not so sure. You see, the survivors had already made some very effective alliances. Rad, Sunny, Shadow, and Ocho look out for one another, and Sham and Whitey are a team.:

:What about Mako?:

:I look out for Mako, and Wasp doesn't need anyone to protect her.:

Dai floats there, looking so alone. :Who looks out for you?: I ask.

:My father, I guess. He considers me his greatest achievement.: Dai's mouth twists in a sarcastic smile. :He spent years trying to create the perfect human to rule the seas, and he's sure I'm it. The other kids know he'd have them killed if they seriously hurt me.:

I shudder at the matter-of-fact way Dai speaks of life and death. He once told me things were different in the world he came from. Now I'm starting to understand what he meant.

:I'm sorry,: I say, and I am. His dad seems so ruthless, and Dai must have lost so many friends over the years.

:The last thing I want is for you to feel sorry for me,: Dai says, his dark brows drawing together. He spins away and drives off on his skimmer, Ton following him.

I stare at the marks his skimmer left in the sand. After the way Dai lied to me—and to us all—I can't still like him. So why do I want to burst into tears?

~ ~ ~

As soon as we return to Atlantea, I go to Robry's room to see if he and Tobin have made any progress hacking into Kuron's computer system.

:Yeah, I'm in,: Robry says, looking smug. :I even got access to some of Kuron's personal files.:

:How'd you pull that off?:

:He figured out that Kuron's password is 'Poseidon,' plus the first four digits of pi, in about ten minutes.: Tobin shakes his head.

:The guy has to be into his Greek and Roman mythology,

based on the fact that his sub is named 'Triton' and this fortress is named 'Atlantea,': Robry says, his eyes dancing. :I bet he even helped to name the Neptune Project. And he's such a perfectionist, his use of pi is evident throughout his design of Atlantea.:

:Sometimes I have *no* idea what you're talking about.: I roll my eyes at Robry. :Guess I'll have to take your word for it. So, what'd you find out?: I ask.

Robry's expression sobers. :I haven't found a way to disable our collars yet, but I did discover that Kuron has been watching Safety Harbor closely. In his notes, he writes stuff like, 'Neptune subjects appear to be more emotionally stable and better socially adjusted than my own.':

:If he's talking about Sham, Wasp, and Whitey, I have to agree with him,: Tobin says.

:Some of the time, Kuron sounds like a brilliant scientist who truly cares about the future of the world,: Robry plunges on. :Then he goes off on these crazy rants about how he wants to build a new and better civilization under the waves, a civilization that only he is fit to rule. But this is the scariest part. I found all kinds of photos and maps of Safety Harbor in his personal files. Looks like Kuron's been spying on our home base even more carefully than Dr. Hanson's observers have been spying on him.:

I gaze at Robry's computer screen, my belly tightening in fear. Someone has created a perfect chart of Safety Harbor, including its caves and depths, and the bubble wall and tidal generators.

:This isn't good,: I say.

:I doubt he's planning to stop by for a friendly visit,: Tobin adds grimly.

:Robry, keep looking through Kuron's files when you can,: I say, :and if you find any evidence he's actually planning an attack on Safety Harbor, we'll send one of the dolphins back to warn them right away.:

I can't bear to think of what might happen if Kuron turns his shredders loose on Safety Harbor.

~~~

We tell Kalli and Ree what Robry found in Kuron's computer and divide up the list that Robry made of the most likely hiding spots. When we're not in the school room, we constantly search for the c-plankton. We know cameras follow our movements, so we do our best to look like we aren't looking for something, which isn't easy.

:Kuron's so into his labeling, we're probably going to find a drawer labeled 'c-plankton cultures,': Tobin says one afternoon when the five of us have a rare moment together while Wasp is off hunting.

:The problem is finding the right drawer,: Kalli says, shaking her head. :This place is mongo, and it has a ton of labs, cabinets, and drawers. And too many of them are behind doors marked 'Prohibited Area.':

:So what happens to us if we're caught in one of those areas?: Ree asks, a gleam in her eye.

:Best guess, we get a scary lecture and a zap from the bossman,: Tobin says.

I swallow and try not to think of the nasty zap the keepers gave me when I touched the shredders' tank. :I've been wondering if we should ask some of Kuron's kids to help us,: I say. :I'm afraid Safety Harbor may be running out of time.:

:If they understand what's at stake, I think Shadow or Sunny, or even the sparkhead, might help us,: Kalli agrees. We've all started picking up some of the slang and nicknames Kuron's kids use.

:I don't know,: Ree says, shaking her head. :That's asking a lot, considering how badly Kuron can punish them.:

:But the ocean is their home, too. If it dies, their future dies,: Tobin points out.

:For now I think we should keep searching on our own,: I decide. :Try not to think about c-plankton whenever Wasp is around, and keep your mental shields up.:

:Yeah, we saw her right after we finished checking out a lab down on Deck Two yesterday,: Ree says. :I think maybe she was following us.:

:I hope we can find those cultures soon.: Kalli rubs her arms. :One of these days Sham, Mako, Whitey, or Wasp could lose it, and someone here is going to end up dead.:

chapter twenty-one

AFTER DINNER THAT NIGHT, Tobin and I hurry off to search for the c-plankton cultures in that Marine Chemistry lab I found on the way to Mako's greenhouse, but it's full of empty shelves and workstations—a total dead end.

:Do you get the sense Kuron has big plans, but many of them never really get off the ground?: Tobin asks me as he glances around the barren lab.

:Yeah. It's weird how there are just fourteen of us and only twenty keepers rattling around in this huge place.:

Glancing at my dive watch, I realize it's getting late. :Guess we'd better head back to our own rooms,: I say uneasily, and Tobin agrees.

On our way, we run into Whitey, Sham, and Mako. My heart skips a beat when I see that Sham is holding Mako's arms, and Whitey is pounding him with his fists. Mako twists and turns, frantically trying to wrench himself from Sham's grasp, but the bigger kid is too strong for him.

:Keep hold of the little freak,: I hear Whitey order Sham. :If he gets away, you know we'll never catch him again.:

:I got him,: Sham grunts, his wide face contorted with effort.

:This is what you get for messing with my speargun, Twitchy. Don't you ever touch my stuff again.:

:I didn't touch it. I just looked at it,: Mako protests.

:You don't even *look* at my stuff,: Whitey says, and hits him again.

:Tobin, we've got to do something,: I cry. I start down the corridor, but Tobin grabs my arm.

:Call Dai if you want, but we can't help. These guys could tear us apart.:

I struggle against Tobin's grasp, but then I realize he's right.

:Dai!: I shout, but Wasp is blocking us again.

Desperate, I change tactics. :Wasp, they're hurting Mako,: I yell at her telepathically. :I know you can hear me. You've got to do something.:

:Do you think I care?: Wasp drawls. :Whatever the little fish turd did, he probably deserves what he's getting now.:

Whitey pulls his fist back and drives it into Mako's rib cage. This time I think I hear something crack.

:No one deserves that.:

I wrench free of Tobin's grasp and sprint down the corridor. :Stop it! You're hurting him,: I yell at Whitey.

Whitey spins around. He grins at us, showing off rows of wickedly sharp teeth. The savage hatred in his face chills me. Right now he looks more shark than human.

He raises his hand and lunges toward me, clawlike nails

sweeping toward my head. I throw up my arms to protect my face.

Before Whitey can slash me, Mako gasps, :You hurt her, the bossman will fry your brains. He wants her here. He wants them all here.:

Whitey hesitates. The bossman seems to be the one threat that everyone fears equally.

Tobin's beside me now. He shoves me behind him, which makes me furious.

:Mako's right,: Tobin says quickly. :The bossman knows he needs some Neptune kids.:

:We don't want any Neptune kids here, and we sure don't need you.: Whitey lowers his hand and glares at us. :I won't forget this, Princess. Don't even think about telling the bossman about this, or I'll tear you both to pieces.:

Whitey turns and swims down the corridor.

Sham lingers a moment longer, his thick lips curled in a sneer. :And if you go crying to Ice,: Sham says to Mako, :you know what we'll do to you later.:

Sham follows Whitey. Before they turn the corner, Whitey looks back at me and gives me one last look so full of cold hatred that it makes me tremble. I turn to check on Mako. He's just floating there, curled into a ball. Afraid he may be seriously hurt, I swim closer.

:Nere, you gotta be careful.: Tobin catches my arm again. :He's pretty freaked right now.:

:We can't just leave him like this.:

Mako's eyes are closed and his shoulders are shaking. I'm pretty sure he's crying. :Hey, Mako, you okay?: I ask him gently, still staying out of his reach.

Mako's pain-filled eyes focus on my face. His tic is worse than ever. :Are th-they gone?:

:I think so. Mako, we need to get you to the infirmary.:

:No! D-don't take me there. The keepers hate it when they have to treat us. They'll do something awful l-later to get even.:

:But someone should make sure you don't have any broken ribs,: Tobin says, backing me up. :Whitey was slugging you pretty hard there.:

Mako's gaze flickers hopefully to Tobin. :Y-you could check me out. Bria said you're a medic.:

:I could, but I know you don't like to be touched. I really don't want you to bite off my fingers.:

Mako reaches down and shakily unstraps the dive knife on his calf. I'm relieved when he doesn't take it out of its nylon sheath.

:I promise if I bite this, I won't bite you.:

:That works for me,: Tobin says.

Mako slips the knife between his teeth and slowly straightens up. The first time Tobin touches his rib cage gently, Mako jerks, but he lets Tobin continue his exam.

:It hurts worse there, and there,: Mako says.

Tobin lowers his hands and shifts away. :I'm fairly sure

you have two cracked ribs. If you get them strapped up, you'll feel a little better.:

Mako takes the knife from his mouth, reaches out his arms, and twists his body experimentally. :Everything hurts right now, but they've done a lot worse to me. I heal so fast, I'll probably be okay again in a few days.:

:They've done this to you before? Oh, Mako . . .: I reach out to touch his arm, only now he doesn't have a knife sheath in his mouth. Mako flinches again but doesn't try to bite me. Instead, he stares down at my hand for a moment and then raises his gaze to mine.

:I don't like to be touched, but I guess I don't mind if it's you.: He looks so young and wistful, for a moment, he reminds me of Robry again.

My eyes prickling with tears, I reach out and smooth his tangled hair away from his face. I wonder if anyone ever hugs these kids. All at once, I miss my dad. I'm never again going to take his hugs for granted.

:It doesn't have to be like this,: I say as I lower my hand. :Kids don't have to treat each other this way.:

:That's what Dai's been trying to tell us,: Mako says, :and Ocho and Shadow believe it, too. But I don't think Sham or Wasp or Whitey can be different. We've got to get away from them and the bossman and this place.:

I stare at Mako. :Have you thought about trying to escape?:

:Only all the time.:

:But what would you do about your collar?:

:Turn it off through the master control panel in the bossman's private rooms,: he replies promptly.

:Is that possible?:

:It might be. There's definitely a 'kill switch' for the collars. I've seen it.:

:What do you mean, a kill switch?: Tobin asks him intently.

:It's one of the bossman's nastier jokes, only I think it's kind of an experiment, too.: Mako grimaces. :We can flip a switch that will deactivate the collars and free us, but that switch is rigged. The person who flips it will get permanently fried. I think the bossman wants to see if one of us is willing to sacrifice his life to free the rest.:

:Has anyone ever seriously considered doing it?: Tobin asks.

:We're all still here with our collars, aren't we?: Mako shrugs. :Rad and I snuck up there to look at it one day, and that's as close as we got. I think we're always going to be here, and now you're stuck with us, too.:

The hopelessness I see in his eyes makes me want to hug him.

:Maybe you should go up to your greenhouse for a while,: I suggest. :I bet your plants would make you feel better.:

:Yeah, maybe. And Nere, thanks for helping me. No

one ever does that except Ice and Shadow.: Mako's restless gaze meets mine. :But don't do it again. I can take whatever Whitey dishes out better than you can.: With that, Mako swims off, as stiff as an old man.

I glance over at Tobin. He looks furious, and it takes a lot to make him angry.

:You know why they only hit his body, don't you?: he asks.

:No.:

:If Whitey or Sham had hit his face, someone would see the bruises the next day. No wonder Mako has a tic. They could have been beating the crud out of him for years, and none of the other kids like Dai or Shadow would know unless Mako actually said something to them.:

:The keepers must know.: I shake my head. :But I'm starting to wonder if the keepers ever do anything to help these kids.:

:Well, if that story Dai told you is true and Mako crippled one of them, I guess I can see why they don't go out of their way to protect him.:

I'm glad Mako has a place he can escape to, at least for a little while.

chapter twenty-two

TOBIN AND I describe to our team the brutal beating Sham and Whitey gave Mako and tell them about the kill switch in the bossman's rooms. The next day, Mako almost seems to be himself again. He even starts wrestling and hanging out with Sham and Whitey. I notice now how often he's on the receiving end of the nastiest of their teasing, and we are more careful than ever to try to steer clear of the shark crew as we continue to search through countless labs and storage rooms looking for the c-plankton.

After lunch, Ocho says that the bossman wants to see us right away. My stomach twists at this news. Dai is off conducting one of his deep-water experiments, which means we'll have to face his dad without him. Even Kuron's kids are quiet as we make our way up to the bossman's conference room, and I sense the tension growing in all of us.

Kuron's waiting for us, dressed in another simple dark suit, his hands clasped behind his back. As we climb out of the water and line up before him, he smiles at us all pleasantly. It's like he's completely forgotten how angry he became when he found out we weren't collared yet.

The metal band around my neck feels colder and heavier

than ever as he strolls over to where my team and I are standing together.

"I'm very pleased with the way you Neptune subjects have been settling in," he says to us. "It's clear from your intelligence tests that your intellectual abilities, except for brilliant young Robry's here, are on a par with my own specimens. I'm curious, too, about your physical capabilities, and I've designed a series of experiments to explore them."

My skin crawls at the way he refers to us as specimens and subjects. What happened to us being his "guests"? I'm starting to wonder if he really sees any of us as human. Shadow is standing near me. Her face appears as impassive as ever, but when I touch her mind, I can tell she's seething with resentment.

"Octavian," Kuron continues, addressing Ocho, "I want you to take them to the Maze, conduct a level-one blind directional and memory test on all the Neptune subjects, and enter their results into the computer. I will have you run some other tests on them in a few days."

"Yes, sir," Ocho replies.

My friends and I look at one another uneasily.

"Very well. You're dismissed," Kuron says with a curt nod and strides from the room.

"Guess we'd better head to the Maze now," Ocho tells us, and he dives back into the water.

:What exactly is this maze?: I ask as we follow him.

Wasp, Whitey, and Sham move up so they are swimming all around me. :The Maze is just what it sounds like,: Wasp replies before Ocho can, :and we have *such* fun playing games in there.: She looks so excited, my heart sinks.

:I hate going in there,: Shadow declares. :It makes me feel just like a lab rat.:

:Aw, the Maze ain't so bad,: Sham says with a mean, toothy grin.

:Particularly when we get to play 'hunt and seek,': Whitey adds and sends me a long, challenging look.

:We are not going to play 'hunt and seek' with the newbies today.: Ocho looks back over his shoulder at the shark crew.

:It's really not too scary. One of us will lead you into the Maze,: Sunny explains, :and then we see how long it takes you to find your way out.:

:But you have to do it with the lights off,: Sham says, a gleam in his eyes. :The bossman wants you to do a blind test, and that's the best kind.:

:So why do you guys like blind tests so much?: Ree asks.

:Because I can echolocate,: Sham replies, :and Whitey and Mako here have the ability to sense electrical fields just like sharks can.:

Goose bumps rise all over me. No wonder they like to play hunt and seek in the Maze. With the lights off, Sham would be able to use his personal sonar system to find other people, but the kids with shark senses would have an even bigger advantage. I've seen sharks find prey buried under inches of sand just by sensing the electrical currents their bodies generate.

Between their taunts and having to swim with the shark crew right next to me, I'm pretty wired by the time Ocho leads us through the doorway to the Maze. It's labeled with a plaque that reads DIRECTIONAL AND MEMORY TESTING FACILITY.

:Guess Kuron couldn't just call a maze 'a maze,' could he?: Tobin says so sarcastically that I smile, but once we're all inside the small control room for the Maze, I don't feel like smiling anymore. Whitey, Wasp, and Sham still look *way* too eager about our tests. Wasp spins around and hits a set of light switches beside the door. The small room is plunged into complete darkness. I bite my lip and wonder if Whitey is sneaking up to tear a chunk out of me.

:You could have waited five more minutes,: Ocho says, resignation in his tone.

:They might as well get used to the dark, Ochy,: Wasp says sweetly.

:Sunny?: Ocho asks.

:I'm on it,: she replies. Moments later, her hands begin to glow. The light emanating from them grows brighter and brighter until the control room is illuminated as brightly as it was before Wasp turned off the lights. I stare at Sunny's hands. The light shines right through her skin, just the way it does in bioluminescent fish.

:That is just sooo cool,: Robry says, shaking his head.

Sunny smiles at him. :You never need a flashlight when I'm around.:

:All right, Kalli and Ree, you guys are up first,: Ocho tells them. :Shadow and Sunny are going to lead you into the center of the Maze. They'll leave you there and see how long you take to find your way out. If you can't do it in fifteen minutes, we'll send someone in to get you.:

:This should be interesting,: Kalli mutters as Shadow slips a wide, thick blindfold over her eyes.

When both Ree and Kalli have blindfolds on, I ask, :Can you see anything?:

:*Nada*,: Ree replies.

:Take 'em in.: Ocho nods to Shadow and Sunny, and turns on a dozen different screens that display the interior of the Maze.

:We'll be cheering for you,: Rad calls after them.

We watch on the screens as Shadow and Sunny lead Ree and Kalli into the heart of the Maze.

:Time starts NOW,: Ocho declares after Sunny and Shadow return.

Sunny switches off the light she's been generating, and the only illumination in the booth comes from the screens. We watch as Kalli and Ree start trying to find their way out. The shark crew laughs as my friends take a series of wrong turns and head farther into the southeast corner of the Maze.

After fifteen minutes, Kalli and Ree still haven't found their way out. Sunny lights up her hand again and swims into the Maze to lead them back.

:So here are your test results,: Wasp taunts them when Kalli and Ree return. :You have no sense of direction and your memory stinks.:

:Like you could find your way out of there.: Shadow shakes her head.

:Wasp gets lost in the Maze all the time,: Rad tells us with a smirk while Wasp glares at him.

Ocho nods to Tobin and Robry. :You're up next.:

:Can't Nere come with us?: Robry asks.

:Nope. The bossman left express orders that she has to go solo.:

That news makes my skin prickle. I still manage a smile for Robry before Shadow helps him put on his blindfold.

After Sunny leads them in, Sham snickers. :I bet they get more lost than the first two.:

:I think you're about to get a big surprise,: I say. Sure enough, as soon as Ocho tells them to start, Robry begins to lead Tobin along the shortest route out. The shark crew swears in disbelief as Robry chooses the correct turn again and again.

Our guys return to the Maze's entrance in less than three minutes.

:What took you so long?: I ask Robry after he takes off his blindfold.

:I had to feel my way along.: He grins. :If the lights had been on, I could have had us out of there a whole lot faster.:

:Not bad. How'd you do that, squirt?: Rad asks.

:Robry has an amazing memory,: I say proudly.

Ocho enters their results into the computer. :Pretty impressive, kid. You guys should head back to the school room now. Sunny and I will come after we finish up Nere's testing.:

I hate whenever our team gets split up, but I'm pretty sure Rad and Shadow will keep an eye on my friends. I catch Wasp and Whitey exchanging a conspiratorial look that I don't like at all, but they leave with the others.

:It's your turn next.: Ocho sends me a smile when the door closes behind Whitey. :Remember, if you can't find your way out, it's no big deal. We'll just come find you in fifteen minutes.:

I stare at his kind, round face until Sunny slips the blindfold over my eyes. *You're in a huge space—there's no reason to feel claustrophobic just because you can't see*, I keep telling myself as Sunny leads me into the Maze.

I'm so busy taking deep breaths and trying not to panic,

I have no idea where I am when Sunny finally leaves me. Floating there in the dark, I fight the urge to rip off my blindfold. Already I *so* can't wait until this test is over.

A lifetime later, Ocho says, :Nere, your test starts NOW.:

Reaching out, I feel my way along the wall. It's cold and smooth under my fingertips. I come to the first turn. Right or left? Taking a wild guess, I turn left. At least the shark crew isn't watching me fumble around in the dark. Slowly, I work my way toward where I think the entrance is. But for all I know, I could be heading deeper into the Maze.

I've just reached a dead end when Sunny says, :Hey, what are you guys doing back here?:

:We just wanted to see how Nere's doing with her test,: Wasp says. :Oh, isn't that too bad? It looks like she's lost wayyy back in that corner.:

My face burns and my stomach starts to churn.

:Sham, let go of me!: Ocho shouts.

:Hold him, and if you don't want to get inked, keep that hood over the ink sacs in his neck,: Wasp orders.

Then Sunny swears and says furiously, :Get this bag off me, you big blubberhead!:

:Sorry. Can't let your light show mess up our game,: Sham replies.

:Whitey, is the door locked?: Wasp asks.

:Yeah, and now it's time for some serious hunt and seek.: The menace I hear in Whitey's voice fills me with dread.

I rip off the blindfold and stare wildly all around me. All I can see is blackness. How can I possibly escape when I don't even know where I am?

:Wasp, you promised me you wouldn't do this,: Ocho pleads with her.

:I'm sorry, Ochy, but we just couldn't pass up this chance to show Nere how much we like to play in here. Come on, Whitey, let's go.:

:She's in the southwest corner,: he tells her.

Thanks, Whitey. At least now I know roughly where I am. I swim as fast as I can, trying to head north and east, back toward the entrance. I keep my left arm extended straight ahead of me and my right out to the side, fingertips brushing the cold, smooth walls. I can't afford to miss an opening.

Here's one! Praying it's not a dead end, I turn right and sprint ahead. Within seconds, my left hand slaps into a new wall. I follow it left, and then get a chance to turn right again, in the direction I want to go. I think.

:If you hurt her, Ice will never speak to you again,: Ocho calls after Wasp.

:Like I care about what he does?:

:You can lie to everyone else, but don't lie to me. It's always about him,: Ocho says bitterly.

As I race through blackness, I hear my own pulse beating in my ears and the sob of my breath. This is worse than my nightmares when something terrible hunts me in the dark.

I reach out to see if I can read Whitey or Wasp and get some sense of where they are, but I touch only blankness. Wasp must be shielding their thoughts.

:Tsk tsk, you're trying to cheat, reading our minds like that,: Wasp goads me.

:Whitey can sense electromagnetic fields, and you say *I'm* cheating?:

:It's not cheating to use the abilities our creator gave us. I'm looking forward to teaching you that lesson, along with another one. You never should have come here.:

:You have to catch me before you can teach me anything,: I gasp as I dash up a long, straight corridor.

:That shouldn't take us very long. Whitey tells me we're very close to you now.:

I sense her rising elation. It's so totally dark in here, I won't know they're near until it's too late. I turn and sprint down another corridor. My outstretched hand hits a wall ahead of me. I lunge to the right and then to the left, but there's no opening.

It's another dead end! I'll have to swim back the way I came. Fighting down my panic, I whirl around and kick as quickly as I can. My legs and lungs are burning. Several kids argue and shout over by the entry room. I can feel Wasp's growing excitement, which means she must be close.

I may be about to plow right into her and her poisonous fingers.

:Sunny, light up so Nere can see them coming!: Ocho yells.

Light begins to trickle through the small gap between the divider walls and the ceiling. I glimpse movement out of the corner of my eye.

I twist around just in time to see Wasp dart through an opening behind me. She charges at me, her ungloved hands raised. Whitey's right behind her, but I have no weapon. Desperately, I bring my feet up and kick out. The edge of my right fin hits her nose, hard, and she reels back from me.

She clutches her face. :I think you just broke my nose. Whitey, take her apart.:

:With pleasure,: he says. He starts forward, his clawlike hands raised. I see such hatred in his eyes that I think he plans to kill me.

Seconds later, a dark shape streaks over Whitey's head, and all of a sudden, Dai's between us, holding a loaded speargun.

:Back off, Whitey. Wasp, you know my father wants Nere here.:

:But we don't,: Wasp cries.

:You sting her, or me, and I will tell him this time,: Dai says in a hard, implacable tone. :You know what he said he'd do if you *ever* touched a member of our family again.:

Wasp gasps and turns even paler.

:We were just playing a little game with the princess here,: Whitey says with a shrug. :I don't see why you're so bent out of shape, bro.:

:Sometimes, *bro*, you two get carried away with your games. Nere and I are leaving, and Wasp, you're *not* going to block us from talking to each other.:

Dai takes my hand and leads me away. I feel Wasp's and Whitey's angry stares burning into my back.

:You okay?: Tobin asks me when we reach the entry room. Everyone is glaring at Sham.

:I—I'm just a little shook up. Guess I'm not a big fan of hunt and seek.:

:Nere, I'm really sorry,: Ocho says, wringing two of his hands.

:You should be,: Dai says and leads me past the others to the main door.

I blink when I see the door handle is melted and buckled. :W-what happened to this?:

:Rad melted the lock for me so I could get to you in time.:

:You thought Whitey and Wasp really might hurt me?:

:Yeah.:

So it wasn't just a nasty joke. I start to shake. Wordlessly, Dai slips an arm around my shoulder and leads me to the nearest entry bay, where he calls a keeper to get permission to take me outside.

:I thought you might want to call Densil and Sokya,: Dai says while we wait. :I know they're around here somewhere. Ton's been hanging out with them. Maybe the dolphins will help you feel better.:

:Th-thanks. Just going outside for a bit would be g-great. I don't understand why I'm shaking. I feel like such a big chicken,: I admit, staring down at my dive fins.

:You're hardly that. I think you're the bravest girl I've ever met.: Dai reaches out and gently lifts my chin so I have to meet his gaze. :You kept it together when it mattered, and now you're just having a delayed reaction.:

The look in his eyes makes my face heat. :Yeah, well, whatever I'm h-having, I'm going to be glad when it's over,: I mutter. He drops his hand again, but my skin seems to tingle where he touched it.

When the keeper gives us permission, Dai and I swim down through the entry bay together. As soon as I'm out of sight of the looming gray fortress, my trembling starts to ease. I even manage a smile when Densil and Sokya streak toward us, Ton right behind them. I hug my friends and give them rubs. I'm surprised when Ton sidles up to me, asking for a rub of his own.

:He likes being scratched in front of his dorsal,: Dai tells me.

:How'd you find me so fast?: I ask Dai as I give Ton a gentle scratch.

:Let's just say I've spent a lot of hours in the Maze, and I know Wasp pretty well.:

:What is it with her? She's *crazy*.:

:What my father did to her was worse than what he did

to the rest of us, since she can't touch anyone. Because of her tentacles, we didn't want to be near her when we were little. Most of us still don't.:

:But she's so angry all the time. I don't get it.:

When Dai looks up from Ton, his eyes are haunted. :I think what really warped her was the day she killed my little sister, Maiya. You asked once about the black coral ring Maiya made for me.: Dai tugs a small dark ring from beneath his seasuit and shows it to me. I remember on our journey to Safety Harbor, he told me about the ring and said he'd had a little sister who'd died.

Dai curls his fingers around it. :One day Maiya got into Wasp's room and started playing with her things. Wasp lost her temper and slapped Maiya on the cheek. Wasp didn't really mean to hurt her, but sea wasp venom is deadly to small children. Before my dad could get a dose of anti-venom into her, Maiya was gone.:

:Oh, Dai, I'm so sorry.:

:Yeah, I'm sorry, too. Maiya was the best. She was a funny, smart little kid, and super sweet despite the way we were raised. She used to follow me everywhere, and I did my best to look out for her. But I didn't protect her that day. Everyone loved Maiya, and we all blamed Wasp for her death, me most of all.:

:But you guys were just kids.:

:Yeah, but looking back on it, it wasn't fair to Wasp.

She used to be pretty nice, and she felt awful already, and then we all made it worse. Over the years, Wasp's grown more twisted. She's decided I'm her personal property, and that's why she hates you. I've been afraid she'd kill you, or find a way to provoke Whitey into killing you. Today, she came close.:

:Can't you tell your dad about her?:

:I've been trying, but he doesn't listen to anyone anymore. He's always been so brilliant and so stubborn. My mom was the only one who could make him see reason.:

:Dai, what really happened to your mom?:

:She drowned when her research ship went down in a sudden storm,: he replies, his mental tone cooling.

:But my dad said there wasn't a storm in that area when her boat went down.:

:Her death really isn't any of his or your business,: he says so abruptly that I draw in a breath. I search Dai's face, but all I see is the closed, angry expression he wore so often when I first met him.

:Right. Well, I think I'm ready to head back now,: I say. :The others will be worrying about me. Thanks for saving me from your friends' fun little hunt-and-seek game.:

Before he can see how hurt I feel, I turn away and head back toward the entry bay. Now I know that Dai cares enough to keep me alive, but he doesn't trust me enough to share the whole truth about his family.

chapter twenty-three

AFTER OUR TESTING in the Maze, the tension between our two groups grows. Wasp scowls at me past the big swollen lump on the bridge of her nose. Whitey often stares at our team as if he'd like to tear us all apart. We're hurrying as quickly as we can through the list of labs that Robry found, but we still haven't discovered any trace of the c-plankton.

When Ocho announces at lunch the next day that the teaching computers will be down in the afternoon, I cheer along with everyone else. Our rigid routine in the school room plus searching for the c-plankton is starting to get to me. If we ever manage to escape this place, I'm going to tell my dad that he needs to give the kids at Safety Harbor some breaks from Vival's precise schedules. So, when Kuron's kids say they are going to take their skimmers out, Tobin and I decide our crew deserves a brief break, too.

:The keepers have orders to allow us a ten-mile range today, which means we can show you some really fierce places.: Rad grins at us.

As we head down to the entry bay, I warn my dolphin friends to stay clear of Wasp and her crew, who are going off to hunt together. Shadow, Rad, Sunny, and Dai end up joining our group.

Dai stays near me as we launch our skimmers. I get the impression that he's keeping a close eye on all of us, and me in particular. I want to tell him I can look after myself, but I'm not really sure I can protect myself against Whitey or Sham.

It must be a calm day topside because the water is incredibly clear and green. Sunlight from the surface brings out the brilliant reds and yellows in the soft corals that grow in profusion along the floor and steep rock walls of the sound. We race one another, driving our skimmers as fast as they can go while Sokya, Densil, and Ton swim alongside us.

We stop to hang out with a friendly school of Dahl's porpoises, a larger cousin of my dolphin friends. Two young calves are particularly curious and swim over and all around our group.

:Hey, guys, we gotta hurry if we're gonna hit the tide just right at the Ride,: Rad says, glancing at his dive watch.

:Um, exactly what is the Ride?: I ask Rad.

:It's this great channel that has an amazing tidal bore. Bodysurfing it is one of the best rushes ever.:

Kalli and I exchange glances. Back at Safety Harbor, we were told to stay away from tidal races and bores, places where tides surge inland at high speeds, because they can be so dangerous.

:It'll be okay,: Dai assures me. For once I don't mind that he's read my mind. :The Ride's in a wide channel,: he explains to all of us. :If you stay in the middle, there's not much chance you'll get mashed against the rocks along the sides.:

:That's nice to hear. I think,: Kalli says, looking unconvinced.

I feel like pointing out there'd be no chance of us getting mashed against rocks if we didn't do this, but clearly the rest of Kuron's kids are psyched. Even Shadow looks excited, and that reassures me a little.

A quarter mile from the mouth of the channel, we park our skimmers on the ocean floor and swim toward shore.

:We timed it just right,: Dai says with satisfaction. :Low tide ended less than an hour ago, which means the first big waves should start building any time now.:

We coast to shore on tidal currents. Rad leads us to an eddy behind a huge rock where we all wait for the first really large waves to form. All of us except Dai climb out of the water and stare at the channel.

As the slack tide turns to flood, the power of the water flowing past us is almost frightening. A huge amount of seawater is being pushed inland by the incoming tide, but here the narrow mouth of the channel forces it higher and faster, creating a truly fierce tidal bore.

"We're going to catch the first set," Rad says eagerly.

"You guys probably want to wait for the second. It won't be nearly as high, but it'll still be a good ride."

"I think we're fine with catching the second set," I say after glancing at my friends. They're all staring at the growing waves.

"Aren't you going with the others?" I ask Dai when he pops his head out of the water. Rad and the rest are already scrambling their way to the top of the big rock.

"I'll go with your group."

"You don't have to look after me every second."

"I know. I just want to see if you can bodysurf half as well as I can," he says with a smirk that makes me want to hit him.

"I can bodysurf just fine, thank you very much."

Dai ducks back into the water to breathe. The rest of us scramble up the rock and look down into the roiling water. As the first wave set crests and gathers speed, Rad, Shadow, and Sunny take a running leap off the rock. Their timing is perfect. They catch the crests of the first big wave and it flings them forward. Seconds later, they're flying up the channel, screaming their heads off.

I have to admit, bodysurfing this tidal bore looks insanely cool.

"A smaller set is forming up here pretty fast," Dai says from right beside me. "Get ready, you guys."

"Robry, you go first. I'll be behind you," I tell him.

I'm not brave enough to jump first, but if Robry goes, I'll have to leap in, too, just to keep an eye on him. Looking down at the frothing, foaming water, I sense the power of the incoming sea behind it. My stomach curls tighter than a nautilus shell. Moments later, Robry jumps. I suck in a breath and jump after him. I fall, and the tide grabs me.

Stroking forward hard, I catch the wave. I can look into its curving green wall and see the sides of the channel rocketing past. The force of the water carrying me upstream is awesome, its thunder echoing off the steep walls.

I hear Robry, Kalli, and Ree yelling like crazy. It's not hard to stay in the center of my wave, away from the sides of the channel, and I realize I'm yelling along with the rest.

Too soon, I spot Rad and Sunny waving at us from a gap on the seaward side of the channel. Robry and I strike out toward them, fighting against the tide still pushing us inland. We manage to reach the edge of the eddy where they're waiting. Robry kicks his way free of the current, but I start to get sucked back into it. Rad grabs my hand just in the nick of time.

"Whoa, Nere, the Ride stops here," he says and pulls me free.

"Thanks," I tell him breathlessly.

"No problem. Didn't want to lose you inland," he says with a smile. Then we all stand around laughing and panting. Dai surfaces to grin at us while he holds on to a dead tree.

"Some ride, huh?" he says to me, his dark eyes dancing with excitement.

It hits me then. I've really missed this Dai, the one who can laugh and loves the sea as much as I do.

"Yeah, some ride." I smile weakly.

Agile as a sea otter, he ducks back into the water and swims into the eddy behind us.

"So how do we get back?" Tobin asks. "It's still hours before the tide changes."

I watch the water surging inland. How *are* we going to fight our way back against that?

"This is the genius part," Sunny explains. "Last year Rad and I found this stream that leads out to the sound." She points to a cut in the channel wall that heads back out toward the sea. "The mouth's small, and then it widens, so the force of the tide coming in isn't too strong. And it's kinda cool looking at all the tidal stuff that grows in it."

She dives into the eddy, and we all follow her. Dai comes up beside me, and as we swim through the narrow, twisting channel, we do see some pretty cool stuff. We pass dozens of big purple starfish and yellow sunflower starfish preying on mussels, while mint-green anemones, scarlet gooseneck barnacles, and spiky maroon sea urchins dot the channel's floor and sides.

Soon we're back out by the mouth of the inlet again.

:I'm starving,: Rad announces.

:You're always starving.: Shadow rolls her eyes, but then

Robry admits he's hungry, too, and we decide it's time for a picnic.

:We're going to eat at the Wall Garden. It's one of my favorite spots,: Sunny declares happily. :I've spent hours photographing that place, and every time we hang out there, I find something new.:

We start up our skimmers again, and Sunny leads us to the west where a steep wall drops away into one of the deepest areas of the sound. That wall, we discover, is covered with an incredible variety of species. Feathery white plumose anemones provide shelter for shy red Irish lord sculpins, rainbow-colored nudibranchs, and all kinds of rockfish. Fat, squat Puget Sound king crabs pick their way through the anemones.

We eat inside a large cleft in the wall that gives us some protection from the strong current. As I look at Shadow, Sunny, and Rad, I realize I'm coming to really like these kids. Remembering the way Rad made sure I didn't get sucked back into the tidal bore, I think I'm starting to trust them, too.

After we finish, Dai looks at me. :There's something I'd like to show you down there,: he says and motions to the dark waters beneath us.

:'Kay, I'll tell everyone.:

:Actually, I'd like to show it to just you, and we need to talk.:

Has he finally figured out how we can escape despite our

collars? :All right,: I say after a moment and tell my friends I'm going off with Dai for a little while.

Rad and Sunny grin at us knowingly, Shadow's expression is as unreadable as always, and Tobin looks worried.

:We won't stay down there for long,: I reassure Tobin on a private send.

:Hey, *mi amiga*, you know that advice I gave you once about Dai?: Ree calls after me, a note of warning in her tone. :Now I know I was dead wrong about the first part and dead right about the second.:

My cheeks heat as Dai glances back curiously at Ree. During our trip north from the southern sector, she thought I should flirt with Dai but that Tobin would be better boyfriend material for me in the long run. I try to shield my mind as I remember her words.

I really don't want Dai hearing those particular thoughts right now.

chapter twenty-four

AS I SWIM DOWNWARD after Dai, I try not to think about the last time he took me to see something special below the sunlit zone. He kissed me that afternoon, and said that he really liked me, but now I have no idea how Dai feels.

Sometimes I wish I could use my telepathy to read other people's minds any time I want. But my mother warned me that was a bad idea, and mostly I think she was right. I don't really want to know what my friends are thinking about me.

Right now, though, it's *way* tempting to peek into Dai's mind.

:This isn't so terrible, is it?: Dai asks abruptly. When I glance at him, the intense look in his eyes makes me uneasy.

:What d'you mean?:

:I mean, couldn't you see yourself getting used to living with us? My friends are cool. Sunny, Shadow, and Ocho really like you, and Rad has a whale-size crush on Ree.:

I stare back at him. How clueless can he get?

:Dai, Safety Harbor's our home, and I can't imagine I'll ever get used to wearing a collar that shocks me like I'm an animal.: Or get used to living with the shark crew and Wasp.

:A home that you lived in for what, all of two weeks?:

:And whose fault is that?:

:My dad's, not mine. You're not being fair if you blame me for what he does.:

:I'm not blaming you for his actions, but I do blame you for not telling us who you were and why you found us.:

:So we're back to that again.: Dai stops swimming and turns to face me, his eyes simmering. :How many times do you want me to say I'm sorry for something I had to do? I didn't have any choice.:

:But you did have a choice. You could have chosen any time during those five weeks while we fought our way up the coast to tell us who you really were.:

:You still don't get it. If I don't do exactly what my dad tells me to do, he takes it out on them.: Dai jerks a thumb back toward his friends.

:I don't understand.:

:He's decided they're all defective.: Dai throws his hands wide. :I'm the only one he thinks turned out perfectly. He only keeps the others alive because he knows I care about them.:

A chill steals down my back when I realize what he's saying.

:They're the way he controls me. They're the reason I don't have a collar.:

:Oh, Dai, I'm so sorry.: My dad and I have our own

issues, but I can't imagine what it must be like to grow up with a father willing to blackmail me like that.

:Don't be sorry for me. That's the last thing I need from you.: Dai turns away, sounding so angry and miserable that my heart twists.

I swim up behind him and touch his shoulder. :Then I won't feel sorry for you. I'll just stay really mad at you instead.:

He turns to face me. :I guess that's better,: he says, his lips lifting in a hint of a smile, :but I don't want you to be mad at me, either. Maybe this will help. I know you'll like what I want to show you down here.:

:'Kay.:

He takes my hand and leads me deeper down the wall until the light from the surface fades completely. I try not to notice how nice it feels to hold hands with him. We pass several large white cloud corals that grow in random patterns and shapes, looking like ghosts and small snow-covered mountains in the dark.

Then we come to dozens of orangish-red Gorgonian corals. Anchored to big boulders, they reach outward with their arms, filtering their food from the water flowing past. Shaped like large fans, and with their feathery polyps open, they almost glow in the darkness. Small rockfish swim behind them, using the corals as shelter from the current.

:Wow,: I breathe.

:They grow so slowly in these dark, cold waters, these corals are probably hundreds of years old. I like lots of species that live below the sunlit zone, but I've spent hours researching and studying these in particular.:

:They're beautiful. Thank you for showing them to me.:

Dai turns to face me. :I didn't want you to come to Atlantea, but I'm glad now that you're here.: He pulls at one of his braids, looking uncharacteristically unsure of himself. :I've missed you,: he says, and he almost sounds angry about it.

:I've missed you, too,:

He swims closer, and I think maybe he wants to kiss me. But everything's so complicated between us now, I'm not sure I want to kiss him back.

Suddenly, Sokya, Densil, and Ton come racing down from the surface to find me, whistling and sawing.

:you have to come! they are hurting her. she is very scared. if they wish to eat her, they should just kill her.: Sokya's words tumble over one another.

:Slow down. Sokya, I don't understand.:

:the other humans with tows, they have a young orca trapped in an inlet,: Densil explains more calmly. :but they do not kill her. they hurt her instead.:

I grab Sokya's dorsal, and she tows me upward toward the rest of our group.

:What's upsetting your dolphins?: Dai asks, swimming so fast that he keeps pace with Sokya.

:It sounds like your adorable friends have caught a young whale, and instead of killing it for food, they're torturing it.:

:They're just playing with it,: Dai says impatiently. :They will kill it eventually. Tell your dolphins I've seen Ton play with fish dozens of times before he eats them.:

I relay his words to the dolphins.

:she is different from fish,: Densil replies promptly. :the orca thinks.:

Densil has cut right to the heart of the problem. Marine mammals are incredibly intelligent, and I know some of them do think.

When I relay Densil's protest to Dai, he shrugs. :It's just an orca. There are hundreds of them in these waters, and some hunt dolphins. Your pod should be glad my friends are about to kill one.:

:Orcas are cousins to your Ton,: I retort. :And you know how smart he is.:

Sokya leads me straight to Tobin. :he wants them to stop, too,: she tells me. :please, you both go make them stop.:

Tobin shakes his head. :I don't like what the shark crew's doing, and I'd like to help, but I doubt it's a good idea. Whitey and Sham hate our guts already.:

:Believe me,: Dai says, breaking in on our conversation, :it's better if they let off some steam this way.:

:Dai's right,: Rad says. The rest of the kids have gathered

around us now. :Just look the other way and let them do whatever they want to that poor orca.:

:What, exactly, are they going to do to it?: Tobin asks Shadow.

:They'll probably torment it for a while longer,: Shadow admits sadly, :and then they'll kill it.:

:That's just wrong. Take me to the orca,: I tell Sokya. If Dai won't stop them, I'll find some way to do it myself.

chapter twenty-five

I DART DOWN to the ledge where we left our skimmers. Ignoring Dai's shouts, I jump on my skimmer and crank the handles back until I'm racing through the sea, determined to help that poor killer whale the shark crew is torturing. Sokya and Densil lead me back toward the fortress, and soon we skirt the western edge of a small island.

On his powerful skimmer, Dai catches me and stays at my side, his expression grim. He doesn't try to argue with me anymore.

The moment we round the island's northern point, I hear the distressed whistles and squeals of the captive orca. The calls of her pod tear at my heart. My anger surges when I start hearing the shouts and laughter of the shark crew, too.

:Whoa, it almost got past you that time!: Whitey yells.

As I draw closer, my throat tightens. They've stretched a section of fishing net across a tiny inlet. The trapped orca rushes back and forth inside, frantically trying to find a way out. Orcas in this area spend their entire lives traveling in family groups. Separated from her pod, the young whale must be terrified.

I park my skimmer on a rock ledge and swim toward

the net. The killer whale has a spear dart in her back and bleeds from two other cuts. I reach out with my mind, hoping I might be able to calm her. I find the orca's awareness quickly. Her mind feels very foreign, and I'm overwhelmed by her fear and pain. Even though I try to send her an image of the net being torn away, I don't think I'm reaching her.

The shark crew is spread out along the net, waving their arms to scare the frantic orca and keep her from leaping over it. Sham's inside the net, trying to line up a good shot.

Wasp laughs with the rest. :Come on, Sham, ten points if you can hit its dorsal.:

Mako's closest to me along the net. He waves at the frightened killer whale when she darts in his direction.

:Mako, don't do this,: I cry. :How can you?:

Mako spins around. His gray gaze meets mine for a second, and then he looks down, his eye twitching. :Nere, you shouldn't watch this. Just go away.:

Dai parks his skimmer and swims up beside me. Whitey and Ocho spot us. Now that I've created the mental link, the young whale's fear and pain beats at my mind.

:This isn't right. You've got to stop them!: I turn to Dai, fighting back tears. :They're just using her for target practice.:

Dai looks at me for a long moment. :All right,: he says with a sigh. :I'll do my best, but this could get ugly.:

He swims to the edge of the net.

:Come on, guys, finish this or let the orca go.:

:He's right,: Ocho says, looking over at Wasp. :We should stop. You should stop. You're better than this.:

Wasp's eyes widen, and her cheeks flush. :I have no idea what you mean. I'm having a great time,: she says carelessly. :Ochy, you can just leave. No one needs you here anyway.:

Ocho's face tightens, but he stays near her side.

:Jeez, Ice, you used to think stuff like this was fun,: Sham says angrily.

:Yeah, back when I was ten maybe, and I didn't know any better.:

I'm aware that Sunny, Shadow, and my team are gathering around us, carrying loaded spearguns. Rad swims closer to Dai and stays right beside him. I'm glad he's there, just in case Whitey or one of the others loses it.

:I can't believe you're taking her side over ours,: Whitey says to Dai and gestures to me.

:I'm not picking her side,: Dai replies, his voice even. :I just don't want us to do stuff like this anymore.:

:Of course you're picking her side. It's like we're not good enough for you anymore,: Wasp hisses.

:Bro, you've been seriously messed up ever since you got back,: Sham says sullenly. :I wish you'd never met these Neptune kids.:

:This has nothing to do with them. Just because we were raised like animals doesn't mean we have to act like them.:

Whitey swims to the front of the kids confronting Dai, his charcoal eyes colder than sea ice. :I *like* acting like an animal. I'm proud of the shark genes in me,: he says, :and I think it's pitiful that you're ashamed of the ones in you.:

I look from Whitey to Dai and back to Whitey again, my stomach churning.

:Oh, you mean he didn't tell you?: Whitey says to me with mock surprise. :Pretty-boy Ice here is just as much animal as the rest of us, thanks to a whole bunch of shark genes his daddy had spliced into him.:

Dai sends me an unreadable look and darts away, faster than I've ever seen him swim before. He grabs the top of the net, and with a massive heave, tears it free of the heavy cables that they've used to anchor it.

Seconds later, the terrified orca flashes past us.

Sham flings away his speargun in disgust. :Now you've done it. We'll never catch it again this afternoon.:

:And you ripped our best net.: Wasp glares at Dai.

Suddenly Whitey is face-to-face with him.

:Don't *ever* come between me and my kill again,: Whitey growls, :or not even the bossman will keep me from tearing you apart.:

With that, one by one, the shark crew leaves the inlet, Ocho bringing up the rear.

~ ~ ~

I stare after them, feeling numb. So Dai has shark in him, just like Mako and Whitey. It explains so much. I remember how little sleep Dai needs, and how restless he can be. Sharks can't stop moving, or they'll die. Dai's crazy strong and fast, like a shark. And he's uncomfortable around blood.

Finally, I think to look for Dai. He's yanking down the cables at the other end of the inlet now, fury showing in every line of his body as he systematically tears the net apart.

:Hey, guys, let's leave them to talk,: Shadow tells the rest, and then Dai and I are all alone.

Swallowing hard, I swim closer to him.

:Great. Now you're scared of me.: Dai bites out the words as he slices the net apart with his dive knife.

:No, I'm not. I know you'd never hurt me.:

:I'd never mean to hurt you, but I could, just the same.:

:But why didn't you tell me?:

Dai glances up from the net. :Maybe because I didn't want you looking at me the way you are now.:

:My parents spliced some fish genes into me, too. Where do you think my gill filaments came from?:

:Your gill filaments don't make you want to attack people or make you crazy when there's blood around.:

:Let's not fight. I don't care what genes your dad mixed into you. I just want to thank you for letting the orca go.:

:How many times do I have to say it?: he says roughly.

:I don't want your pity or your gratitude,: he says as he flings a section of net away from him.

:I don't feel sorry for you, but I am grateful for what you just did.:

Dai sends me a charged glance. :Maybe you shouldn't be. Today may have just changed everything.:

:I don't understand.:

:Bria and Robry and the rest, they're like your family now. Shadow and Ocho and Whitey, they're all the family I've got. I've been trying to keep them together, but I don't think I can do it much longer, and today just made things worse.:

I picture the way Kuron's kids always divide into two groups, and the tension between them has only gotten worse since we arrived. :I think they want different things,: I say slowly, :and they are so different, I doubt you can keep them together much longer.:

:I know, but it was better before you came.: He sighs and sheathes his knife.

:We didn't exactly want to come here,: I say, irritation rushing through me.

:I realize that.: Dai raises his hands to rub his face. When he lowers them again, he doesn't look angry anymore. He just looks tired and worried. :Nere, promise me you'll be extra careful around Whitey from now on. You've crossed him twice now, and you don't want to cross him a third time.:

chapter twenty-six

DINNER IS incredibly tense that night. The members of the shark crew look daggers at us, and they only speak to one another during the meal. Mako sits close to Dai, his tic worse than ever.

After dinner, my team members retreat to my room. Robry heads straight to the computer. He's been working harder than ever to find a way to disable our collars. While he searches through files and reads us bits about Kuron's experiments and his concerns over losing investors, I tell everyone what Dai said about the growing divide among his friends.

:It feels like we're sitting on a bomb, and it could explode any time now,: Tobin says.

:I really don't want us to be here when that happens,: Kalli says.

:Which means we've just gotta find that c-plankton and find it soon,: Ree declares with a resolute look.

:Whoa, this is *not* good news. Guys, check this out.: Robry looks up from the computer screen, his face pale.

:What have you found?: I ask him quickly.

:I was looking around in Kuron's personal logs again,

and I—I think he's planning an all-out attack on Safety Harbor soon. You gotta read this entry.:

We crowd around Robry. I'm relieved that the surveillance camera in the corner of my room is set at the wrong angle to cover the computer monitor. Along with the others, I begin to read:

I'm now convinced that I have to add more subjects with marine adaptations to my program. I need them to help to build the new order under the waves that I, and my son after me, will lead. If we kill the adult staff supervising them, these young specimens will naturally look to me for shelter and safety. I expect some losses on both sides, as my shark mutates are regrettably imprecise weapons.

I will give the subjects at Atlantea the option of joining this attack as a test of their loyalty to me. Those who will not participate will be eliminated. . . .

We stare at one another in horror.

:He's talking about us and Safety Harbor, *sí*?: Ree says uncertainly.

:Yeah, he is,: Robry says. :There's even a chart of Safety Harbor right below this entry.:

:But how can he expect us to attack our own friends and our own home?: Kalli cries.

:Now I know this *hombre* is completely *loco*,: Ree says, shaking her head.

:Do you think the other kids know about this?: I ask my team.

:I can't believe Shadow or Sunny or Rad would have anything to do with attacking Safety Harbor unless Kuron forced them,: Kalli replies.

:I can't, either, but I bet Whitey, Sham, and Wasp would go on a raid like this in a heartbeat,: Tobin says.

:Does Dai know about this?: Ree asks me the question I think we're all wondering.

:I don't know, but we have to assume for now that he does,: I force myself to reply calmly, even though my heart feels like it's about to shatter. :I've got to send one of the dolphins back to Safety Harbor to warn everyone. Does Kuron say when he's planning this attack?:

:At the highest tide this month,: Robry responds. :He's planning on taking his sub inside the perimeter, and he's worried about grounding it in some of the shallower areas of the colony.:

:When's the next king tide?: I ask him, trying to hide my panic.

:I'll check,: he says, his fingers racing over the keyboard. He stops after he pulls up the tide table. When he looks away from the screen again, his eyes are wide and worried. :The next one will be exactly four days from now.:

A cold wave of dread rushes over me. :That means we have less than four days left to find the c-plankton and figure out a way to disable these collars.:

~ ~ ~

I can tell everyone on my team is as stunned by Kuron's log entry as I am. We talk briefly about Kuron's plans and decide to redouble our efforts tomorrow to find the c-plankton.

We all jump when a keeper pounds on my door. Curfew begins in ten minutes. Their faces grim, my friends leave my room.

The keeper, though, stays by my door and stares at me. I can just make out the red scar over his eye. It's the same man who shocked me at the shredder tank. As the moment stretches into forever, I consider touching his mind, but I don't want to know what he's thinking. The hatred radiating from him is clear enough. At last, he closes the door and locks it.

Letting go a shaky breath, I call Sokya and Densil and explain to them what we just found out. Densil agrees to swim as fast as he can back to Safety Harbor to warn my father through Bria.

:Be careful,: I tell him. It's dangerous when a dolphin swims alone without a pod to protect it.

:I am always careful,: Densil says and breaks off contact. I look out into the twilight sea, hoping he'll be safe.

:You need to be careful, too, Sokya,: I say.

:I will be fine. I swim with the big dolphin,: Sokya assures me. I do feel a little better knowing she's with Ton.

Taking a deep breath, I lean forward and rest my forehead against the cold window glass. Now that everyone's gone, I can stop trying to be brave. I wish Dad was here. He'd know what to do. I just want to go home. But I can't go back to my old home down south, and my new home's in danger. And Ran Kuron is going to "eliminate" my friends and me if we don't agree to attack Safety Harbor.

Wrapping my arms around myself, I burst into tears.

My dad's colony has so few real defenses. I keep picturing starving shredders storming through the bubble wall and attacking kids, dolphins, and helper staff. I can see the shark crew helping Kuron, but would Dai really be a part of it? He's such an amazing fighter, he'd be like an army in himself.

:Nere, what's wrong? Are you hurt?:

I twist around in surprise. As if my thoughts had summoned him, Dai is floating inside my door, his expression worried. The image of the shredders, the shark crew, and Dai attacking Safety Harbor is still vivid in my mind. Hastily, I raise my mental shields, but I can tell from the shift in his expression that I'm too late to keep him from reading me.

His face cold, he swims farther into my room. :So, my father's planning to attack Safety Harbor, and you think I might be in on it. I guess that doesn't surprise me. He's capable of unleashing his sharkheads on a colony of innocent kids, and you obviously believe I'd help him. How'd you find this out?:

I just stare at him, shielding my thoughts as tightly as I can.

Dai's mouth twists. :Not going to tell me, are you? I bet I can guess. Somehow Robry hacked into his personal files. Ocho's going to be impressed. He's been trying to break into them for years.:

:Why are you here?:

:It doesn't matter now.: Dai just looks at me. When I reach out and try to read him, I sense waves of anger and hurt leaking through his shields.

:So you wouldn't help your father,: I say miserably. :I—I didn't really think you would.:

:But for a moment, you thought I might. That's what counts. Good night, Nere.: He leaves and locks my door quietly behind him.

~ ~ ~

Dai doesn't appear at breakfast, which is almost as tense as dinner was the night before. The shark crew continues to glare at us, and I'm relieved when we get through our classes without a fight. The moment school is over, Tobin and I head off to search for the c-plankton in a far section of the fortress.

:If we promised to join him, do you think Kuron would buy it?: I ask Tobin as we swim quickly down a long corridor.

:We'd have to say the right things,: Tobin replies, :like how much we love Atlantea and *want* to be a part of his program. He's such a megalomaniac, I think he just might believe us.:

:I'm afraid Wasp could tell we were lying, though.:

All at once, the red alarm lights along each corridor begin to flash, and a shrill siren rips through the water.

I jump and glance up and down the corridor. :I *really* hope some shredders didn't get loose.: We don't even have dive knives to protect ourselves.

:Hey, Nere,: Ree calls me a moment later. :I think Kalli and I just set off an alarm. We found a big lab, and I opened a drawer in a cabinet, and the next moment, all these lights were flashing like crazy. I closed the drawer and we got out of there *muy* fast.:

:Did anyone see you guys?:

:Well, no one was in the lab, but maybe someone saw me on a camera.:

:Head back to your room, but try to look like you're not hurrying. We'll meet you there.:

Tobin and I say little as we swim swiftly through the stark corridors, and I call Robry and tell him to meet us in Ree's room. Finally someone shuts down the alarm, which was making my head ring. By the time we get back, Ree, Kalli, and Robry are already there.

:I'm really sorry, boss,: Ree says the instant she sees

me. :I swear there weren't any prohibited area signs on the door to that lab.:

:It's okay. We had to start taking some chances.:

:That lab looked promising, too,: Kalli says. :There were all kinds of tanks growing stuff in there. I'd like to go back and check it out.:

Seconds later, Sham storms in, his broad, flat face flushed with anger.

:Nice job, morons. The bossman got back just in time to hear the alarms, and he's mad at everyone now. He wants to see us in his conference room pronto.:

My team and I exchange worried glances.

:Yeah, you guys should be worried,: Sham gloats. :The keepers know you set off the alarm, and when the boss-man finds out, someone's gonna get fried big-time.:

:Lay off them, Sham,: Rad says. He and Shadow float in the doorway, faces tight.

:Sure thing, sparkhead. Just thought your Neptune buddies ought to know what's coming.: Sending us a nasty, toothy smile, Sham leaves the room.

:Guess we'd better go,: I say and kick for the door, touching Ree's shoulder as I pass her. :It's going to be okay.: But I wish my words didn't sound so hollow.

As we swim for the conference room, the rest of Kuron's kids join us, all except Dai. I keep looking down the various corridors we pass, hoping he'll show up.

:Dai's not here,: Shadow tells me on a private send. I wonder, not for the first time, if Shadow is a strong hereditary telepath, too.

:The bossman sent him to deliver a message to your father at Safety Harbor,: she explains. :Dai tried to reach you, but Wasp blocked him. He told me he'd get back here as fast as he could. He didn't want to go, but we promised him we'd look out for you.:

My stomach clenches even tighter. I *really* wish Dai were here. I know he has been looking out for us, and he may be the only one who can reason with his twisted, crazy father.

All too soon, we reach the deck access where we have to leave the water. One by one, we climb up into Kuron's conference room.

I spot him immediately, standing in front of the big plasma screen. He's dressed in a black suit again, and he's completely still. His expression appears to be cool and calm, but when I see the muscle ticking in his jaw, I realize he's furious. When we're finally all lined up in front of him, he begins to speak.

"I understand one of our guests trespassed in a prohibited area and set off the alarm," he declares in a cold, hard voice.

Ree squares her shoulders. Before I can stop her, she steps forward. "I did, sir, but I didn't know that lab was off-limits. There wasn't any sign on the door."

"Of course Enviro Lab Three is a 'prohibited area.'"

I sense a surge of satisfaction near me, and I whirl to stare at Wasp. "You took the sign down," I accuse her. Wasp looks so smug, I want to strangle her.

"Me? You're crazy. I never break any rules around here," she says aloud in a sweet, girlish voice, and then mentally she adds, :or when I do, I'm smart enough to not get caught, unlike your idiotic friend Ree.:

Wasp turns an innocent face to Kuron. "Whether or not there was a sign, why did Ree and Kalli go into that lab in the first place? Were they looking for something?"

Panic floods me. Wasp must know about our mission. She probably overheard enough of our thoughts to guess why we're here.

"Wasp raises a fascinating point," Kuron says, turning his icy stare on Ree. "Maria, what were you doing in that lab?"

"I was lost," Ree replies stonily.

"Do you always go through drawers when you're lost?" Wasp retorts.

"I know you ran with some rough types after your parents died," Kuron declares, "but I will not tolerate thievery here at Atlantea."

"I'm not a thief," Ree says, her cheeks turning red.

"Your actions contradict your words." Kuron shakes his head. "We're going to punish you for attempted theft. And Kallisandra, you will be punished for ignoring the prohibited sign on the lab door."

"There wasn't any sort of warning sign on that door," Kalli contradicts him, her voice amazingly steady.

Desperately, I reach out and touch the minds of the kids standing near us. Most of them don't want Ree or Kalli hurt. And they all loathe Kuron. Since Wasp is probably about to reveal our mission anyway, maybe it's time to take a gamble.

Kuron strides to a nearby computer terminal. I'm sure he's about to send a command to Ree's and Kalli's collars.

I step forward beside Ree. "Please, sir, don't punish them. Ree was just following my orders."

Kuron stops in his tracks and turns to face me. His dark eyebrows draw together, and the sudden fury in his face is terrifying. I forge ahead anyway. "We d-did come to free Bria and Robry, but we also came to find the c-plankton cultures your brilliant wife created."

As I speak, I probe his mind as strongly as I can. I'm hoping my words will make him picture where the c-plankton is stored. Instead I pick up a storm of violent emotion erupting inside him at the mention of his wife: anger, guilt, and regret, along with an image of a beautiful woman with a sad face and long black hair. Then it all vanishes, as if Kuron smothered his emotions entirely.

Before he can interrupt me, I hurry to explain our real mission to the others. "Idaine Kuron genetically engineered a form of plankton that can absorb huge amounts of carbon dioxide. Our Neptune scientists believe if we can sow enough of this plankton in the oceans around the world, we'll finally have a real chance to reverse global warming."

"It doesn't matter what happens to the foolish people who persist in trying to survive on land," Kuron declares impatiently. "Clearly mankind's destiny lies in the sea."

"But if the planet continues to heat, the oceans are in huge trouble, too. Already coral and kelp forests around the world are dying, and phytoplankton is starting to die off, too. The whole foundation of the ocean food chain is in danger."

"The oceans have warmed before." Kuron dismisses my argument with a wave of his hand. "As the most superior species on the planet, we will adapt and make their resources serve us."

I remember Dai once said to me that dolphins exist to serve us. Now I know where he picked up some of his attitudes.

Obviously I'm not getting anywhere convincing his father. "If the seas continue to warm," I say to the others, "there'll be nothing left down here but jellyfish, sea slugs, and some tube worms—"

"Enough of this nonsense," Kuron says, cutting me off. "I'm tired of this discussion and I'm very disappointed to hear this fruitless mission is why you came to us. Now Maria and Kallisandra will be punished, and then you Neptune subjects have four days to decide. Either you swear to become loyal members of my community here, or I'll feed you to my shark mutates." He starts toward the computer panel again.

My mind is racing faster than a tidal bore. First I've got to stop him from shocking Ree and Kalli. Then we'll decide what to do about his crazy ultimatum.

"If you have to punish anyone, you should punish me," I say, fighting to keep my voice steady. "I'm their team leader."

Kuron looks at me for a long moment. His eyes are so intense and his face is so cold again, my whole body prickles with dread. "Very well." He nods and then glances down at his watch.

"Sir, would you like me to take care of disciplining her?" Wasp asks sweetly.

"I leave the matter of her punishment in your capable hands, my dear." Kuron gives her an approving smile before he strides from the room.

Suddenly I'm short of breath, and it's not from being out of the water. Wasp hates my guts, and now she's in charge of punishing me. *Oh, Dai, I wish you were here.*

"I-Ice isn't gonna like this." Mako is brave enough to speak up.

"He's right. If you hurt Nere, you'll have to deal with Dai when he gets back," Tobin tells Wasp, sounding fiercer than I've ever heard him.

"I don't plan on hurting our darling Nere in any physical way." Wasp smiles unpleasantly at Tobin.

Then she turns to me, and her smile widens. "You see, I've listened in on your thoughts enough to know exactly why you don't like the room we've assigned you. I know

259

you dread the moment the bolt slides home each night. I know you don't like small, dark places because . . . you're claustrophobic."

Fear floods through me, leaving me nauseated and shaky.

"So, Whitey, how should we punish a girl who is severely claustrophobic?" Wasp asks him, clearly savoring every moment.

"Lock her away in the smallest, darkest closet we can find around here," he replies promptly.

"And I already have a perfect one all picked out for her." Wasp drops her playful act. "Back in the water, everyone," she orders. She dives in first, and we follow with Sham and Whitey right behind us, joking and snickering.

My team clusters closely around me as we swim.

:Nere, you'll be okay,: Robry tries to reassure me. He's the only one who knows just how bad my claustrophobia is. :You just gotta think about stuff you like and keep your mind busy.:

:Thanks, but I'm more worried about you guys,: I reply, fighting to sound cool and calm. :You've *got* to stay out of trouble. Don't do anything to set off Whitey or the rest of them. Dai should be back in a few days, and I know he'll look out for you all.: At least I hope he will.

Wasp halts outside of a door labeled SENSORY DEPRIVATION LAB.

:Here it is. I've been hoping I'd find a way to arrange a stay for you in here.:

Wasp throws open the door with a flourish. Icy fingers seem to trace down my back as I gaze at her small, dark prison.

It looks like an empty storage closet, maybe seven feet tall, seven feet deep, and not much wider than the door. There's a sea toilet built into a small compartment along one side, much like the ones in our rooms. There's definitely no porthole that looks out into the sea, which is the only thing that keeps me from panicking after they lock me into my room at night.

I refuse to show Wasp how much this small space freaks me.

:Looks fine to me,: I tell her coolly.

:Which is why you're already starting to shake like a jellyfish,: Sham says gleefully.

Tobin slips an arm around my shoulder. I can't help leaning into him. :Nere, you'll be okay.:

:Why, I think Tobin wants to go in there with you,: Wasp says. :That's how worried he is for you.: A crafty look steals over her face. :And that's a lovely idea, now that I think about it. Are you willing to be shut up in here, too?:

Tobin nods instantly.

:Tobin, no, you don't have to do this,: I protest. :The rest of our team needs you more than I do.:

:Being in there won't bother me at all,: he tells me, his face earnest, :and I might be able to help you get through this.:

:Righty-o, in you go.: Wasp grins at us. Before I can say good-bye to the rest, Whitey shoves me inside, and Tobin gets pushed in after me.

Then Wasp slams the door closed, the lock clicks, and we're shut in.

chapter twenty-seven

I STARE INTO blackness so total that even with my genetically altered vision, I can't see the hand I raise in front of my face. The silence is so dense, all I can hear is the blood beating in my ears. Trying not to lose it, I breathe in and out. I want to pound on the door. I want to scream at Wasp to let me out. But I'm too petrified to move.

I don't want to remember, but here in the total dark, I'm afraid I'll be swallowed up by that other time when I was shut in and couldn't get out. But then I was alone.

This time, Tobin is here.

:Tobin?: I reach out with my mind but touch only blankness. Wasp is blocking us. I clench my hands. If she keeps blocking our telepathy, I'll still be all alone in the dark.

I breathe faster and faster. My heart is pumping so hard, I'm afraid it will burst. Wrapping my arms around my chest, I shake so much that my teeth chatter. I haven't had a full-blown panic attack like this in years.

Feeling a touch on my arm, I can't help but jerk away, my heart pounding faster yet. But then the touch comes again, and this time Tobin finds my hand and grips it firmly. His other hand finds my shoulder, and he pulls me close until my head rests against his chest.

I try to push away from him, feeling more trapped than ever, but then I hear a warm, deep rumbling. Any sound in this awful silence is comforting, but this sound is wonderful. The rumbling ranges higher and lower again in a sequence that somehow seems familiar. Then I realize what Tobin's doing. He's humming.

I press my right ear closer to his chest and concentrate on the notes. I recognize "Hymn to Joy," a beautiful old hymn he sang once at the graveside of Sara, the girl who died during our trip north.

Way to go, Tobin! He's found a way to communicate with me, despite Wasp. We can't speak aloud underwater because sound gets too distorted for us to understand each other's words. But he can hum, and I can listen, and the song helps me focus on something besides the smothering dark.

I remember my pain and anger from the night we buried Sara. The lyrics of the hymn were all about fields and forests, the sun and "the flashing sea." I picture times I've seen sunlight dance and shine on waves. Gradually my breathing slows and my trembling stops.

Tobin starts humming another tune, and I recognize "Pop Goes the Weasel." The song reminds me of long afternoons on the beach playing with Lena and Robry and his big brother, Cam. I let my mind drift, and I think of days I spent sailing and fishing with Cam on his tiny boat and how he loved tinkering with its sails. I picture his smile and how happy he was on the water. I hope with all my heart that he's still alive, and that someday he'll have a chance to sail again.

After another two songs, Tobin squeezes my hand and shifts back from me. He touches his dive watch and light gleams from the data displayed there. He holds the watch near his face so the dim light illuminates his features.

You okay now? he mouths clearly.

Better, and I nod. At least I'm not totally freaking.

Still holding my hand, Tobin raises his watch. By its dim gleam, we search every inch of our prison, making sure there's no way we can escape. Finally we give up and float again in the center of the cramped space.

Had to try, Tobin mouths at me, his lips lifting in a familiar smile.

I can't believe he can smile in here, but that smile helps me fight the panic that wants to suck me under.

I touch my own dive watch and lift it close, illuminating my face. *Thank you.* I shape the words as clearly as I can and gesture to the walls of our prison.

Tobin shrugs, as if being shut up in a small, dark cell is no big deal. Staring at his calm, good-natured face, I wonder what I ever did to deserve such an incredible friend.

Better than hanging out with Whitey, I think he says. When he scowls and bares his teeth in a great imitation of Whitey, a laugh bubbles up inside me.

But then the walls and the darkness close in on me once again. I kick upward, but almost instantly, the ceiling traps me. I pound my fists against it, my breathing crazy fast.

Tobin's beside me and pushes my head against his chest again. This time, he hums a series of light, popular songs. I picture myself back home in Goleta, watching my parents dance. My mother was always so graceful and my father hopelessly clumsy. He danced with her anyway because he knew it made her happy.

When my breathing slows to something near normal, Tobin touches his watch to create a glimmer of light once more.

We should try to sleep, I think he says, and he motions toward the floor. He sits, pulling me gently with him, and then lies down. Awkwardly, I lie down next to him. He pats his chest, and before my claustrophobia seizes me again, I lay my head just below his collarbone.

Tobin goes back to humming, and I'm amazed at all the different kinds of melodies he knows, from church music to nursery songs to hard-core glacier rock.

When he starts on old lullabies, I wonder if he'd like me to go to sleep so he can finally stop humming. I smile sadly when he begins one my mother used to sing to me. Squeezing Tobin's hand, I try to project my gratitude. Even though Wasp will block my words, I hope some of what I'm feeling will reach Tobin. He squeezes my hand in return, and I close my eyes and listen to my childhood lullaby.

Exhausted from fighting fear, I finally slide into sleep.

~ ~ ~

I'm exploring the cabin of a small boat all by myself. In the floor of the bow there's an open compartment. Long and narrow, it almost looks like a coffin. Wait till I tell Cam about this! Grinning, I climb down into it and stretch out on my back. A wave rocks the boat and the heavy door to the compartment slams shut.

I stare up into total darkness. The air stinks of fish and engine oil. My heart begins to pump faster and faster. I push against the hatch with my hands . . . but it won't open. I push my feet against the door with all my strength. It still doesn't budge.

I call Mariah and tell her I'm trapped. She rings and rings the bell at the end of the dolphin dock, but no one comes.

I can't breathe. I pound against the door. Tears trickle down my hot face into my hair and ears. I don't want to die! I raise my hands and hit the door again and again as I fight to pull the stinky air into my lungs . . .

Someone is shaking my shoulder. :Hey, Nere, you're just having a nightmare. Wake up.:

I sit bolt upright, my chest heaving. Tobin reaches out, and I cling to his hands like a lifeline. I'm not suffocating in the hot, fishy bow compartment of that boat anymore. Instead I'm shut in a tiny dark cell inside Kuron's fortress.

It occurs to me that I just heard Tobin's words clearly in my mind. :Did Wasp finally fall asleep?:

:I guess she must have.:

:What time is it, anyway?:

:Just after midnight.:

I breathe deeply, and my heart rate slows a little. I don't want to think about my nightmare. Instead I ask, :When do you think they'll let us out?: I'm painfully aware that our time to find the c-plankton is slipping away fast.

I feel Tobin shrug. :If Kuron wants us to help attack Safety Harbor, then he'll have to let us out of here in three days.:

I start shaking again. I don't know if I can last three days in here. I rest my head on my arms. :Our mission was a total failure.:

:Hey, this mission isn't over yet. You know Robry will keep looking for a way to deactivate the collars, and the others will keep searching for the c-plankton when they can.:

Only if Wasp and Kuron's keepers aren't watching them every second now. I think Tobin realizes his words have a hollow ring to them because he's quiet after that.

:I wonder when they'll get around to feeding us,: he says eventually. :My stomach's so empty even a sea cucumber is starting to sound good.:

:I bet Shadow and the rest will make sure they bring us some food first thing in the morning.: At least I hope so, anyway.

:Shadow really looks out for everyone. In her own way, she's just as much a leader as Dai is.: The respect I hear in Tobin's tone makes me a little jealous.

:Do you like her?:

:A lot,: comes his prompt reply. :She has the guts to stand up to Whitey and Wasp, and I'll always be grateful to her for taking care of Bria.:

:She's pretty, too,: I say, thinking of her beautiful long black hair. I've always wished I had hair like hers.

:Yeah, she is,: he says. He shifts and shines his watch on my face. :But I guess I've always liked blond hair better.: His tone is light and he's smiling, but there's a wistful look in his eyes.

:Tobin, I—: I'm not even sure what I'm going to say, but he cuts me off before I can say it.

:It's all right, Nere. I get it,: he says with an unusual edge in his mental voice. :Do you want to talk about your nightmare now? They say talking about your nightmares can help keep them from coming back.:

I don't want to talk about my nightmare, but it's better than Tobin talking about my hair. I do really like him, but I'm *so* out of my depth when it comes to guys. Back home, I think I was starting to fall in love with Cam. But he wasn't a part of the Neptune Project, which means I'll probably never see him again, and that still makes my heart twist.

Then there's Dai, who makes me happy and frustrated and crazy all at once. And he's part shark, as well as a liar.

I always like being with Tobin, and I know other girls think he's cute. He has a nice face, his eyes are as green as the waters of the strait on a sunny day, and I love the copper color of his hair. He's so much more patient than I am. In fact, he's still waiting patiently for me to answer his question.

:But my nightmare is just going to sound stupid to you.:

:Nightmares are never stupid, especially when they make you punch me.:

:Did I really?:

:Just once, so I tried to get out of your way, but then you hauled off and kicked me. That's when I decided I'd be safer if I just woke you up.:

I raise my own watch and see there's a glint of humor in his eyes now that makes me smile.

:So I figure if you tell me your nightmare,: he says, :maybe you won't have it again, and we can get back to sleep.:

:Okay then.: I draw in a breath. :My nightmare's from this time I climbed into a boat, got shut in a dark compartment, and no one found me for a long time. I-I thought maybe I was going to suffocate in there.:

:How'd you get out?:

:Mariah and the rest of the pod rang a bell for an hour until my father came up from his lab and heard them. The dolphins were so upset that even though my dad's not telepathic, he realized something must be really wrong. The pod kept circling a particular boat, and eventually he figured out I had to be on it.:

:No wonder you don't like small spaces.:

:I had nightmares about that afternoon for years. The nightmares finally stopped, but I guess being in here brought them back.:

:Yeah, well, I understand how that could happen. I feel a little smothered in here myself, and I'm usually okay with small places.:

Probably to distract me, he asks me to tell him a story about my life before the Neptune Project. Even though I'm glad to be distracted, it takes me a minute or two to come up with one.

:My eyes were so weak,: I tell him at last, :that I always had to wear some kind of dark glasses, but my parents were clueless about getting me ones that looked okay. I had one pair I LOVED that James bought for me on the black market using most of the money he'd earned over the summer spearfishing. The glasses were white and had little rhinestones along the edges, and I felt like a movie star when I wore them. But then Rend, a total bully in my class, smashed them on purpose, and I was heartbroken. James and my friend Cam beat the crud out of him later, but it was too late for my poor glasses.:

:So then what happened?:

:So then my dad decided to make me a new pair. He spent forever gluing some rhinestones on an old set of lab goggles, but the goggles made me look like a human fly with bulging eyes. Dad was so proud of them, I wore the horrible things to school every day and took them off the moment I got inside. Then I walked around squinting. I was so relieved when a wave knocked the goggles off our zode into the water, and I begged Mariah not to find them for me.:

:That sounds like your dad,: Tobin says, and I can hear the smile in his voice.

:Yeah, he's always been good at making something out of nothing,: I say lightly, :and that's probably a good thing when you're trying to start a colony in the middle of nowhere.:

But the story I told Tobin still stings. Somehow we had money for state-of-the-art research equipment for Gillian's secret lab, but my parents couldn't afford to buy me and my messed-up eyes a decent pair of dark glasses.

As Tobin and I talk, I try not to think about the small space around us. Sokya checks in with me. I do my best to reassure her we're fine, and warn her, once again, to stay far away from Whitey and the rest.

When another panic attack starts to claim me, Tobin lies down, offers up his shoulder, and hums me to sleep again.

~ ~ ~

Early the next morning, someone throws our door open. I raise my head from Tobin's shoulder. Compared to the complete darkness, the corridor's lighting seems painfully bright. I have to squint to see who's hovering there.

:Well, aren't you two cute, all cuddled up there together,: Wasp says spitefully.

I push myself upright. Shadow and Ocho are floating right behind Wasp, looking worried.

:These guys:—Whitey jerks his head toward Shadow and Ocho—:seem to think we need to feed you. If it were up to me, you two would go hungry for a week or two. But Shadow's a real softy, so here you go.: He pitches a parcel at us, hard, and I have to duck to keep it from hitting my head. Before we can talk to the others, Whitey slams the door in our faces.

:Shadow!: I shout. :Can you hear me? Are Ree and Kalli and Robry okay?:

I hear only blankness. I swim to the door and press my cheek against its cold, hard surface and draw in deep breaths, trying to fight my rising panic at being shut in again. Tobin comes to float beside me. He lifts his watch near our faces.

You okay? he mouths.

Yeah. I nod and try to smile. If Wasp is listening in on my thoughts right now, I don't want her to know how much I hate her prison. I manage to slow my breathing after a few minutes, and I even eat some fish fillet and wakame from the bundle Whitey threw at us.

But as that endless day crawls by, the panic attacks

return, and the only way I can keep from flipping out completely is to listen to Tobin's humming.

That night's even worse. Twice I wake from my old nightmare, thrashing and screaming. After the second nightmare, we realize Wasp has finally fallen asleep, so Tobin and I just sit up and talk. He tells me more about his mother, who was a nurse and died in the last famine. For the first time, he also talks about his father.

:My dad was a genetics professor. When they took him away, we were so little that Bria doesn't remember him. But I do. He loved to tell stories and play the guitar, and he collected folktales and folk songs as a hobby. He told me once that he was afraid too many small but important things, like songs, were getting lost in the wars and famines. And he was always singing when he was in a good mood.:

:So we know where your music genes came from.: I smile at him.

Then I picture my own father and how worried he looked that last night I talked with him at Safety Harbor.

:I keep thinking about my dad and what a good parent he is compared to Kuron,: I tell Tobin. :My mom could get so caught up in her research, she'd hardly speak to us for days, and she was always traveling.: As I stare into the dark, it occurs to me: maybe most of that research and travel I resented so much was for the Neptune Project, and it was her way of loving James and me.

:Anyone would look like a good parent compared to Kuron.: Tobin shakes his head. :But you're right. Your dad loves you, and I think he really cares about all the kids at Safety Harbor. We're just a bunch of lab specimens to Kuron.:

:I know my dad loves me, but while I was at Safety Harbor, I couldn't forgive him for lying about his death and changing me in the first place.: I hug my knees tighter to my chest. :I'm starting to realize that he thought he had to do those things to keep me safe and to give me a better life, but a part of me is still mad at him.:

:That's pretty understandable.:

:Yeah, but I'd like to tell him that I do get some of the choices he made. I-I'm afraid I may never get back to Safety Harbor and have that chance now.:

:You're going to get out of here,: Tobin says firmly, :and I know you'll have a chance to tell your dad everything you're telling me.:

I rub my arms. :Between all those shredders and Whitey and Wasp, I'm not sure we are gonna get back.:

Tobin reaches out and takes my hand. I have another fear I don't want to bring up right now. What if we have to face Kuron tomorrow and he makes us promise to be loyal to him? Wasp is such a strong telepath, I *know* she'll sense that we're lying.

Tobin offers to hum some old sea songs to me. We lie down together and I nestle into his shoulder again. Somehow everything seems a little less grim and scary when I'm next to Tobin like this. Eventually I start to feel sleepy.

:Tobin?: I say as my eyes flutter shut.

:Yeah?:

I want to thank him for being here and helping me through this. I want to thank him for being one of the best friends I've ever had. But sleep is pulling at me, and all I can manage in the end is, :Hey, thanks for everything.:

:Hey, you're welcome. You're always welcome,: he says, a world of Tobin warmth in his reply, and I think I feel him kiss my cheek.

I wake up sometime later when our door crashes open. Raising my head from Tobin's chest, I blink against the bright light. The first thing I focus on is Dai's face.

I see his surprise. Then his expression turns to ice.

chapter twenty-eight

:SEE, YOUR SWEET little Nere hasn't been suffering while you've been gone,: Wasp tells Dai gleefully as she floats next to him. :Tobin's been taking very good care of her.:

Despite the coldness of Dai's expression, I see the pain in his dark eyes.

:I drove a skimmer all night and all day,: he says to me tightly, :just to get back and make sure you were okay. I was so afraid my father might do something terrible to you while I was gone. But I can see now that I didn't need to worry. Clearly you're just *fine*.: He spins away from the door.

:Dai, please don't leave,: I cry.

I reach out to him, but Wasp darts between us. Too late, I see her raise her ungloved hand and swing it toward me.

Instantly, Tobin is there and catches her wrist. Instead of stinging me, she deliberately strokes her fingers across his hand. Tobin gasps and jerks back.

:Dai, she just stung Tobin!: I shout, lunging past Wasp. :Dai, please, don't leave us.: But even as I hurl my words at him, I sense Wasp has raised her stifling wall of silence between us. Dai flashes away down the corridor. Either he doesn't know what's happened to Tobin, or he's too angry to care.

Whitey blocks my path, and he shoves me roughly back into the cell. I fight him with all my strength, hitting at his arms and kicking hard, but he's too strong. Sham is there, too, and he's already pushed Tobin back inside our prison.

Wasp slams the door shut on both of us. I try not to panic, but I know that Tobin's in real trouble.

:If Tobin dies, your bossman is going to be furious with you,: I yell at Wasp. :He wants every Neptune kid he can get.:

:He may want you here, but we don't.:

:But he'll know why Tobin died.:

For a moment, I think I sense a flicker of concern in her mind, but then it vanishes. :It was an accident,: Wasp says mockingly. :Accidents happen all the time here in Atlantea.:

:How can you just let him die? Tobin never did anything to hurt you.:

I strain my telepathy, trying to understand why she's doing this, trying to see if there's anything I can say to change her mind. For an instant, I succeed in pushing past her shields. In the brief moment I'm linked with her, I sense Wasp is desperately lonely. She's angry with both Tobin and me, but she's even angrier with Dai for not liking her.

:Ah, but *you* did hurt me,: she says after I withdraw hastily from her bitter mind, :and I know you care about Tobin. So this is a perfect way to get back at you, and through you I get back at Dai. But I don't know why you're so upset. The idiot will probably be happy to die in there with you.:

:Wasp, don't do this. PLEASE.:

She laughs, but she doesn't reply again. I whirl away from the door to check on Tobin with the light from my watch. I bite my lip when I see he's curled on the floor holding his hand. His eyes are closed and his whole body shakes.

Frantically I try to remember everything my mother taught me about sea wasp venom. Sea wasps are a species of jellyfish that kills more people each year than sharks and all the other dangerous ocean creatures combined. Tobin will be dead in hours unless I can find some way to get him help.

I kneel beside him and lift my watch to shine on our faces. Gently, I touch his shoulder. *How are you?* I mouth.

It hurts, I think he replies, but his teeth are clenched so tightly, I can't be sure.

Let me see, I say. I wince at the angry red blisters across the back of his hand.

I rack my brain trying to think of some way I can help. Any living tentacles left behind on his skin will just inject more poison if I try to remove them. I think people use vinegar to kill them, but of course I don't have any. What Tobin really needs is a shot of antivenom. I'm guessing the keepers must have some, since Wasp has such a vicious temper.

Even as I watch, Tobin starts breathing faster. He lurches upright, heads for our tiny bathroom, and vomits up what little he has in his stomach. Then he staggers back and collapses to the floor. Feeling completely useless, I sit down next to him.

I help him shift so his head is resting on my leg instead of the hard floor. I stroke his hair, but he's in so much pain I doubt he'll even notice. He's panting now, and his trembling is getting worse. When I check his pulse, it seems frighteningly fast and fluttery.

He reaches out and takes my wrist. Somehow he manages to shine my watch on his face.

Sorry, he mouths and gestures to our cell, his eyes glistening with pain.

I know what he really means. He's sorry that he may be about to leave me alone in here. It figures. Even though Tobin might be dying, he's still worrying about me right now.

Then he takes my hand and deliberately brushes it with his lips.

Oh, Tobin. I lean over and kiss his cheek. He smiles for a half second, and then he's gritting his teeth again.

I straighten up, curling my hands into fists. I'm not going to let Tobin die. Wasp may be a strong telepath, and her blocking is powerful, but I'm a strong telepath, too.

:Dai, we need you. Wasp stung Tobin. He's dying!: I shout again and again. Dai's such a sensitive receptive telepath, I hope he can hear my shouts even through Wasp's dampening field. Precious minutes crawl by, but I don't receive a hint that Dai's heard me.

I close my eyes. Hot, angry tears leak past my lids. My head pounds from my psychic shouting. There *has* to be someone I can reach. Shadow's never spoken about the strength of her telepathy, but the fact that she often picks up thoughts I don't purposely send her means she may be a powerful hereditary telepath. And I think she truly cares about Tobin.

I look down at Tobin and swallow a sob. I care about him even more.

Building my fear for him into a single focused, desperate call, I force my way through Wasp's telepathic barrier, trying to find Shadow's mind.

I suck in a breath and focus harder. :SHADOW!: I shout with all my mental strength.

Abruptly, I can sense her awareness. :Nere?: Her mind connects with mine in a link so strong that we can hear each other despite the thick interference Wasp projects.

:Nere? What's wrong?:

:Wasp stung Tobin. He's dying!:

:We'll get meds to you as soon as we can. Tell Tobin to hang on.:

:Thank you.: I gasp, and then Shadow breaks off the link.

I lean down near Tobin's face and shake him gently. *They're bringing meds,* I try to tell him, but his eyes barely open.

His chest heaves rapidly as the minutes crawl by. I check

Tobin's pulse. His heart rate is beginning to slow. What if his heart stops before the others come?

:Tobin, you've got to hang on!: I yell at him telepathically, despite Wasp's dampening field. I take his uninjured hand, squeeze it hard, and will him to stay alive.

Finally someone throws our door open. Shadow darts into our cell with Sunny right behind her. They kneel next to me.

:Where was he stung? Oh, I see,: Shadow says. It's hard not to see now that light is flooding in from the corridor. Tobin's hand has already swollen up like a red, angry ball.

:Sunny, you give him the shot of antivenom. I'll clean the back of his hand with these vinegar pads.:

I move out of the way so the girls have more room to work on Tobin. They seem to know exactly what to do. I notice they're both wearing gloves.

:Looks like you've been through this before,: I say to Ocho, who is floating in the doorway.

:Yeah, way too many times,: he replies with a bleak expression.

I glance past him and see my friends are also there, along with Rad.

:Are you okay?: I ask Ree.

:Yeah, we're fine. These guys have been looking out for us,: she replies.

:Which is a good thing. I think Whitey's waiting for a chance to rip us apart,: Kalli says.

:Make sure you don't give him one,: I say. Wasp's telepathic block seems to have disappeared. :Hey, how come I can hear you again?:

:Wasp left the fortress a few minutes ago.: Shadow glances up from Tobin. :I think she's trying to find Dai. He went storming off, which is strange because he just got back, and I know he's been really worried about you.:

On a private send, I explain quickly. :Tobin's been humming songs to me to help me fight my claustrophobia. Wasp made sure Dai saw us together, and I think it made him furious.:

:That explains a lot,: Shadow says. Carefully she places the pads that she used to clean Tobin's hand into a bag. :I'm sorry we can't let you out. The keepers might turn the shredders loose on us.:

:We're trying to reach the bossman to let him know what happened,: Ocho adds. :We're pretty sure he'll let Tobin go to the infirmary when he finds out.:

:It's good you reached Shadow when you did,: Sunny says, shaking her head. :Wasp stung him pretty badly.:

:Here's a cold pack,: Ocho offers. :We'll bring you a new cold pack every hour. That's the only thing that helps the pain.:

:Thank you all so much,: I say.

:We're just sorry this happened,: Rad replies. :Tobin's a good guy.:

:How could Wasp be like this?: I ask.

:I stopped trying to understand her a long time ago,: Rad admits.

:Imagine never being able to touch anyone,: Ocho counters, his brown eyes sad, :and always having to worry if you might kill someone. It twisted her when she was little.:

:And she's only gotten more twisted,: Rad says with much less sympathy in his mental voice.

:Nere, you doin' all right in there?: Robry breaks in.

:Tobin's been doing a great job of distracting me.: He's still doing it. Now I'm much more worried about him than I am about being shut in again.

:H-he's not going to die, is he?: I ask Shadow and Sunny.

:That antivenom should work fine.: Shadow tries to reassure me, but I sense she's still anxious about Tobin.

From the way Rad keeps glancing at the nearby camera, I know he's anxious about the keepers. I force myself to move back into our prison.

:We'll be back in an hour with a new cold pack,: Ocho says, looking apologetic as he pushes the door shut.

I hear the lock click, and Tobin and I are in the dark again.

chapter twenty-nine

I TAKE A DEEP BREATH and turn away from the door. Staring into blackness, I kneel beside Tobin and find his right arm by touch, carefully wrapping the cold pack around his poor swollen hand.

:That feels better,: he says weakly.

:Hey, nice to have you back with us.: I check his pulse. I'm encouraged to see it's already stronger and steadier.

:How's my heart rate?:

:It was getting scary slow, but it's picking up again.:

I sit down beside him, and Tobin shifts until his head rests on my leg.

:You could always smooth my hair again. That made me feel better, too,: he says, a hint of his old humor in his mental tone.

Relieved that he can make a joke, I smile and start stroking his hair. But I can feel that he's clenching his jaw, and tremors still rack his body.

:Hey,: Tobin says after a long moment, :if I don't get out of here, please t-tell Bria I love her.:

.They said that antivenom is going to fix you up just fine. You'll have a chance to tell her that yourself.:

:Yeah, well, just in case,: he insists, and I sense the pain he's trying to hide.

:Just in case, you know I will,: I promise.

As Tobin dozes off, the dark presses on me, but I do my best to ignore it. Tobin needs me, and I can't start freaking out again. I miss his humming. But the others are coming back in an hour, and just knowing that our cell door will open soon makes a huge difference.

His breathing is more labored than normal, but I check his pulse every ten minutes, and it's definitely stronger.

:Nere, you need to get ready.: Robry's mental touch startles me just a half hour later. :We're about to break out of this place.:

:Huh?:

:Dai led the shark crew away and then circled back to help us escape. You're not going to believe this, but he brought a bunch of Sea Rangers back with him from Safety Harbor. They're mining the supports to the fortress. They know Kuron wants to wipe out Safety Harbor, and their orders are to destroy Atlantea. But they're going to wait to make sure we're out safely with the c-plankton first, and Dai's pretty sure he knows where it's hidden.:

:You're right. I don't believe it,: I say dazedly. :But won't the keepers know the Sea Rangers are out there and turn the shredders loose on them?:

:We sent all the keepers to shore, and I don't think they'll be coming back.:

:How'd you pull that off?: I ask, struggling to keep up with him.

:Ocho and I took the surveillance cameras offline.: Robry sounds so smug, I have to smile. :Then we showed up topside with plenty of spearguns and Rad. The keepers are terrified of Sham and Whitey, but they're really scared of the sparkhead, too. Rad gave one of the keepers a nice little zap. We told them he would fry their brains if they didn't leave Atlantea, and they almost jumped into the boat. A bunch had been thinking about quitting anyway. Kuron's a pretty scary employer.:

:What about our collars and the c-plankton?:

:We've got a plan for them, too.:

:Great,: I say, still trying to wrap my head around the idea that we're going to try to escape right now.

:Tobin, wake up.: I shake his shoulder gently. :We're about to get out of here and go home.: I hope Tobin's strong enough to survive the next few hours. Somehow I don't think we're just going to swim away from this awful place.

When the door swings open, I'm surprised to see Dai and Mako are there, along with Rad, Sunny, Ocho, Shadow, and my friends from Safety Harbor. Dai's expression is cool as he gazes down at Tobin and me.

:You'd better get him up,: he says. :We don't have much time before Wasp and the others come back.:

Tobin tries to swim, but he's so weak, Ocho has to help him from our cell.

:First we're going to try to deactivate the collars,: Dai explains to me, :and then we're going down to the Enviro Lab on Deck One. Based on the tanks and plankton rotators I've seen in there, I'm pretty sure that's where we'll find the c-plankton strain you've been searching for. I spoke with your dad, and he told me why you guys really came here.:

:I can't believe you talked with him,: I say, trying to imagine Dai and my dad together. :And are you sure you want to help us take the c-plankton? Your father is going to be furious with you.:

:Nere, I'm not a moron. I know the seas are in serious trouble. If the c-plankton my mother engineered can help cool the planet, you should use it. And I don't plan to stick around to see how my father feels. We all want to come to Safety Harbor. Your dad said we can live there.:

:If we help you escape and then we stick around,: Ocho adds, :the bossman will feed us to his sharkheads for sure.:

:We've always wanted a real home,: Shadow says quietly.

:I think you guys would really like Safety Harbor,: I say, still struggling to absorb the news that they all want to leave. I knew they were unhappy, but somehow I never pictured them coming back with us.

:All right then, we move to phase two of our plan,: Dai declares. :Mako, you and Rad are up next.:

Rad glances at Ree. :Hey, *chica*, you take care of yourself, okay?:

:You get yourself permanently fried doing this, I'm never talking to you again,: Ree says fiercely, but I hear the worry in her mental tone.

:I'll keep that in mind.: Rad sends her a cheeky smile, and then he and Mako dart away.

:Where are they going?: I ask Dai, afraid I already know the answer.

:Rad and I have talked about this a bunch of times,: Dai replies somberly. :We think there's a good chance he could survive the big zap if he hits the kill switch.:

:Are you guys crazy?:

:Just think about it,: Shadow replies. :His body is designed to generate large amounts of electricity. He thinks it would take some serious voltage to really kill him.:

:Then why didn't he try to flip the kill switch before?:

:We didn't have any place to go before,: Sunny says with a shrug, :and now we do. And we all want your dad to get that c-plankton.:

:Come on,: Dai urges us. :We can watch Mako and Rad from Control Room Two.:

Dai leads us to the nearest control room. He and Ocho pull up a shot of a long corridor on a dry level and display it on a dozen screens around the room.

:This should be the right feed,: Dai says, and moments later we see Mako and Rad running down the corridor.

They pause in front of a wide door to enter a code, and the door swings open. Dai switches the feed, and then we see Mako and Rad burst into a stark black-and-white bedroom. They run straight to a wall covered with screens and controls and stop at a bright red lever. That, I realize with a shiver, must be the kill switch.

The camera shows us Rad's profile. His hand hovers over the lever. Then he scans the room and finds our camera. He tries to send us a smile, but even from this distance, I can see his face is pale.

:He's *muy estúpido*, but he's even more brave,: Ree says quietly. Kalli slips an arm around her shoulder.

I look back at the screen. The next instant, Rad jerks the lever.

chapter Thirty

RAD'S BODY convulses as his collar shocks him. He falls to his knees and then to the ground as his muscles seize and jerk. Mako watches Rad, and even from here I can see his eye is twitching.

:Mako, you gotta stay clear of him!: Dai shouts telepathically.

:Why?: I can't help asking.

:Mako can't touch him,: Dai explains. :That voltage is so strong, it would flow right into him from Rad and stop his heart immediately.:

My eyes sting with tears. Oh, Rad, thank you for risking this, I think. Like Kalli, I slip my arm around Ree, who is trembling now, and we stay by her side. Seconds seem to crawl by, and finally Rad's body goes slack. Now he's sprawled on his back and he's clearly unconscious. But is he dead?

Mako waits for an endless minute. At last he leans over and gingerly checks for Rad's pulse. He turns toward the camera and gives us a big grin. He picks up Rad like he weighs nothing, slings him over his shoulder, and dashes out of the room.

Now I understand why Dai chose Mako to help. He's

strong and fast, and he can handle staying out of the water better than the rest of us.

We glance at one another uncertainly.

Ocho reaches for his collar first. He finds the release catch with his fingers, rips off the collar, and throws it away from him. :Way to go, Rad!: Ocho pumps several fists at once. :He really did it.:

Seconds later, we're all reaching for our collars, but I can't seem to get mine off. Tobin can't get his off, either, with his right hand so swollen, but Shadow helps him.

Dai is beside me. :Lift your braid,: he says, and he presses the catch for me. He pulls off the collar and tosses it away with a look of pure loathing. Instantly I feel lighter.

:Thank you.: I turn to Dai. :Thank you for everything.:

:You can thank me after we get you guys out of here in one piece.: He turns to Ocho. :Let's check the camera feed and make sure that jammer Kalli and Ree placed next to the shredder tank is still working.:

:You know about the jammer?: I ask in surprise.

Dai nods to my friends. :They told me about it.:

:The moment I heard we were going to try to escape, I thought of the jammer,: Kalli explains. :I figured we should take it to the shredder tank to make sure no one could send them after us.:

:What happened when you turned it on?:

:That happened,: Ree says, and points toward the screens. :Guess the prototype worked okay after all.:

I stare at a screen full of red water and floating bits of shredder. Occasionally there's a flash of gray in the red murk. I look away from the screen, my stomach lurching.

:They're still tearing each other apart in there,: Dai says grimly. :I'm guessing a few dozen will survive, but they won't be hungry for a long time.:

:It's more merciful this way,: Shadow says, her eyes haunted. :They were too human to be happy as sharks, and too sharklike to ever be human.:

:Right,: I say, but I can't help shuddering as Dai leads us out of the control room, with Ocho and me helping Tobin along.

We reach Entry Bay One just as Mako arrives towing Rad in a lifeguard hold. Gently, Mako lays Rad down on the deck, and Ree hurries to his side. As she checks his pulse, Rad's eyes flutter open and his gaze focuses on Ree's face.

:Hey, *chica*, do I have frizzy hair?: he asks her weakly. :I got a pretty big zap.:

:You got some nasty electrical burns around your neck, but your hair's looking good.:

:That's the first nice thing you've ever said to me,: Rad says, struggling to sit up. :Maybe I'm finally getting somewhere.:

I glance away from Rad and Ree and realize Dai and the others are busily unlocking a variety of skimmers we can use to make a quick escape.

:Nere, are you okay in there?: A familiar mind contacts mine.

It's Rohan! :Yeah, we're okay.:

:Great. We've got the mines set to bring the whole place down. They're rigged so we can blow them in sections. Let me know the moment you're safely out of there.:

:We should be leaving in a few minutes. I'll keep you posted. Dai, we'd better go find that c-plankton *now*.:

:Yeah, I just want to get this unlocked.: He motions to his own powerful skimmer.

I reach out to my dolphin companions. :Sokya, Densil, you guys close?:

:yes, and we are happy to see our friends from Safety Harbor,: Sokya replies excitedly. :my mother and her little one are here—:

:the other young humans return on their skimmers,: Densil says, breaking into our conversation, :and a sub comes quickly from the south!:

:Rohan, some of Kuron's kids and a sub are heading for Atlantea,: I warn him. :You've got to hide and send your dolphins away.:

:Roger that,: Rohan replies coolly.

:We'll tell you when to blow those mines,: I add.

I really hope we don't have to fight our way out of here, but I have a nasty feeling Wasp isn't going to just let us walk away. And I bet Kuron's on that sub.

I warn the others that the shark crew will be here any moment.

:I still think we should ask Wasp if she wants to come with us,: Ocho says.

I stare at him in disbelief. Wasp is the last person I'd want swimming around Safety Harbor.

:Bro, she's so broken and twisted now, she'll never be happy.: Dai shakes his head.

:She would have let Tobin die without a second thought,: Sunny adds indignantly.

:I think she'd be different away from here. We'd all be different,: Ocho says, looking stubborn.

My heart sinks when an angry mind touches mine and I see a blur of movement behind me. Wasp and the others are parking their skimmers on the deck.

:Just what do you think you're all doing?: Wasp asks, her pale cheeks flushed, while Sham and Whitey flank her.

:We're leaving,: Dai replies steadily. :And we're never coming back.:

:Rad flipped the kill switch to disable the collars, and now we're all free,: Shadow adds, moving up beside Dai, her face cool and watchful. Rad and Sunny gather around Dai. Ocho and Mako hover on the sides. I've seen this divide between Kuron's kids before, but it's never felt this ominous.

:So, this really doesn't work anymore, huh?: Sham reaches up and quickly tugs off his collar. :Isn't that too bad? Now the keepers can't zap us if we misbehave.:

The menace I hear in his tone makes the hair rise on the back of my neck.

Whitey pulls off his collar, too, his cold, slate gaze never leaving me. :Princess, you're the reason everything changed around here. Maybe if we feed you to the sharkheads, Ice here will get his act together, and we can go back to the way things were before.:

:We were one big ol' happy pod and doing fine until you came along,: Sham adds.

Dai shifts until he's floating in front of me. :You really think we were doing fine? I'm glad Nere and her friends showed me there's another way we can be.:

:Most of us have never been happy,: Shadow declares defiantly. :We've been treated like lab specimens ever since we were little.:

:Hey, it worked for me.: Whitey shrugs.

Wasp gasps, and her gaze goes distant. :There are dozens of Neptune kids outside. They've come to destroy Atlantea, and Ice brought them here.:

She turns on Dai, her mouth twisted in a strange smile. :You really want to tear everything apart? We mean so little to you? Then let's have some real fun.: She raises a hand and pulls out a knife.

:No!: Ocho cries.

He lunges for her, but he's too late. Wasp slices the palm

of her hand, and blood blossoms like a scarlet flower in the water in front of her.

Whitey, Mako, Dai, and Sham stiffen as if the keepers just zapped them.

chapter thirty-one

WHITEY IS THE FIRST to move. He lunges for Wasp, rows of sharp teeth bared, but Ocho darts between them. The water fills with a blinding cloud of dark ink that Ocho shoots from his neck. I think I see Ocho grappling with Whitey inside the cloud, trying to keep him from killing Wasp.

When Sham charges straight at me, Dai slams him aside. Sham whirls around to charge me again, but Rad dashes up behind him, and Sham stiffens as Rad shocks him.

:You'll pay for that, you stupid sparkhead.: Sham snarls at Rad and goes after him instead.

:many shark people follow the sub,: Densil warns me.

Rohan contacts me seconds later. :Nere, a bunch of shredders are heading for your entry bay. We cut off a dozen, but the rest got past us by hiding behind that sub.:

:HUNGRY SHREDDERS HEADING OUR WAY FAST!: I broadcast desperately to everyone in the entry bay. I dive for the wall and grab the closest speargun and quiver.

:Mako, you take Robry, Tobin, and Nere and head for the lab,: Dai orders. :Find the c-plankton, and I'll meet you at Entry Bay Two.: Ocho and Whitey are still fighting each other, but the rest of Dai's friends race to get their spearguns.

I glance at Mako. Although his eye is twitching horribly, he seems to have himself under control. :You got it, Ice,: Mako says.

:What about Kalli and Ree?: I ask Dai.

:We'll look out for your friends,: Shadow snaps. :You find the c-plankton. Now go!:

Seconds later, the first wave of shredders rushes into the bay. Mako grabs my wrist with one hand and Tobin's with the other and tows us away as fast as he can. Robry, a speargun slung over his shoulder, fights to keep up with us. I glance back to see Shadow squirt a cloud of ink at a charging shredder. Moments later, through a gap in the dark cloud, I see Shadow has her arms around its neck, and she's literally choking it to death.

Mako pulls Tobin and me down a long corridor so quickly, his legs are a blur of movement. He turns and turns again, and then we're in front of a door marked ENVIRO LAB THREE, PROHIBITED AREA, which explains why we've never been in here before. Mako opens the door and we rush inside. Instantly, lights begin to flash and an alarm siren sounds. Large tanks of greenish water fill the lab. At one end, four tall, narrow machines slowly rotate dozens of small metal canisters.

Robry heads straight for the machines, ignoring the lights and sirens. :I'm pretty sure this is what we're looking for. To keep a really dense culture of phytoplankton alive, it would help to keep rotating it so the plankton doesn't pile up and get crushed on the bottom.:

He reaches out and snags a canister off the carousel. :Hey, Tobin, you were right. Kuron did label it.: Robry shows us the canister. It reads C-PLANKTON STRAIN 52.

:I'm just glad we found it,: I say shortly, then I unsling my quiver and toss out most of the darts. :Let's grab as many canisters as we can and get out of here.:

Swiftly, Mako and I take dozens of canisters from all four machines and stuff them in my quiver. In the meantime, Robry sweeps up several small notebooks and shoves them into his seapack.

:Guys, we have a problem.: Tobin's pain-filled mind touches mine.

I spin around. One of the keepers hovers by the door in full scuba gear, his speargun trained on Tobin. I look into the man's mask. There's a familiar long red scar over his right eye. Somehow Rad and the rest must have overlooked him when they sent the other keepers to shore.

He motions for Robry and me to dump out my quiver. Then he jabs the tip of his speargun into Tobin's side. If we don't do what he wants, it's clear he's going to shoot. Trying not to panic, I reach out and touch the keeper's thoughts.

The boss will give me a big, fat bonus for saving his precious plankton, he's thinking with satisfaction.

:Once he shoots, we can get him before he reloads,: Mako says.

:Yeah, but that first dart's going into Tobin.: I have to

fight to keep my mental voice steady. :Mako, help me unload this quiver slowly.:

As we lean over it and start pulling out canisters, Tobin curls up as if his injured hand hurts, and I see him inching for the dive knife on his right calf.

:Don't,: I yell at him mentally, :it's too dangerous!:

Robry hears me and glances at Tobin, who's still reaching for his knife. Moments later, Robry takes his seapack and makes a big show of trying to shake out the notebooks. He reaches an arm deep into his pack and acts like one of the notebooks is stuck.

Numbly, I watch them while my heart beats in hard, fast strokes. I can sense the keeper's rising impatience.

There's a flash of movement as Tobin twists about and slices through the keeper's air hose. The keeper fires at Tobin, and silver bubbles flow from the hose, making it hard for me to see. Mako darts across the room in a blur of motion and wrenches the speargun from the man's grasp. Then he clubs the keeper unconscious with the butt of the weapon.

I launch myself at Tobin. :Did he hit you?:

:J-just missed me,: he replies. He's shaking hard again. Gently, I take his knife and slide it back into the sheath on his calf.

:Um, Nere, this guy's gonna suffocate in about two minutes,: Robry says as he looks at the unconscious keeper floating there with bubbles still streaming from his air hose.

:Switch him over to his backup hose. Mako, help me gather up all these canisters again. We gotta get out of here.:

:If this guy doesn't wake up before his oxygen runs out, he's still gonna suffocate,: Robry points out as he quickly adjusts the keeper's breathing rig.

:At least we're giving him a chance. That's more than he'd give us,: I reply.

The moment we finish gathering up the c-plankton canisters, Mako grabs our hands and pulls Tobin and me out the door. As he tows us down the corridor toward Entry Bay Two and Robry sprints alongside us, I realize I'm trembling from our encounter with the keeper. Red lights flash and the alarm siren continues to sound. Where are Kalli, Ree, and the rest? I hope they're doing all right against the shredders.

We've only made it halfway down the corridor when Sham's threatening voice fills our minds. :Hey, little buddy, it's time to play some hunt and seek again.:

I glance back and spot Sham. He's closing on us fast. His thick lips are pulled back in a fierce grin. Mako sprints forward, towing us so quickly that my shoulder burns.

:Tobin and the Neptune princess are just slowing you down, Twitchy-boy. You let go of them, and you could get away from me no problem.:

:I'm *not* gonna leave them,: Mako says, and he swims even faster.

:Then I'm gonna catch you. And you're gonna wish you'd stayed to play with those sharkheads instead of with me.:

:Sham's right,: Mako tells us on a private send. :He's gonna catch us before we can reach Entry Bay Two, and then we'll be in big trouble, but he gave me an idea. Let's duck into the Maze. We've got a better chance of losing him in there. I can't use my speed against him while I'm dragging you around out here.:

:'Kay,: I reply, fighting a surge of nausea. Entering that maze again is just about the *last* thing I want to do.

:Robry, once we're in there, I'll lead Sham away from you guys, and you can guide Tobin and Nere back out,: Mako says.

:I'll try,: Robry replies.

Mako pulls us around a corner to the door to the Maze. He dashes inside with me, Robry, and Tobin right behind him. Mako slaps off the lights. Instantly I'm staring into total darkness. At least the Maze is bigger than the cell I just left.

Mako takes my wrist again. :Grab my leg,: I order Robry. :Otherwise, you might get left behind.:

:Good idea,: Robry says, and I feel him grip my left leg just as Mako jerks me forward again.

My shoulder and arm muscles quiver from the extra strain of towing Robry as Mako darts and weaves through the Maze. After the first three turns, I've completely lost my sense of direction, but Mako never hesitates as he pulls us deeper and deeper into the heart of Kuron's labyrinth.

:So you wanna play shark versus whale in here. That's never gone so well for you,: I hear Sham taunt Mako. I shiver when I realize Sham must be in the Maze now.

:I wasn't playing for keeps before,: Mako says, surprising me with the steel I hear in his mental voice. :Now I am.:

:That's supposed to scare me?:

:It should,: Mako replies steadily as we turn and turn again. :I'm faster than you, and before, I still wanted to be your friend. Now I know you're a coward. You just left your best friend to be chewed up by those sharkheads.:

:I'm just smarter than everyone else. I plan to get out of here alive, but first I have a little unfinished business with the princess and her friends. She needs to pay for messing with my pod.:

Mako suddenly comes to a stop. :You guys stay here,: he tells us on a private send. :I'm going after Sham. When I tell you, head for the door as fast as you can.:

I risk lighting my watch and shine it on Mako's face. :Sure you want to do this?:

:I'm sure,: he says as he checks his speargun. He looks amazingly calm, and his tic is gone. :Head for Entry Bay Two. I know Ice will meet you there if he can.:

:Thanks, Mako,: I say, my throat gone tight.

:No biggie,: Mako says as he darts away. :I owe you, and I owe Ice.:

I raise my watch to check on Tobin. He's cradling his swollen hand, and he's still shaking. :We'll get you out of here soon.:

:D-don't worry about me.:

I load my speargun. :Robry, let's float back to back with Tobin between us, just in case.:

:You got it,: Robry says. We shift around so that we're facing different directions. After a long moment, Robry asks in a small voice, :Do you think Sham really wants to kill us?:

:If I catch her, I'm gonna kill her and her little buddies, and then maybe things will go back to the way they were around here,: Sham calls out. :I'm not looking for you, Twitchy; I'm looking for them. So you can just stay out of this.:

:Guess that answers your question,: I tell Robry.

I strain my eyes, peering into total darkness. Mako's faster than Sham, and I hope that his shark's senses will be more effective than Sham's ability to echolocate.

Over the pounding of the blood in my ears, I hear a low-pitched series of clicks to my right. I grip my speargun tighter. Sham is definitely using his personal sonar system as he prowls the maze searching for us. He can't sense us through the thick dividers, but if he turns on to our row in the Maze, he'll find us in seconds.

Raising my speargun, I keep my finger on the trigger. I don't hear anything now. Is Sham sneaking up on us? I can sense his rising excitement, but he's shielding his thoughts so tightly that I can't read him directly.

Suddenly, I hear a burst of clicks straight ahead.

:Did you hear those?: I ask Robry and Tobin on a private send.

:Yeah,: Tobin replies. :Mako'd better make his move soon.:

:I think Sham's right in front of me.: My heart races faster and faster. I stare into the darkness. Should I fire? But what if I miss? It takes at least ten seconds to reload, and Sham could be on us by then.

I start to tighten my trigger finger, but then Sham's psychic shout roars out.

:OW, YOU LITTLE FREAK! I can't believe you shot me. I'm gonna make you pay for this.:

:I got him from behind. Nere, Robry, go!: Mako shouts on a private send. :If Sham can still swim, he's gonna chase me first. I'll lead him away from your route out.:

:Make sure he doesn't catch you,: I tell Mako.

:He won't, not with a spear dart through his thigh,: Mako replies. Then I hear him call out to Sham, :Hey, you big moron, I'm back this way.:

:Help me pull Tobin,: Robry says breathlessly to me. :We can't get separated in here.:

I sense Tobin stiffen in pain as we grab him, but he doesn't say a word as we sprint away from Sham for the door.

:Left, and then a right, and then another right,: I hear

Robry murmuring to himself as he leads us through the dark. I can't believe he has any idea where we are. I hear Mako taunting Sham again, and Sham swearing angrily as he tries to chase him.

:One more left should do it,: Robry declares.

Seconds later, we turn left again and swim hard until I hear Robry's hand smack into a wall. :The door's gotta be around here somewhere.:

I risk using my watch for a half second to scan the wall. :There's the door handle.: I almost sob with relief. I twist the lever, and moments later, we burst into the corridor. I check both directions for shredders, but the hallway's clear for the moment.

:Kalli, Ree, where are you guys?:

:We're in Entry Bay Two, waiting for you. No one else is here yet.:

:Don't wait for us. This is an order. Go find the Sea Rangers. We'll follow you as soon as we can.:

:'Kay, but we'll be right outside. Call us if you need help,: Ree replies. :Rad's with us.:

At least two of my team are safe now. Robry and I sprint down the corridor, pulling Tobin along as fast as we can. I hope Mako's going to be okay, too.

Dai dashes out from a corridor on our left. The right side of his face looks swollen, and there's a makeshift bandage wrapped around his forearm.

:You guys all right?: he asks.

:Yeah. Sham came after us, but Mako hid us in the Maze and shot him in the leg,: I reply.

:Did you get the c-plankton?:

:This is crammed full of the stuff.: I pat my quiver.

There's motion on my right, and suddenly Mako's swimming beside me.

:Sham's not too happy with me right now,: he tells us with a shaky grin. :My spear dart won't kill him, but he's gonna have to stop and patch himself up, and that should slow him down some.:

:Nice job, bro,: Dai says.

:I'm glad shark beat whale this time,: I tell Mako.

:Yeah, me too.:

:Let me and Mako take Tobin. We'll go faster,: Dai says, and we transfer Tobin over to Dai and Mako as gently as we can. We still jostle Tobin's hand and he groans.

:Just keep going,: Tobin urges us.

:Hang in there,: Robry tells him. :We'll have you to a medic soon.:

As we kick as fast as we can for the entry bay, I say to Dai, :I was surprised you came back. I thought you were furious with me.:

:I wasn't too thrilled to see you with Tobin, but you did hand me a good excuse to go storming off and lead Wasp away while the Sea Rangers set their mines.:

:You really want them to destroy Atlantea? This is your father's dream.:

:They can bring it down around his ears. My dad wanted to help the world, but he's too warped and twisted now to help anyone. I have to make sure you'll be safe from him . . . and I have to prove to you that I want to be different.:

:What about Wasp, Whitey, and Sham?:

:They're just too violent for Safety Harbor. I hope I'm not, also,: he adds darkly.

Seconds later, we reach Entry Bay Two. A small sub is moored along the bay's southern side. Kuron glares at us through its large porthole. He's wearing a full wetsuit, and I shudder when I see anger in every line of his taut body. Dai freezes when he spots his father. Then he squares his shoulders and swims on into the bay.

Wasp kneels on the deck next to a torn and bleeding Ocho. Whitey hovers behind them, a loaded speargun in his hand. His face looks strained. Sunny and Shadow are working over Ocho feverishly. I wince when I see he's missing at least one of his arms, and Sunny has a bandage tied around her leg.

I sense Whitey is fighting to keep himself under control, and in his cold way, he's sorry for hurting Ocho.

:It got pretty ugly back in Entry Bay One,: Dai tells me on a private send. :Whitey hit Ocho, and then a sharkhead ripped off his injured arm. Whitey got himself together, and once we shot enough of the sharkheads, they turned on one another, and we slipped away. Whitey and Wasp must have overheard me telling the rest of us to meet up here, and wanted Shadow and Sunny to help Ocho.:

:Ochy, I'm so sorry,: I hear Wasp say, tears in her voice. :I never meant for you to get hurt.:

:I know,: Ocho says. He reaches up one of his unhurt arms to touch her cheek. But then his eyes roll back in his head, and his hand slips from her face as he passes out.

Her face stricken, Wasp looks up at Shadow. :You have to save him,: she says. :Please, I don't want him to die.:

:He's going to bleed out unless we can get him to their medics,: Shadow says sternly and motions to us. :There's no one left here who can help him.:

Wasp glances at the sub. Kuron has vanished from the window. She draws in a deep breath. :Then take Ochy and go,: she says. :I don't care what the bossman says.:

Shadow looks away from Wasp and meets my gaze, her eyes full of concern.

:Good luck, Nere,: she says as she and Sunny gently pick up Ocho. Moments later, they swim out of the bay, towing Ocho between them.

Once they're safely away, I realize that Whitey is staring at me malevolently, his loaded speargun pointed right at my gut.

:Robry and Tobin, you guys should go, too, if Whitey will let you,: I tell them.

:Yeah, go on and get out,: Whitey growls. :We never wanted any of you here. It's all about the Neptune princess now. She's the one who messed with Ice's head.:

Robry shoots me a worried look.

:You've got to get Tobin to a medic,: I say quickly. I'm dying to pass Robry my spear-dart quiver, but I'm afraid to draw too much attention to it.

:W-we can't leave you here,: Tobin protests, his eyes glazed with pain.

:Dai and Mako will look out for me. Go!:

Robry doesn't waste another second. He grabs Tobin, and an instant later, the two of them disappear over the deck's edge into the sea.

"Mako, Dai, and Nere, drop your spearguns now," I hear a familiar male voice through my ear receivers. "Whitey, if she so much as twitches after she puts her weapon down, shoot the Hanson girl."

I turn, shivers tracing down my back. Kuron is hovering by his sub in full dive gear. Through his wide dive mask, I can see his expression is cold and set.

chapter Thirty-two

:WE'D BETTER DO what my dad wants,: Dai says reluctantly.

I lay my speargun on the deck, and Mako and Dai do the same. Wasp is still gazing after Ocho, but abruptly, she seems to remember herself.

:This is all your fault.: She turns on me, her mental voice tight. :Just because you came here to get that stupid c-plankton, everything's ruined.:

The moment she says c-plankton, I can't help picturing the canisters I'm carrying. I try to guard my thoughts, but when her eyes narrow, I know I'm a second too late.

:So you found it after all, and now you're planning to take it to your daddy. Isn't that sweet?: she says coldly, and quickly keys the com-pad on her wrist. I'm almost certain she's telling Kuron about the c-plankton.

I watch his face, and I can tell the moment he's read her message on the tiny screen built into his mask. His brows draw together and his dark eyes focus on me.

"Drop that quiver now, or I will tell Whitey to shoot you in the heart this instant."

The frozen menace in Kuron's tone makes me tremble.

When Dai deliberately swims between Whitey and me, Kuron's expression tightens.

Swiftly, I unsling the heavy quiver and lay it on the deck. I don't want to give Whitey an excuse to shoot either of us.

"Nere Hanson, how dare you try to steal my wife's research?" Kuron's voice is controlled, but I hear the anger vibrating in it. "You, Mako, and my son must be punished for defying me. And Whitey and Wasp, you two have disappointed me as well by letting the other Neptune subjects escape." He reaches for a small square device on his dive belt.

:Nere, cover your ears!: Dai cries.

I see Wasp pale, and she, Mako, and Whitey clap their hands over their ears. Before I can cover my own, Kuron pushes a button on the device.

Instantly, pulses of sound fill my brain. They are so loud and piercing that they feel like they're going to tear my head apart. I cover my ears, but that doesn't help. The sound builds until I'm afraid my eardrums are going to explode.

I curl into a ball as wave after wave of agony radiates through my head.

Just when I'm sure I can't stand the pain a second longer, it vanishes. I stay curled up, panting and gasping and wondering if the pain is going to come again. I open my eyes and look around. Wasp is uncurling herself and looking just as white and shaken as I feel.

:W-what was that?: I ask Dai, but he's angrily keying

his com-pad. Whitey, I realize with a sinking heart, appears to have recovered the quickest from those sonic pulses and once again has his speargun trained on the three of us.

:The bossman triggered a sonic emitter on his sub,: Mako answers me bitterly. :We call it 'the Screamer.' Originally he designed it to drive orcas away from his research sites, and then he realized it was a great way to punish us, too.:

"Now I have your full attention," Kuron declares, "I'm returning to my sub through the smaller airlock. You will follow me inside through the larger airlock immediately, or I will punish you again."

Kuron swims for a small round hatch at the bottom of the sub and disappears inside. Dai glances at the edge of the entry deck.

:Don't even think about trying to make a break for it, bro,: Whitey warns him. :I'd shoot you in the leg to keep you from going, and then your princess wouldn't have anyone but Twitchy here to look out for her.:

After a long, tense moment, Wasp sends us a malicious smile, swims to a large round hatch at the base of the sub, and enters the airlock first. Dai takes my hand and follows her, careful to keep himself between us. Mako follows me, and Whitey brings up the rear with his loaded speargun.

The airlock is about eight feet long. Inside it looks like a big, round steel pipe with a heavy, watertight door at each end. Whitey swings the outer door closed and seals it shut.

The space is small and tight, particularly with five kids fill-ing it. But this is no time for a panic attack. I force myself to take long, steady breaths. I miss Tobin and his humming, but at least the airlock is well lit. Dai squeezes my hand.

:My dad can't use the sonic emitter on us in here,: Dai tries to reassure me. :That's mounted on the outside of his sub.:

Moments later, the water begins to drain away as pumps push air into the chamber. The pumps stop when the water is sloshing around Dai's shoulders and my neck.

"We figured this out years ago," Dai explains. "If my dad really wants to talk to me, this is one of the few ways I can still breathe, talk, and hear him at the same time."

Kuron appears at the window in the middle of the air-lock. His expression is still cold, but I can sense the waves of fury radiating from him.

"You've removed your collars." His deep voice issues clearly from a nearby speaker. "How did this happen?"

"Rad threw the kill switch," Dai replies. "And though I doubt his life matters to you, he managed to survive your nasty little experiment."

"So he cared enough about the rest of you to risk his life," Kuron muses. "I thought he was so unremarkable. There's little in the boy's psychological profile to suggest he would be capable of such sacrifice."

"I guess that just goes to show how useless your profiles are," Dai taunts him.

The moment Rad reached for the kill switch replays itself in my mind. "If you'd taken the time to get to know him," I retort, "you'd know how *remarkable* Rad is. He's one of the kindest and bravest of all your kids."

Kuron looks at me as if I'm some kind of insect. "Wasp is right. This Hanson girl is a dangerous instigator."

"Sir, when we returned just now," Wasp interjects, "Dai was about to run away with her to her father's colony."

"Is this true?" For the first time, Kuron appears startled.

"Absolutely," Dai flings at him.

"You would leave me and everything I've built for you here?" The surprise in Kuron's eyes is quickly replaced by rage again. "You're my perfect prototype. The others all have defects, but in you, I finally succeeded in creating the ideal human to rule the ocean."

"I've got some news for you, Dad," Dai drawls. "I'm not perfect and I really don't want to rule anything. I'm leaving now with Nere and her friends, and I'm not coming back."

"You dare to defy me?"

"Not us, sir," Wasp breaks in. "Whitey and me, we're with you all the way."

I do *not* like the way this conversation's going. Suddenly, I remember the Sea Rangers and their mines. Reaching out to Rohan, I say, :We could really use a diversion to help us get out of here. Could you blow the mines on the landward side of the fortress right now?:

:You got it. We'll set those off, but they shouldn't put you in any danger,: Rohan responds immediately.

Seconds later, I feel the airlock shake.

"Sir, they're detonating the mines I warned you about," Wasp cries, "and *she* told them to do it."

"But they can't strike against me," Kuron says wrathfully. "Don't they understand? My son and I are the future of the sea. We are the future of the world."

I stare at him in disbelief. Is Kuron really such an egomaniac that he can't believe his fortress is under attack?

"We're not the future of anything," Dai says, shaking his head. "You're crazy and I'm a half-shark mutate who's almost as dangerous as those sharkheads you created."

"How dare you speak to me this way? She's the reason you've become even more stubborn and intractable." Kuron points at me, his expression wild. Another wave of mines detonates, knocking Kuron off his feet and making the airlock shake so much that the water inside it slaps our shoulders and faces.

"I—I have to save the research in my lab." Kuron staggers to his feet, looking agitated. He hurries away from the window. "Leave this airlock, kill the Hanson girl, and seize my son," he calls back to Whitey and Wasp.

"With pleasure," Whitey says. His hard, slate gaze is focused on me.

"Dad, you can't go to your lab," Dai cries out. "They're

about to bring the whole place down!" But Kuron doesn't hesitate, and moments later, he vanishes into the control room of his sub.

"Looks like your daddy doesn't care about what you have to say anymore," Wasp goads Dai as Whitey opens the door to the airlock. He motions us out but keeps his speargun trained on me as Wasp closes the door again.

Everything seems to be moving in slow motion. I feel numb from my lips to my toes. Are they really about to kill me?

:Dai?: I reach out with my mind, but I touch only blankness.

Wasp sends me an evil smile. Clearly she's blocking us again. Seconds later, the sub roars out of the bay, buffeting us with currents generated by its propellers. Whitey raises his speargun to his shoulder, tracking me carefully despite the currents. Mako stays close by my side. I glance at my quiver. It's lying on top of our spearguns, just a few feet away.

Wasp swims toward me with her tentacle-covered fingers spread wide. I sense Dai can't decide whether to protect me from Whitey or from Wasp.

All of a sudden, the lights in the bay flicker and die. The Sea Rangers must have just blown the main generators.

Instantly, I dive to the deck. A spear dart burns across the top of my shoulder. I flinch but still manage to grab the quiver. A strong hand grasps my own, and Dai pulls me out of the bay and into the sea.

:Bro, I'm not going to let you leave with her!: Whitey roars.

:Then you're going to have to kill us both,: Dai yells as he tows me away from Atlantea, his legs kicking incredibly fast. When the lights went out, Wasp must have been distracted enough to drop her mental block, because I can hear Dai clearly now.

:I smell blood. Whitey get you with the speargun?: Dai asks me.

:Yeah.:

:Is it bad?:

:It looks like a graze.: Now that we're out in the water below the fortress, I can see again.

:At least he has to reload now.:

Out of the corner of my eye, I see a blur of gray hurtling toward me. I forgot about Mako and the fact that I'm bleeding. Instinctively, I raise my right hand to ward him off. A second later, I hear a terrible thud as Dai throws Mako away from me.

:Stop it, Mako. You're not an animal!: Dai shouts.

Mako flashes around to face us.

:I wasn't gonna hurt her, Ice. I was gonna help you protect her.: The stricken expression on Mako's face tears at me.

Hastily I lower my arm. :I'm sorry, Mako, I should've known.:

:But you didn't and Ice didn't. I'm *not* an animal.:

With a determined look, he turns back toward the bay.

Whitey charges out, his speargun loaded. There's no sign of Wasp yet, but I know she can't be far behind.

Mako launches himself straight at Whitey.

:No, Mako!: I cry.

:Go on, Ice, you and Nere get outta here,: he calls to us.

Whitey fires at him, but Mako twists out of the path of the speeding dart just in time. He strikes Whitey's face with both of his fists and then flashes away before Whitey can grab him.

:We can't leave Mako to fight Whitey all by himself,: I shout at Dai.

:I'll circle back to help him, but I want you out of here first.: Dai starts towing me away from the fortress again. Bright flashes flare in the distance, and deep thunder from the Sea Rangers' mines rumbles through the water.

:The dolphins can take me. Sokya, Densil, I need your help!: I call them.

:we come.:

I glance back just in time to see Wasp fly out of the bay on a powerful skimmer. She spots Mako speeding toward Whitey, and she heads directly for them.

:Watch out for Wasp!: I yell at Mako, but I'm too late. Wasp rams the skimmer into Mako's back. Mako tries to struggle away, but Whitey grabs him and slams him into a nearby fortress support. Then Mako simply floats there, his eyes closed, looking terribly broken.

Whitey grabs the edge of Wasp's skimmer, and they head straight for us.

As fast as Dai can swim, that skimmer is faster. Helplessly, I watch them close the distance between us. Wasp reaches out with her ungloved hand, trying to rake my face with her poison-tipped fingers.

Sokya arrows out of the green sea and rams her beak into Wasp's side. Wasp tumbles away from the skimmer. Seconds later, the waters around us fill with angry dolphins.

:Don't let her touch you!: I shout at the pod.

:we know,: Densil reassures me.

A dozen dolphins descend upon Wasp and Whitey. Sokya and Densil must have told them about the orca. I've never seen the pod attack so violently. I spot Ton fighting with the rest.

They slam into Wasp and Whitey again and again, never giving Whitey a chance to reload. At last he drops his empty speargun and hurries away, clutching his side as the dolphins continue to swoop and dive furiously around him. In the meantime, Wasp manages to climb aboard the skimmer again.

:Nere Hanson, you won't get away with ruining everything I care about,: Wasp shouts at me, :and I swear you'll *never* be safe at your precious Safety Harbor!: Then she speeds off before the dolphins can ram her again.

I draw in a shaky breath. :Thank you,: I say to Densil

and Sokya and send feelings of gratitude to the rest of the pod as they swim in agitated circles around me. :Watch and make sure they don't return. Please, Densil, take me to the boy back there.:

Densil flashes to my side, and I grab his dorsal.

:his heart struggles,: Densil warns me. :I think he is dying.:

My throat tightens after Densil leaves me by Mako's side. He's floating on his back, staring up at the surface. His chest rises and falls jerkily as he fights to breathe. I don't like how pale his face looks.

:Hey, Mako,: I say gently. :How you doing?:

He can't seem to turn his head to look at me, so I lean in closer. :I think I'm all busted up inside, but it doesn't hurt. You safe now?:

:My dolphins attacked Whitey and Wasp and chased them away. They're both going to be hurting tomorrow.:

:I'm glad you're okay,: he says, and then his eyes droop shut as if he's tired. :I wanted you to see my cereus bloom,: he says with a painful sigh.

:I wanted to see it, too,: I say, tears burning in my eyes.

Dai reaches my side and looks down into Mako's face. :Mako, I'm here.:

Mako's eyelids flicker open again. :Ice, did you see that? I didn't run this time. I didn't leave her.:

:No, bro. You didn't run.:

:You saved Tobin, Robry, and me from Sham,: I tell him, :and just now, you kept Whitey away from us until my dolphins came.:

:Kimi'd be proud of me, don'tcha think?: Mako says, his silver gaze never leaving Dai's face.

:She'd be really proud.:

Then Mako looks at me. I reach out and gently stroke his thick bangs away from his face. Mako sends me one of his sweet smiles, his chest falls, and it doesn't rise again.

Blinking back my tears, I close his eyelids. I glance up at Dai, and I see grief in his face that mirrors my own.

:Nere, there you are!: I'm startled when a familiar mind touches mine. I turn to see James swimming hard toward us in scuba gear. Rohan, Kalli, Rad, Robry, and the rest are right beside him with a dozen Sea Rangers at their backs.

:We're about to blow the supports on this side of the fortress,: Rohan says quickly. :You guys need to move back from here.:

Together, Dai and I pull Mako away from the fortress. I warn my dolphins that more mines are about to detonate, and they speed off.

:We should bury Mako on land under a cedar tree. I think he'd like that,: I tell Dai, but he's not listening to me. Instead, he's looking at the fortress, his face strained.

:Nere, I gotta go back and find my dad. I thought I could leave him, but I can't. Not now.:

:But it's too dangerous!: I protest, glancing at Atlantea. Another wave of mines detonates, giving off flashes of orange light and sending a thunderous roar through the water. A cloud of sediment rises up and engulfs the base of the fortress. Odd dots are starting to gather around the edges of my vision. I blink. Some sediment must have gotten into my eyes.

:You reminded me what it means to care about people,: Dai says quickly. :My dad may be crazy, but I still love him. He could be dying right now.:

:Dai, please don't do this,: I say, suddenly feeling dizzy.

:I'm sorry, Nere. Look after my friends. They deserve a real home.: He leans forward and kisses me, and then flashes away toward the fortress. I see a streak of gray, and Ton's beside him. After Dai grabs his fin, they disappear into the cloud.

I stare after Dai, his kiss still tingling on my lips. I can't stop him now.

:I'm sorry I gave you such a tough time about lying to us,: I call after him. :I understand now why you had to do it.: I think of his cold, cruel father and how hard Dai fought to protect his friends and to keep them together. I finally do understand what Shadow meant. Dai never had a choice.

:Uh, Nere.: James swims up to me, but he sounds like he's speaking from far away. :We need to get a medic to look at your shoulder. You're bleeding pretty badly.:

Moments later, the right side of the fortress collapses, filling the water all around us with more clouds of sand and sediment. With a cry, I start after Dai, but the dots prickling around the edges of my vision seem to spread across my eyes, and the world goes dark.

chapter thirty-three

THE NEXT TIME I open my eyes, I see a black rock wall over my head instead of gray steel beams. And it feels like someone sliced my shoulder open with a dull dive knife. I glance around and spot Tobin sleeping in a berth next to mine, his blistered hand raised in a sling above his body. I must be in Safety Harbor's sickbay. Looking in the other direction, I see Lena floating next to my berth, beaming.

:It's about time you woke up. You've been out of it for two days. How do you feel?:

:My shoulder hurts, but the rest of me is okay, I think. How's Tobin?:

:Stronger, but he's still in a lot of pain. That sea wasp venom must be nasty stuff. Bria's been waiting on him hand and foot. They even let her sleep in here.:

I close my eyes, and a wave of sadness washes over me when I think of poor Mako, and Dai, and Ocho.

I decide to ask the safer question first. :Did Ocho make it?:

:Somehow he pulled through. I guess his octopus genes helped him survive. He's missing an arm now, but he's already making bad jokes about how handy it is he has some spares and changing his name to 'Siete.' His berth is over there behind that curtain. Kuron's kids kept popping in to visit him so often, we hung that up to give you and Tobin a little more privacy.:

There's no use in putting it off any longer. :Do you know what happened to Dai?:

Lena's eyes are full of sympathy. :We didn't find Dai's body or Ran Kuron's, and apparently some guy named Sham is still missing, but Atlantea is such a mess, we couldn't get very far inside it. There's still a chance Dai made it.:

:But if he was alive, Dai would've found his way to Safety Harbor by now,: I blurt. :I know he wanted to be here with his friends.:

Lena touches my hand. :I bet he still turns up. Dai's a survivor.:

:I hope you're right,: I say, fighting back tears.

Bria swims into sickbay and hurries to my berth, her face lit up with a smile. :Nere, you're finally awake,: she cries. She nestles up to my good side, and I give her a one-armed hug.

:I hear you've been taking good care of your brother.:

:It's not too hard,: she says, rolling her eyes. :All he does is sleep and ask for more cold packs. I'm never going to be a medic. Sick people are boring.:

:I guess we probably are.: I smile at her. Then I'm surprised to find myself yawning. :I wonder why I feel so tired.:

:They say you lost a couple of pints of blood before we got you back here,: Lena explains. :That kind of blood loss wipes you out, and it sounds like they didn't feed you too well while that awful Wasp girl had you shut up. Speaking of which, I'm supposed to get you to eat something.:

Lena and Bria scold me into tackling a salmon fillet. While I eat, they catch me up on Safety Harbor gossip, but the moment I finish the food, my eyelids grow heavy, and I drift off again.

The next time I wake up, my dad is looking down at me, wearing his scuba gear. He reaches out and squeezes my hand.

"I'm glad you're back with us," he says simply.

Me, too, I key into my com-pad. I'm surprised by how much even Safety Harbor's sickbay feels like home now. I'm *so* glad to be out of Atlantea and its endless, cold, gray corridors.

How are my new friends settling in?

"They've got good hearts, but those are some wild kids you brought home with you."

They're definitely going to keep Vival on her toes, I reply, thinking of the way Rad and the rest love their tidal surfing.

"We've had some interesting moments. Rad almost shorted out our generators his first day here, and Sunny scared the heck out of some of the younger kids when she decided to put on a light show for the Sea Rangers at dinner last night, but they're trying to get along with everyone. That Shadow is a remarkable young woman."

They're all pretty remarkable. Thanks for taking them in.

"It's the least we could do. I understand they're part of the reason your team made it back alive. Your friend Dai was the most remarkable of all. When I first saw him, he looked so much like his father, I didn't want to believe a word he said. He still managed to convince me that we had to send the Sea Rangers back to help rescue you all before it was too late."

The way my dad's looking at me makes me wonder how much he knows about Dai and me.

"Shadow's told me how hard he tried to protect them all from his father," he adds. "I think young Dai may be one of the bravest people I've ever known. I hope we see him again."

I do, too.

I'm relieved when my dad changes the subject and goes on to share more Safety Harbor news. I'm too weak and tired to add much to the conversation, but just having him here is nice. After my dad leaves, I look over and realize Tobin's eyes are open, and he's watching me.

:Hey over there.: I smile at him.

:Hey yourself. Getting claustrophobic in here yet?:

:Nah, not really. I had a friend who helped me face my phobia, and I think it's a lot better now. In the end, all he got for his trouble was some really nasty sea wasp stings.:

:I think he got more than that.: Tobin sends me a

quizzical smile, and I blush when I think how he helped me in our tiny prison. :That's good news, though, about your claustrophobia being better.: He closes his eyes. :I don't want to have to hum that many lullabies to you ever again.:

~~~

The next afternoon, the medics finally let me leave sickbay with orders to take it easy. I head off right away to visit the pod, but they mob me before I can reach Dolphin Bay. Mariah makes sure that ten excited dolphins don't jostle my hurt shoulder.

:I missed you,: Sokya says, flipping her head. :it was boring while you were in the sick place.:

:we all missed you,: Densil says in his more serious way.

:I am glad your shoulder is better,: Mariah says. :you must be careful with it.:

I give the other dolphins rubs as they each send me visual images of what they've been doing.

:missed you.: I hear a new dolphin voice in my mind, one I *know* I've never heard before. I feel an insistent tug on my right fin and see Tisi there, grasping my fin gently with his teeth, eyes shining with mischief.

:Tisi, you can talk to me. I'm so proud of you!: I lean over and rub his favorite spot on his melon.

:missed you, missed you, missed you.: He lets go of my fin and swims tight circles around me.

:Hm, I guess we may need to teach you some other words now.: I smile at him.

:we are happy to be back here, away from that bad place,: Densil says.

Sokya rests her beak on my shoulder. :I am, too, but I miss the big dolphin,: she says, referring to Ton.

And I miss his friend.

My human companions are psyched when I arrive in the mess cave in time for dinner. Thom, Penn, Lena, Ree, Kalli, and Robry all gather around me as we eat. I'm happy when Shadow and the rest of our new friends from Atlantea come join us, too.

:How's it going, Shadow?: I ask her across our chattering group.

She sends me a brilliant smile. It's the first time I've ever seen her smile like that, without any sadness in it. :I like Safety Harbor, and your father's been very kind. He's even going to get some tubing so Ocho and I can build another water organ. I think it will be a good home for all of us.:

Two younger boys come up to Sunny. :Hey, can you do your light-up thing?:

:You mean like this?: Sunny holds out her palm, and her hand gives off a brilliant pulse of light.

:Whoa, that's just so cool. Thanks, Sunny,: the first boy says.

:I hope they don't bother you too much,: I say to her.

:I don't mind. It's really nice to be around some younger

kids,: Sunny says, her eyes bright. :I'm going to teach art classes for them, and one of the helpers is already letting me use her dive camera to take pictures.:

:There aren't too many work sessions around here for you guys?:

:Not after where we've been,: Shadow says with a shrug. :And it's cool they're letting us choose where we want to work.:

:Getting to choose makes all the difference,: Rad says with unusual seriousness.

:Except they're not going to let you choose to play games on the computer all day long, bro,: Shadow teases Rad with a grin.

:It's more fun to build real stuff in engineering anyway,: Rad replies with a good-natured shrug.

Even though I'm still feeling kind of shaky, I need to talk to my dad without scuba masks or keyboards between us, so after dinner I head topside. I have to climb the ladder one-handed, and I'm panting by the time I reach the top. I walk slowly to his cabin, breathing in the scents of cedar, moss, and earth. It feels like so much has happened since I was last here.

I stop when I notice my brother is sitting under a nearby spruce tree, very involved in talking to Roni. He grins when he finally notices me and jumps to his feet. He nods to Roni and then jogs over to my side.

"How's that shoulder feel?"

"Better, and I'm *way* glad to be back. Atlantea was one scary place."

"We're glad to have you back. You did a good job on your mission, little sis."

"Thanks. How's it going?" I'm relieved to see James looks less skinny, and he doesn't seem as tense as he did before.

"Dad's put me in charge of my own research team, and the work we're doing on ocean acidification is fascinating."

"Uh-huh. I don't suppose Roni's on your team?" I tease him.

"Yeah, and she's great. Turns out she's got such strong mental shields, she doesn't bombard me with her thoughts. It's nice to hang out with someone and not know what she's thinking every moment."

"And she's cute, too."

"I hadn't noticed," James says with such a straight face, I crack up.

" 'Kay, well, I really need to talk to Dad."

"He's in his cabin. I'll catch you later."

I'm not surprised to see James head straight back to Roni.

My dad's smile is warm when he answers my tap on his door. "Look who's up and about," he says, and I sense his relief that I'm better. "I've been keeping some space clear, just in case you were strong enough to come for a visit."

I head for his bed, sit on the towel he places there for

me, and take a deep breath. "I'm sorry I didn't say this before I left," I tell him, "but I promised myself if I ever got out of Atlantea, I'd say it to you straight away. I'm not mad at you anymore for making me think you were dead . . . and I forgive you for making me a part of the Neptune Project. I understand now that you and Gillian were trying to give me something better."

"My dear girl," my father says, his voice gone thick and rough. He kisses me on the forehead. "Thank you for that."

He leans back and studies me. "And I should have asked for your forgiveness the moment you made it here from the southern sector. At the time I left you, we didn't see that we had any other choice. I had to disappear to begin my work up here, and deceiving you was the only way to keep you safe. As for changing you and your future, I understand that it may be a long time before you really do forgive me or your mother for that. I'm not sure yet we did the right thing. But the world was turning into such a desperate place, we had to try to do something to save it."

My father pauses and looks at my mother's picture on his cluttered desk. "What we didn't realize back then was how hard it would be, once we'd had our children, to commit them to this dangerous path." He sighs and looks at me again. "I want you to understand that you don't have to keep trying to save the world."

"Well, I think I'm pretty much stuck with living in the

sea for the rest of my life." I smile at him ruefully. "And I'm getting more used to that idea all the time."

"But in terms of our larger goals, you've done enough—more than enough—to help the Project. Kuron was a huge threat, and you and your team neutralized that threat quite effectively, and you got Bria and Robry out of there alive. Now it's up to James and me and our Neptune scientists to find ways to cultivate the c-plankton and spread it throughout the oceans of the world."

My father rubs his eyes again and straightens his shoulders. "Your job is to heal as quickly as you can and get back to dolphin training. We had another ten kids arrive while you were gone, plus your new friends need to learn how to work with dolphins, and Seth can use all the help he can get."

"I'm happy to pitch in."

I look at my mother's picture on his desk and take another deep breath. "Maybe not tonight, but sometime soon, will you tell me more about Gillian and how you two got involved in the Neptune Project? Sometimes I feel like I didn't know her very well."

"Your mom was a brilliant, driven, complex person. After all the years we were together, I think there were sides to her I never knew or understood, either. But I'd be glad to tell you more about her and the Project."

"Thanks, Dad."

We talk about James and dolphin training until I grow short of breath, and then I return to the ladder and the sea. As I swim back to the dorm caves, I realize that Safety Harbor really feels like home now. My father, my brother, my dolphins, and my friends are all here.

Except for one.

chapter thirty-four

I MEET SHADOW for an early breakfast in the mess cave. Before our workday begins, she's going to take me to the place they buried Mako. I'm surprised when, one by one, our new friends from Atlantea and my old friends from the southern sector appear, yawning and stretching. Pretty soon they're all here except Tobin and Ocho, who are still in sickbay.

:What are you guys all doing up so early?: I ask the others.

:Guess word got around where you're planning to go this morning.: Ree smiles at me.

:And we wanted to keep you company,: Kalli says.

I already know that Shadow, who was a frequent visitor to Mako's greenhouse, made sure they buried him in a cedar grove. As soon as we finish breakfast and leave the mess cave, I call the pod, and they tow us to the small cove near Mako's grave.

When we surface, morning fog is still thick on the water. Swirling gray clouds muffle everything but the sigh of the gentle surf and the rustle of round beach pebbles under our feet as we leave the water and walk inland.

"It's just here," Shadow tells me and leads us to a grove of ancient cedars. It's even quieter here under the old, tall trees, and the air is filled with the clean, pungent scent of cedar bark.

"I think Mako would have liked this place," I tell the others. They've heaped his grave with moss, and someone marked it with a simple M made out of white sand dollars.

We stand around the grave without speaking. Picturing that last sweet smile Mako sent me, I wish he could have had a chance to start over again at Safety Harbor. I really believe he could have been happier with us. Remembering all the plants he loved and the places he hoped to travel someday, I hope I'll have a chance to see some of those places for him.

"Thank you for my life," I whisper to him, and then turn and leave the grove.

When I reach the shingle beach, rays of early morning sun break through the fog and dance and shimmer on the waves. Even though Tobin's not here to sing his hymn, I'm glad there's still a flashing sea for Mako.

I pause to watch my friends. Rad's talking to Penn and Robry about some computer project. Thom's helping Lena look for seashells for the necklaces she likes to make. Shadow smiles as she watches Sunny taking a picture of the disappearing fog.

If only Dai were here. If only I knew he was safe.

A dark head breaks the surface of the water. I don't think it's anyone I know from Safety Harbor, and then my breath catches. It almost looks like . . .

I take several steps toward the shore.

It *is* Dai!

I race forward, splashing through the small waves. He swims toward shore until he's standing hip-deep in the water and facing me, his black braids shining in the morning sun. He looks tired and more than a little sad. That sadness stops me in my tracks.

"Is this where you buried Mako?" he asks, his gaze going to the grove behind me.

He must have been listening to my thoughts again, but this time I don't mind. I'm just so happy and relieved to see him.

"Shadow thought he'd like being under some cedar trees."

"It seems very green and quiet here," he says approvingly.

Seconds later, Rad, Sunny, and Shadow notice Dai, and they mob him. Rad actually tackles him back into the water. I join them under the surface, knowing it will be easier for Dai to breathe there anyway.

:Did you find your dad?: I overhear Shadow asking him.

:I searched and searched, but I couldn't find any sign of him.:

:I'm sorry,: Shadow says for all of us.

:I'm sorry, too. In his own way, he was trying to save the

world.: Dai looks away from his friends and swims toward me. The others fall back and give us some space.

:How's your shoulder?: he asks, his gaze going to my bandage.

:It's better.:

:I'm sorry I'm a little late. Am I . . . Do you think I'm still welcome here?:

I'm not used to seeing Dai look so unsure of himself. :I know there's still a place for you at Safety Harbor, and for Ton,: I add when I notice my pod is swimming in ecstatic circles around the big dolphin.

:Hey, Nere, you guys coming? We don't wanna be late to our work duties,: Rad calls to me.

:Yeah, we're coming,: I reply with a grin.

I reach out and grab Dai's hand. I'm going to help him and Ton get settled in their new home, and then I have some dolphins to train.

acknowledgments

THANKS SO MUCH to Sue and John Manion of NOAA for sharing their knowledge and experience on a wide variety of marine topics. I'm grateful to Kristin Gonzalez for her botanical suggestions and help with my teachers' guides, and to Cindy Gay for patiently answering my random biology questions. Maria Isabell Cruz, I appreciate your graciously providing Spanish translations. Bill Burton educated me on the topic of how electricity behaves underwater. John Klemzak, Erin Harrington, and Margaret Commins all contributed some much needed salmon expertise.

It was so helpful and exciting to share early drafts of this story with my enthusiastic beta readers: Holly, Maia, Marie, Joselle, Abby, Lou Anne, Lori, and Corinne. Karen C., I'm so very glad we are sharing the dream and facing its dragons together. Doug and Shirley, you two are the best agents ever. Alex A., it goes without saying that you are "bloody brilliant." Lisa Y. and Julie M., I'm so very grateful for your careful and insightful editing that transformed my sprawling manuscript into a much better story. Robert, Randy, Hema, Pam, and Brenda, members of the best little ol' critique group in Texas, once again you helped me to make Nere and her undersea world come alive.